Madison

"UPON THIS ROCK"

A. V. Smith

DEDICATION

To my children, Devan, Naiya, and Christian:
My prayer to The Universe for you has been sent. You are
my life source; greatness awaits you.
I love you.

TABLE OF CONTENTS

UPON THIS ROCK

INTRODUCTION

The chairs and tables were stationary, fastened with faded black steel plates drilled into the grey painted concrete. Two large glass panes were stationed on separate sets of walls for visible access into the area. The tables, also metal, had not been changed in over two decades. The room, typically busier with inmates speaking to their loved ones, was empty with the exception of a lone woman. She wore a navy-blue skirt suit and a matching stretch silk blouse with satin-finish and matte panels.

The two mounted cameras spread throughout the rooms weren't active currently. This first visit, and any other subsequent visits, would never be recorded.

The warden of this Reformatory for Women in Ohio had been ordered by someone much higher up in the pecking order to give access to anything and anyone requested. He obliged fully.

The woman sat expectantly as she heard the loud clicking sound of the security lock opening. She watched the inmate walk into the room wearing standard orange prison attire.

The inmate walked with awareness and slowed down to look over the face of her visitor while choosing to stand a few feet away from the metal chairs.

"Do I know you? Have we met?" Her voice didn't waver.

"I'm pretty sure we haven't, so I can only surmise that this is another level of intimidation from your boss. I will spend another 6 years in and out of the hole, before I take the life of someone because he or anyone else ordered it. I'm done taking orders. I am done with any part of that life." The inmate needed to make things clear upfront. Her first few years in this prison she had the protection of an organization her husband and had been knee deep in with since he was eleven years old. She found out the hard way: alliances were only as strong as the people committed to them.

The first months she had spent in the hole had been terrifying. After being pulled into an altercation with another inmate group, she was singled out and threw into the seven by nine-foot cement room, layers beneath the general population. She found out later that she had been sacrificed instead of other members of the group who she thought had her back.

The first three months she had contemplated taking her own life. She had been isolated, with only her thoughts keeping her company. She relived all the worst parts of her life repeatedly. She came face to face with the worst version of herself. Yet somehow, in the recess of her mind, she understood the separation of the shadow and the body. She shifted her loathing and low self-worth into reflection. Her eidetic memory helped her considerably. She thought back to each self-defense lesson that her daughter had taken and repeated them in her solitary confinement. The training helped her with clarity of not only her mind but her body. When she was released back into the general population, her status had changed.

She no longer had the protection of the group. When others attempted to bully her, she fought back. She had been beaten by a group of three women. She fought hard but, in the end, she was overwhelmed. After three weeks in the infirmary, she was placed back in the hole. It was not only discipline for fighting, but punishment for striking a guard in the process. When she didn't sleep, she trained. Variations of push-ups and sit-ups in which hundreds, turned into thousands. She shadow-boxed, remembering all the information about footwork and angles she overheard Mattie's trainer share. She did solo drills of leg circles and hip-ups. Core guard retention, shrimps, and reverse

3

shrimps, along with other BJJ basic drills. When she escaped the hole for the second time, she took revenge on two of the women who had jumped her.

Her last few years she barely slept for fear of retribution and found the time in the hole more manageable and safer than being in the general population.

"Uhm, Ms. Parks...Dominique...You need not worry about any demands on your time, your money, or your acquiescence to anyone. I don't represent who you think I do." The woman unbuttoned her blazer and motioned for Ms. Parks to also sit.

It was an awkward exchange of movement as the inmate placed her cuffed hands out onto the table as she sat down.

"My name is Camilla Alvarez. My client wanted to introduce herself to you in person, but I advised sending me would be best initially; I am an attorney and better at litigating any last-minute recommendations." Camilla could see the confused expression across the woman's face.

"Your client?" Ms. Parks needed more information before she engaged again. Information was power, the only real power behind these bars. She had a few ideas but would allow her to confirm who she was through conversation.

"This is…" Camilla paused in earnest; she was coming to realize that being the first contact with inmate Parks was much a much heavier responsibility than she had believed initially.

"…different for me as well. You may have noticed that you haven't been bothered by guards or the other inmates since your early release from the hole." Camilla was cut off by the prisoner who now seemed agitated.

"Oh wait! Are you with the government? Is that why you can throw a little weight behind you?" she spoke rapidly, her words tumbling over themselves. Her brain was working faster than her mouth.

"You know, years ago I told another agent I had no information to give them to build a case against that organization…" she paused because she would not say the name after learning the head of the crime family deliberately played a part in the destruction of her family. The women who had betrayed her and sacrificed her to the guards told her firsthand.

"Against him. Even if I did, I'm no rat. I did what I did to save the person I loved most. I will spend another 17 years behind bars if I have to, but I will never go against my morals again." Inmate Parks got up to walk away. She motioned for the only guard who stood on the opposite side of the first double-paned glass door.

"No wait…" Camilla spoke up to slow her. This conversation was not going as she had planned; for everyone's sake, she needed to find common ground quickly.

"Madison… Madison is why I'm here! I represent her… sort of. Please let's start over. I am an attorney for the family who…well…" Camilla blurted out before pausing. Family matters… mattered.

Inmate Parks relaxed and instantly felt more at ease. Her voice seemed less tense as she continued.

"I know who you are. I still have contact with my mother and others; I know it's not ideal to have my daughter somehow tied into the family." She slowed down and made eye contact with Camilla who listened intensively.

"But my mother has spoken to your employer on several occasions in person. I trust my mother, and my mother trusts and has even come to love your employer as family. The letters your employer has sent has helped ease my mind and also made me ampliar mi espanol." Inmate Parks held reservations about Madison and her surrogate family after finding out nearly a decade ago, but that passed with each letter shared with her mother.

"Ms. Parks, it may take some time, but we are working on getting you an earlier release. You've punished yourself enough…" Camilla saw the instant shift in Ms. Park's body and knew she had chosen the wrong words to use.

"Don't tell me what I have done or haven't done to earn my…" her words spilled out in anger.

Camilla interrupted her before she could continue. She was not here for any form of adversarial energy.

"You're absolutely right." Camilla apologized before Inmate Parks could finish. "Well, I can see where Mattie gets that part from and she's always been headstrong in her own way," Camilla finished with a genuine smile on her face.

Mattie's mother looked deeper into Camillas eyes, and for the first time, a smile creased her lips.

"Mattie has gone through a lot. My employer believes it's best for both you and Mattie to be reunited. We couldn't move before now. The latest maneuvering and positioning have shifted more benefits of our family, which you have been a part of for years." Camilla moved her elbows onto the table and set forward. Her next few words were meant to be conveyed with clarity.

Mattie's mom listened attentively as Camilla explained a few additional changes.

"You do not have to fear any repercussions from any past actions against inmate or guard. You now have access to anything you want inside these walls. The minimum sanitary supplies you've been given in the past will never be lacking. We have ensured you will have better access to mental health and healthier food items. We understand that you train. Now when you want to run or shadow box, you can do so outside." Camilla shared that it would take more political maneuvering to ensure that either a pardon or completely overturned verdict was received.

Mattie's mom wasn't sure how much of what Camilla told her was true, but when Camilla motioned for the guard to enter, she was gaining a clearer perspective.

"Correctional Officer Jarvis Johnson, hand Dominique the phone in your pocket and leave until she waves you back."

The prison officer did exactly as he was told.

"The phone is for inbound calls only, a secured line between you and Señora only." Camilla inhaled deeply. She felt the tension released in the space between them.

"If you have any specific requests, we have a courier who will make herself known to you within the next 24 hours. Do you have any questions at all?"

………...

The mahogany wood desk extended into another portion of the office, creating an L shape with enough space behind it that another table was situated with three monitors stationed on it. The various video feeds throughout the prison were shown intermittently.

Framed photos were also spread on each wall showing the modifications this Women's Reformatory had undergone over the previous 30 years.

The rustic orange carpet had small square designs only separated by the beige line boundaries of each geometric design. The air was cool, like the rest of the prison, but the office didn't have a heavy musty smell. The loveseat matched the desk and the upholstery of the two separate wood chairs directly in front of the Warden's desk.

This was the first time these two women had met in person, although the previous three years they had Face Timed each other at least twice a week and nearly every day when Grandma Redd, her mother, had passed. The family had attempted to have Dominique released for Grandma Redd's funeral services, but they had not secured their final political position until recently. Both Senora and Mattie's mom needed reassurance that Mattie was finding her footing after losing the woman who held her together. These video chats also served as bonding moments between Senora Rojas and Dominique, who in time became extremely vulnerable with each other, always speaking the truth. Not all conversations were easy, but necessary if they were going to develop a true familial bond.

Senora Rojas had hugged Dominique as soon as she walked into the Warden's office before kissing her on each cheek.

"Even with all of the correspondence over the last couple of years, my palms are sweating, and my mouth feels dry." Senora Rojas tried to make light of the moment. For nearly a decade, she had taken on the role of "mother" to Madison. She loved Mattie as if she had born her. It wasn't always rainbows and sparkles between Madison and Senora Rojas. They had arguments and screaming matches, but that's what parents and children did, only to make up and find wisdom after tempers flared.

Mattie's mom didn't know what to say initially. She believed Camilla was making the visit today, and she also had no idea that she was being released from incarceration with a full pardon from the Governor of Ohio.

"Your presence over video chat could fill this entire room, but you're much shorter than I imagined," Mattie's mom let out with a smirk across her face.

Senora Rojas laughed. They had found a space where being genuine mattered most and laughter had been part of their bonding over the years.

"It is true, very true." Senora Rojas pulled Mattie's mom to the loveseat and sat down.

"So, let's be serious for a few minutes. We can leave here and go straight to see Mattie and rip the Band Aid off for the scar to be healed. It would be my first instinct to go see my children; as mothers, nothing matters more than our children. We have already secured housing and transportation for you. It takes time to adjust back into the 'world.'" Senora paused and used her fingers like quotations when she said "world."

"This world resembles nothing that you remember, and I will support your decision. We are family."

Dominique stared into Senora Rojas' eyes before standing back up. All of this was hitting her faster than she imagined. On record, she had another 3 years of time to be served, but with the pardon, her life was shifting again.

"We could do that, leave and go see Mattie or…" She paused, waiting to hear the other option.

Senora Rojas had known Dominique was just as much of a stickler for details as she was, so she continued with a separate choice.

"We could get you back up to speed. We have a legitimate passport for you, and we would like you to come stay with us. You can leave anytime you want, and everything you'd require is at your fingertips. I pray I am not overstepping; I love Madison like she is my own flesh and blood, as does the rest of our family. I hope that you come to know us as family and accept any support you need. Once you change…" Senora motioned to a few garment bags in the warden's office.

"You can choose what you feel is best, Dominique." She placed her hand on top of Mattie's mom.

The garment bags contained various styles of clothing; in the end she chose blue jeans, a t-shirt, and hoodie with some low-cut sneakers.

"Our daughter gets her style from you." Senora said lightheartedly. She wasn't certain how the "our daughter' would be received, so she waited.

Mattie's mom looked directly into a mirror positioned on the wall at her ensemble and then back towards Señora."

"So, she still loves her jeans and hoodies…" Dominique paused to turn and face her counterpart.

"I know I need to get my head in a space to see her," Dominique spoke her decision out loud.

"She will have tough questions and may not be ready to accept me back into her life. I need a little time to get things right. So, the second option works best."

YoYo

Chapter 1

Mattie had so many thoughts racing through her mind on the drive to the airport. Was she ready to be a mom? Would she be protective as her mom was? Could she raise a child by herself if Kendal wasn't receptive to being a father? Would her body snap back?

Sheila had offered to drop her off at the airport, but there had been an emergency at work with various departments overlapping as she was promoted to Nurse Manager. Sheila had been interviewing potential staff but was being deliberate in the process.

The only minor speed bump was a two-car accident off to the side of I-71, and commuters slowed down to be nosey. She had packed her bag the previous afternoon and spent the day cleaning Kendal's condominium including putting a few bags of black mulch down around the perimeter of his home and patio area.

Mattie had hoped to catch an earlier flight but waited until the late afternoon to ensure Aunt Penny had everything she would need while she was gone. Aunt Penny couldn't replace her grandmother, but Mattie had accepted her into her life.

Mattie left her BMW in long term parking and, after checking her bags in, decided to get something to eat. Nourishment was more important now that she was carrying a child. She hated taking pills—her phagophobia was legendary, but prenatal vitamins were essential to the development of her baby. She was going to do everything possible to ensure her child was born into this world healthy, which meant she would have to overcome the fear of pills lodging in her throat.

The main corridor had a few people scampering to their gate from connecting flights. The sterile white floors contrasted against the dark carpet in the waiting area.

Sitting at her gate, Mattie looked around at the groups of people, wondering why each person was traveling to New York City. There were the casual sweatpants and hoodies being worn by some. Both women and men dressed in classic business suits using laptop computers and an assortment of women dressed similar in front-slit midi sheath dresses. Groups of what looked to be college students were huddled together either listening to music or texting messages on their phones. Mattie sat across from a family of three—a mom with two children. The male child was young, around six. He was fixated swinging his yo-yo back and forth instead of up and down. His sister, sporting a new cornrows up-do ponytail, was a teenager. She was clearly trying to make herself look older as she crossed her legs, making eye contact with a few older collegiate boys who glanced at her.

Mattie's emotional range was more than just sporadic. She was overwhelmed with joy to be going to see her man. She had come to accept that love had no boundaries, that life could be shared completely between two people, but at times this belief still frightened her. Although she and Kendal had spoken briefly about having children, she also knew children could scare men away. Mattie had seen it firsthand with an older coworker years ago at her company. Her colleague became pregnant with a man she dated for nearly a year and a half, but once she was with child he ran from her, quitting his job. Now the woman was raising a child alone; Mattie didn't want that for herself.

"Sit down and stop swinging that yo-yo." The young boy was trying to do a trick, but the yellow toy kept swinging wildly. The boys' mother grabbed him by the sleeve of his shirt, pulling him into the seat directly across from Mattie.

"But I'm yo-yoing and getting good at it, mama," he squinted his nose in disappointment as he slumped back in the chair.

"There are people walking by, Tyler, and if you hit them, then what? We are not at home so sit yo' little butt there and... and read a book out of your backpack." She finished by handing him his bag and a Gatorade.

Mattie couldn't help but wonder if the child she carried was a male or female. It truly didn't matter; she just continued to pray that the baby would be born healthy. But for the first time Mattie became deeply aware that there was another living being growing inside her, a child that would one day become an adult, and innocent child that she was responsible for, that she would raise to the best of her ability... with Kendal. A distant thought was imagined of raising the baby without Kendal, but Mattie buried that fear.

Many conversations overlapped between travelers while airport workers and the intercom updated travel itineraries. Mattie sat back and opened her social media accounts after smelling someone eating popcorn.

An older woman's voice came through the terminal's intercom system. "Flight 217 to La Guardia Airport will be boarding momentarily. We would like to announce that we do have business class upgrades for only $59. Please see the attendant if you would like to change your accommodations." Some people made eye contact with each other, seemingly measuring their willingness to pay for the upgrade.

"Mom, can we upgrade? Because you are gonna be doing business this week?" Mattie followed the questioning teenage girl as another couple made their way to the counter.

The mother was quick in response.

"No, we are not upgrading, our seats will be just fine…" the mother attempted to convince her daughter.

"Mom, please? We'll have more room, and it's only $59." The young boy sided with his sister as he swung the yo-yo outward again.

"That's $59 per person, add that up! It's almost another $200!" She paused to take her son's yo-yo and redirected her words back to her daughter.

"You wanna shop while we're there don't you? Or would you rather spend the money for six more inches of legroom? We're not upgrading, so leave it alone." The mother sternly looked at her daughter, and her message was understood.

"We are minutes away from boarding, for those of you flying flight number 217 to La Guardia Airport. We would like you to take a minute and view your boarding pass, as each ticket has been assigned a zone number as well as your seating number. When your zone is called, please move forward and welcome to Air Sun. Also, for those passengers still wanting to purchase our business class upgrades, we have a few seats available ensuring you first to board and exit, along with additional beverages and services while in flight." The male counter attendant's voice was heard through the intercom system.

"What's our zone, mama?" the young boy asked politely. He understood that she was losing her patience.

"Brianna, take a look in that folder and tell me what zone we're in." The mother directed as she gathered her belongings and put the yo-yo into her son's backpack.

"Um, row 22 seats A, C, and D... zone five. We don't have all our seats together?" Brianna answered her mother as she stuck her iPad into her personal carryon bag.

Mattie pulled out her ticket to check her seat and zone number. "Damn 22B and zone five." She quickly made her mind up that sitting with the family in the terminal was one thing, but on an airplane, entirely another. One other person had made their way towards the counter but turned around.

Without hesitation, Mattie grabbed her purse and carry-on bag to purchase the upgrade. She received a text message from Sheila apologizing again and asking if she made it on time.

Mattie smiled. She had no doubt that her sister-friends would make the best aunties.

Cindy and Geri had already begun buying baby clothes and diapers. They had taken on the role of being aunts already, even before the first ultrasound. Cindy joked to Mattie that she was going to be mom number two, because she wasn't having no snot-nosed babies on her own.

As Mattie waited in line for the business class upgrade, her phone rang—Kendal.

"Hi baby, I miss you." Mattie hoped no airline announcements would be made to spoil her surprise. She kept her thumb on the mute button just in case.

She truly wanted to share that she was pregnant with him a while ago but decided the best way to give information of this magnitude was in person. She would be able read his facial expression when he received the news to know how he really felt about everything. She was nervous, but his voice was reassuring.

"My lil' sexy queen, just hearing your voice makes my day better. You know I miss you, all crazy like…" he paused to clear his throat.

"…so, baby I was thinking about our computers, phones with video capabilities. You know we could see each other as we talk and have a little on-screen romance going on."

"I was thinking the same thing." Mattie interjected quickly. Kendal chuckled and continued.

"You still staying at the condo, or have you and Aunt Penny hugged it out?" He joked. He adored the older woman because he understood everything was about family to her.

The truth of the matter was that Aunt Penny was still getting on her nerves, but Mattie had eased up and was learning to tolerate the older woman. Now Aunt Penny was teaching her how to crotchet; one part of Mattie felt this honored her grandmother's memory by learning this like all the other women kinfolk. The other part was simply wanting Aunt Penny to stop bugging her about it.

Aunt Penny was treating Madison with a little more respect but every now and then she would crawl under Mattie's skin by snooping into her personal belongings. It was irritating.

"We ain't worked anything out, except..." Mattie muted the call as the airport intercom sounded.

"...what types of stitching and knots she's teaching me. I did stay at the condo last night and ran out of Pepsi this morning."

Kendal chuckled on the other end interrupting her in the process.

"You and your Pepsi," he waited.

"I miss you. How was the performance last night? Y'all still knocking 'em dead? Mattie muted her phone again as the male attendant at the counter reissued her boarding pass.

"Here's your upgrade to business class, Ms. Parks. You can board immediately."

"Thank you." Mattie shook her head and went back to listening to her phone call.

"Last night, well last night was… was ok. Some of the poets decided to try new pieces. Some were good, and some were just downright weird. I stuck to the ones I had been doing, and tonight I'm gonna do a brand new one, but I don't want to talk about that stuff right now. I've been thinking about you 24/7, and I was thinking about flying back for a couple of days before the D.C. shows. What do you think?" Kendal asked as Mattie began boarding her flight.

"You all get a break at the end of the week, right?" she muted her phone as the flight attendant greeted and welcomed her aboard. Mattie handed her carry-on bag to store in the overhead compartment.

"Yeah, Saturday night begins the last few days performing in New York, and the D.C. show doesn't start until Thursday of next week. So, I could fly out after the show and fly into D.C. early Tuesday. I miss you, the best and sweetest, good-good in the world and even that morning breath." Kendal laughing loudly through the phone.

Mattie couldn't help but burst out in laughter because the truth of the matter was, she was addicted to Kendal. He filled her up mentally, emotionally, spiritually, and physically.

"You better miss me, or I'd cut ya…" Mattie paused to adjust her seat backwards before pulling a piece of gum out to help alleviate the pressure when the plane took off, keeping her ears from popping.

"Well, what I'm gonna do, baby, is go online and look for tickets. I will have everything ready by tonight, so you'll know your itinerary. Oh, and Frances called, and said that some of the funding has hit the accounts, enough at least to buy 20 brand new computers and to convert that old storage room into an Information Center. Alonzo has been helping so much lately; I think he doesn't want to disappoint you again. You helped change the course of his life… you've changed my world too, so your ass belongs to me, Kendal Abraham Scott. I've got to make sure Aunt Penny gets to lunch today, honey. She keeps bugging everyone about Golden Corral. And honestly, I can't lie: I love their peanut butter fudge dessert. You guys have the same show times tonight, right?" Mattie asked already knowing she had the answer to the question but was doing everything to keep him unaware.

"Yes, you sexy thing, 7:30 and 10:30, so please, baby, get my ticket because another week of being without you, is just too damn long. Oh, I almost forgot to tell Geri that I made a contact for her. There's an organization that deals specifically with funding publications and magazines, and they're looking to invest some money. I gave them the edition that had my interview in, and they were very interested in speaking with her. So, make sure she gets the message for me, sweetie. I love you so much, and tell everybody I said hi, and make sure you get my ticket to fly back," Kendal added one final time.

"I love you more, baby. I'll call Geri right now, you will have the ticket information when I see…" Mattie had to catch herself, knowing she was half of a second away from ruining the surprise.

"…when I talk with you tonight/ I love being your woman."

"Hmm, ok baby I love you." The call terminated.

Mattie's stomach was filled with butterflies knowing that in less than eight hours she would be watching Kendal perform on stage and a few hours after that her arms would be locked around the man she loved. As promised, Mattie dialed Geri to share the news of the investors. Unfortunately, Geri didn't answer so Mattie left a voice message.

"Tyler!" a voice called out startling Mattie. She looked up to see the family of three again. The young boy had hit the flight attendant with the yo-yo and even with the flight attendant saying no problem, he clearly didn't like being hit. He attempted to smile it off, but his eyes betrayed him as he continued to usher other passengers forward.

"I told you to put that yo-yo away or I'm taking it from you and giving it to someone else." The mom genuinely apologized to the flight attendant.

"I don't want to yo-yo no more. You don't let me do nothing, and Brianna can do everything she wants." He was defiant before offering his yo-yo to Mattie as the family was still waiting to get past the entrance of the plane. Several groups of passengers were trying to locate their seats and put bags in above head storage bins.

"You can give it to your baby." The boy extended his toy to Mattie.

Her facial expression was blank. How he knew she was pregnant she couldn't imagine.

"Out of the mouth of babes." The male flight attendant raised his eyebrows watching the exchange between the two.

Mattie looked over at the young male and then to his mother who was staring with one eyebrow rose higher than the other. Mattie had seen that look before from Sheila when her kids acted out or said something inappropriate. It was the look that said I'm losing my patience, or I'd whoop his butt if no one was around. Unconsciously, Mattie took the yo-yo and said thank you, all the while wondering if these would be some of the traits she would have to develop as a parent. Would she be able to exert patience, as this mother had?

As the plane taxied down the runway, Mattie stared out the window and said a prayer before putting in her earbuds and listening to music for the short trip.

After landing, the taxi ride from the airport was another event with the driver weaving in and out of traffic and running soon to be turned red lights. For some reason he seemed to be in a hurry.

Mattie checked into her hotel and unpacked her bags. She couldn't wait to get out of her sweatpants and long-sleeved top. She felt sweaty and a long hot shower was calling her name. As she undressed in front of the mirror, she stared at her belly button, sucking her stomach in and out attempting to see how her body would be transforming eventually over the next seven months. Mattie couldn't wait to tell her family in Colombia. They would be excited and want to throw a huge celebration.

I'm gonna have to work out twice as much after you're born. She envisioned herself with stroller, pushing her child around the park. She smiled, wrapped her hair up with a hair band, and placed a towel down onto the bathroom floor by the tub before hopping into the shower. The water was perfect; she enjoyed the temperature a little hotter than most. She debated washing her hair, but as soon as the first stream of water hit her head, she immersed herself completely. Drying off and wrapping her hair into a towel, she stared a second time at her belly.

I'm gonna teach you so much, and your daddy is gonna be a great father. She wanted to reassure herself. She walked over to the desk situated next to the window to get her cell phone. She wondered why she hadn't heard back from Geri or anyone for that matter, especially after an investor for the magazine would make the publication go nationwide. It was one of Geri's lifelong dreams.

"Oh damn…" Mattie realized she still had her phone on airplane mode. Now with her phone back on, multiple text and voice messages came through, and then her phone rang. It was her house phone number, so Mattie had no doubt that it was Aunt Penny.

"Hello?" Mattie waited for her aunt's sarcasm.

"Child, I know hell is low, you may want to find a different way to answer the phone instead of cursing at the person on the other end." Aunt Penny paused before continuing. "…anyways, Ms. Charlotte's daughter said her mom wanted us to stop by the house when you get back. I guess she was holding onto something for us. Henry called and wanted to bring something by to you, some type of reward. I told him you wouldn't be back 'til Friday night but I'm gon' let him drop it off today. What type of reward you got? Is it for that Jackson fella? Baby, you gotta be more careful in New York, child. That city eats most people alive and got all types of predators living there… you seen Kendal yet?" Aunt Penny asked.

Mattie hesitated before responding; Aunt Penny had found one more button to push.

Mattie's response needed to be even though she was flustered. In her heart she knew her aunt truly cared for her.

"I'm gonna surprise Kendal at the show, and I'm careful all the time, Auntie. Don't forget, I am a grown-ass woman, not some teenage or 20-something with my nose wide open…" Mattie was interrupted.

"Child, you ain't gotta respond to everything, and you sure don't have to use profanity. I just want you to be safe and… and… I'm gon' tell you something about surprises. Sometimes they backfire on you, and you be the one all surprised, so remember that…" she paused again.

"Geraldine is coming to take me to dinner. I told her that Golden Corral is a good place for me 'cause I like the variety but she says she gon' surprise me. I like that girl, but I ain't eating no sushi or nothing that ain't cooked like that, so she betta keep it simple or she gon' get a piece of my mind, 'cause I done already told her." Aunt Penny was being serious, but Mattie couldn't do anything except her hold laughter in.

Mattie pulled out the outfit she was going to wear tonight as she listened—designer blue jeans with a multi-colored strapless blouse. She bought three-inch stilettos to set the outfit off, because she wanted Kendal to be shocked when he saw her later. Aunt Penny was still talking, but Mattie had tuned out most of the conversation.

"So, this reward Detective Jenkins is bringing over later. You want me to deposit it into your account or just leave on yo' desk, child?" Aunt Penny asked for the second time.

"Ok… uhm, you can deposit it, but I don't remember where my deposit slips are. I think…" Mattie was recalling her memory for where the slips were located when her aunt chimed in.

"They're in my hand right now; you left 'em in the bottom drawer of your desk by the computer. You should keep your stuff more organized. I'll have Geraldine run me to your bank before we go to dinner."

Mattie held the phone to her ear and could feel her blood pressure rising. It was bitterly upsetting that her privacy had been violated. It was one of the reasons she hid her more… adult items in her basement.

"Auntie, I am grateful you're taking care of my house while I'm gone, but you can't be going through my personal stuff like that, that's not cool at all. I have to keep some of my things private. You wouldn't want me all up in your business." Mattie tried being a little diplomatic about it, but the words came out with an attitude.

"It's a deposit slip, it ain't like I read your journal in your nightstand. Now that's private and you may… just a suggestion, child… You may want to consider putting your personal and private items in a safe or sumthin'. How private it gon' be when you got it out where people can get to it easily." Aunt Penny responded with a fact of the matter tone.

Mattie bit her tongue. Had this been while she was in Columbus or some other time, she would have cursed over the phone but right now she was gonna let it go. She was only a few hours away from being with her king.

"That's fine, Auntie. I've gotta go…Cindy's calling me on the other line, so I will check on you later," Mattie said hoping this would be a sufficient end to the call.

"Call back later, bye, child. I love you."

"I love you too."

Mattie answered the other line.

"Oh my God, that woman makes me so angry sometimes! She snoops into my personal belongings and thinks of me as this little girl or something! Child this… child that. I ain't a child no more, I'm about to have a baby! I'm telling you, she can't stay much longer. I've learned to crotchet like she asked, and I'm getting better dealing with grandma being… being in heaven, but sometimes that woman can be hell on earth!" Mattie was exasperated while rambling into the phone.

"Damn, she got you fired up! It won't last forever, and girl, you ain't even here so stop letting her get under your skin. Your flight… how was it?" Cindy changed the subject; she didn't want to harp on the older woman. She was also meeting Aunt Penny while Mattie was out of town.

Mattie told her about the kid with the yo-yo somehow knowing she was pregnant and the cab driver who thought he was racing in the Indy 500, almost getting into two accidents en route to the hotel.

"Well, yo' ass is safe and sound now, and yo' man is going to be surprised to see you…" Cindy began saying before Mattie interjected.

"Oh, that's another thing. 'When you try to surprise someone, you may be the one being surprised.' She speaks to me like I don't know these things already, but I already know in my heart he's gone be happy to see me… right?" Mattie statement was more of a question; somewhere along the line, Aunt Penny had planted a seed of doubt.

"Girl, Kendal ain't seeing nobody else or wanna see nobody else. He ain't that type of man. He's one of the good ones, and there are few and far in between. Relax… oh and let me tell you. Last night, I'm up at Easton Town

Center for happy hour, and I see the usual flunkies doing their thing, making moves on the unsuspected and guess who walks in…" Cindy paused.

"…ok I'll tell you, the general manager of the car dealership. That man is fine. I let him do his thing so I could check out his swag. I'll say this: he knows an awful lot of people and woman after woman tried getting his attention. So, I'm just sitting there, thinking somebody is gonna end up going home with him and giving up some ass, but he blew all of em off… every one of them. So, you know me, I'm thinking he either committed to someone or on the DL." Cindy said.

Mattie chuckled before responding, "You think every man is on the down low, maybe he jus'…"

"He ain't on the down low, Mattie, 'cause he tore my shit up last night and had some cheeks clapping." Cindy waited for a response.

"What… you let him… oh my God! He did go home and get some hookers punani." Mattie couldn't help laughing because her friend had not included herself during the original assessment.

"Well anyways I can't go and take it back now, can I? We're going to dinner this week and then to the Old School concert on Saturday night."

"Hmph, so I guess you… like him like that? That's cool that he's not in the category of one and done. Sometimes you be too hard on men." Mattie added, opening the bottled water left next to the microwave in her room. She drank down half the bottle, realizing she was more parched than not.

"Whateva'. If you can find happiness, it might be possible for me too. Oh, Geri told me about taking Aunt Penny to dinner and she wanted me to tag along. I said hell to the no. Aunt Penny… well… she told me at church I can't serve two houses and lectured me on how to be a woman. I have a once per year chastisement level, and she's over that by two." Cindy laughed hard but was serious about what she said.

"So, you know what I'm talking about when I say she gets under my skin. Listen girl, I need to dry my hair, get a bite to eat, and take a nap before Kendal's show. I'll call you back in a bit, so let me go trick momma." Mattie took another sip from her water bottle.

"OK girl, we'll talk later… and Mattie, Kendal loves you, and he's gonna be ecstatic knowing that you are carrying his child. It will be a great surprise so don't second guess yourself and don't listen to Aunt Penny. She's just mad cause her Depends fit her too tight… holla." Cindy finished before hanging up.

The truth was Mattie believed in her heart that he would be elated to be having a child together.

But… The thought resurfaced.

What if he isn't? What if having a child gets in the way of his dreams? What if it's too much for him? Mattie began doubting herself once again. She rushed the thoughts to the back of her mind, took another gulp of water, and began to get ready to find out for sure what Kendal really thought about having a child with her.

SURPRISE SURPRISE
CHAPTER 2

Mattie arrived at the 10:30 show late. She fell asleep in her hotel room at 6 p.m. and had asked for a courtesy call to wake her. Either they didn't call, or she had not heard the phone ring. Finding her way to the theatre was an event all its own. It took her 15 minutes to hail a cab, and when she arrived to buy tickets, they were all sold out. Luckily for her, scalpers always had extra to hustle. The ticket she had was for the balcony and instead of trying to rummage her way around in the dark she had an usher escort her to her seat. At first, when he was called by the front office, he seemed reluctant but when he laid eyes on Madison his whole disposition changed, trying to strike up a conversation with her.

As Mattie took her seat, she looked at the program guide to scan for Kendal's name, he was slotted right before Kwame.

Good he hasn't performed yet, she thought.

She had missed the first five poets, and the sixth artist was ending his set. The only two remaining were Kendal and Kwame.

Mattie was amazed at how packed the theatre was and how engaged the audience had been. As the poet walked off the stage to the sounds of claps and cheers, the host came on, speaking in a heavy Caribbean accent.

"Give it up for Dali Simons, all the way to the stage from Europe. This has been one of the best crowds we've had all week, and we're gonna keep the energy level sky high as we bring the next artist out. He's the newest poet of the bunch, from Cleveland by the way of Columbus, Ohio. You've read the reviews, his dynamic way with words and concepts of life brings each sentence, phrase, and paragraph into existence, making you think beyond ordinary measures. So, without further ado, Mr. Kendal Scott." the host concluded shaking Kendal's hands as they passed each other on stage.

Kendal stepped up to the microphone and adjusted the height of the mic stand.

"Alright New York City, they say if you can make it in The Big Apple, then you can make it anywhere. Please give another round of applause to the poets that have shared their work so far tonight. You all have been wonderful, and I hope to keep adding to all the hype. This first piece I'm gonna do is brand new, never performed on stage… unless you want to count the bathroom mirror," he laughed genuinely as the crowd joined in with him. He approached the mic stand.

"It's called Moving Concepts, because as we learn in this life, we will begin to see that we are more closely connected than apart." He took a step back from the microphone to let any noise die down in the audience, a trick Kwame had shown him.

"Beyond imaginary friends and unintelligible acts of faith or even frigid revelations of egocentric idiocracy. Past the sands of Iwo Jima and the Hills of Macedonia through the madness of tethered farewells. Within moments of the first agreement performing like hecklers at the last supper or Roman soldiers bending down to carry HIS burden after sipping ale in a pauper's grave, it's strange that oil and wine mix better that blood and holy water. Scattered like atom-bombs, shattering seeds of Hiroshima with speeds still not a tenth of the velocity that Adam hastened through soil and roots or the potency that Eve's voice has as it carried through fallen leaves, broken twigs, and apple fruits. Miscarriages of a prophet's genesis wrapped in linen cloth, calloused by fire and brimstone. Tied together like a bowtie across a bald fat man's belly… posed …cross legged and positioned in the elevation of life. The trumpet's sounds causing mistreated miscreants to be forgiven and then enlightened by 20,000 volts of

lightning. The torrential downpour of spirits masturbating for one breath of life. Three hundred and sixty degrees comprises a circle... are we less majestic in purple skin, less perfect in golden yarn spun from a child's fairy tale because His story was shelled like crustaceans in deep black seas where power is absolutely nothing. Nothing is something in the stillness; still, we wait weightlessly for the last goodbye to have a new beginning. Fractional at best, divided by itself still leaves an answer to the only true question left. Who am I? Existing in a landscape of the absolute artist. Being one in the same yet changed with testament from old and new. Testified with the truth of sins. Spoken with the dialect of a hieroglyph. Digesting conspiracies between the summit of Mt. Everest and the mahogany depths of the Nile River while staring with crow's eyes into the middle of a black hole, past the center of one verse. Wondering if each verse spoken over 14,622 days has more gravity than the weight of the world.

The momentary silence after he completed this first poem was overshadowed by the applause right after. Mattie clapped loudly and realized the depth of her man had not been tapped into and the Creator, as Kendal said, was still working on him. As his performance continued, the crowd listened attentively. This was his arena, a stage to dialogue with the world. He was living his dream; the dream to glorify God with his words. When Kendal's set came to an end, he received a standing ovation. Mattie was proud of him.

Kwame took the stage last, and as usual, his charm and stage presence added to his 30-minute performance. It was more like a one-person play; the content of his work was a wide range of politics, love, war, and peace with a lot of comedy. It was no wonder why this tour, with these poets, had been received as well as it had been.

As the theatre let out, Mattie found herself working against the crowd attempting to get backstage to surprise her man, but by the time she made it, he was already gone.

I'll meet him at the hotel, he should be expecting my call anyways. She flagged down a taxi. Mattie slumped back into the taxi and told the driver her destination.

"You bless my taxi with your beauty! Where are you from?" This cabbie was more engaging than the first one she had used, but she didn't feel like speaking much. Even as he talked, Mattie had a funny feeling that she was being gamed and was driven a longer route than was necessary to get to Kendal's hotel. She felt like he was running the meter up but overlooked it because his driving was much better than before and because she was one step closer to touching, kissing, and holding her man.

As she stepped out the cab, she called Kendal's cell phone so that she could be talking to him, but he didn't pick up the call.

Maybe he's in the shower, she thought as she called him a second time. Making her way into the lobby, she could feel the patron's and staff's eyes looking her up and down, watching her every step. She knew she looked sharp, but the only eyes she wanted watching her were Kendal's. Before stepping onto the elevator, a man approached and asked if she needed any aid attempting to make conversation.

"No, I'm fine, thank you." She was kind in her response but there was a level of firmness. She was getting butterflies in her stomach as she stepped into the elevator.

Going up to the seventh floor, she was nervous. She could feel her hands sweating. Aunt Penny's words attempted to re-surface, along with the dampness between her fingers.

She had intended on getting a room at the same hotel, but with multiple conventions in New York City, they were completely booked.

Don't be acting like a little girl. She felt giddy as she walked down the hall while calling his phone again but no answer and right before she knocked on the door, she heard noises coming from inside the room… sounds she never expected to hear. Her butterflies were gone, to be replaced by being confused and anger. She heard moans of pleasure. A woman's voice was calling out loudly behind the door.

"Oh no… not again, give it to me, daddy, take all this wet, wet and …. oh my god, it's too much," the woman's voice cried out demanding more pleasure.

This muthafucka is cheating on me. He's been cheating on me! The thought flooded Mattie's mind along with experiences from her past relationships, when she gave so much to only be let down again. But this time, this time was different. She had given her hopes and dreams, spirit and soul, to this man. She had given her future to Kendal, and now she was pregnant with his child. She was crushed.

"Fuck that!" Mattie banged on the door with her hands initially and then slammed her shoulder into it. The rage she felt was acute.

"Open the fucking door, you piece of shit!"

Memories flooded her of all the people who had let her down; this time she couldn't control herself. He would experience her full wrath.

Mattie yelled continuously at the top of her lungs as she banged on the door before trying to kick it in, breaking the heels to her shoes. Two other hotel doors opened to see what was happening before quickly closing.

"Fuck you… fuck you, Kendal, you piece of shit!"

"I'm not playing with you or that slut you got inside… open this fucking door, muthafucka, you lying son of a bitch! I hate you… I hate you!" Mattie was enraged, how could he say he loved her and missed her?

How could he want to fly back to see me and have me make plans… "Fuck that shit!" she yelled again.

"You ain't shit, muthafucka, I'll kill you!" she bellowed out before slamming her shoulder into the door again.

"It's over! Don't ever call me or try to see me, 'cause I'll kill you, muthafucka! I will kill you!" Tears poured down her face as she ran back down the hall to the elevator, pressing the down button repeatedly. She felt like a fool to have trusted a man.

"Aunt Penny was right!" she cried aloud as the elevator door opened and two couples already inside stared at her. Her hair was wildly about her face, hanging down her shoulders. She couldn't remember this depth of anger and her irritability followed her onto the elevator.

"What the fuck y'all looking at?"

She was hurting; she was losing herself in the betrayal of another man who was supposed to love and honor her.

No one said anything to her in the elevator, but she could see her reflection and those of the four other people in the elevator door. She didn't recognize herself. She felt like a child again, a little girl waiting for the judge to tell her where she was going. Waiting to see if her mother would be set free, wondering if her mother blamed her for everything. If her father was truly remorseful before passing away.

I will never trust another man again.

All the men in her life had let her down: her father, the boyfriends and now the man she had learned to believe in. Jimmie Fredericks face flashed in the mirror of the elevator door before quickly fading.

I shoulda known better… never again… never again. She thought as her phone rang. It was Kendal calling her. Mattie walked quickly through the hotel lobby as she spoke loudly.

"Fuck you and the horse your rode in on, muthafucka, you think I'm stupid. Don't ever fucking call me or even think my name! You're the worst kind of man because I trusted you and I believed in you. I gave you my everything, and you cheat on me, you gon' have a fucking slut up in your room? You are a whore. If I see you ever again, I'm gonna hurt you, if I find out who the bitch is I'm gonna fuck her up too! I'm gonna hurt you like you just ripped my heart out my chest, and I'm pregnant, you piece of shit, with your child, you damn bastard. I'm pregnant with your child, and you will support this baby, whether you like it or not. I came all the way to New York only to find out you're a self-centered, lying piece of shit. A man who lies about loving me, a man who uses words to make people vulnerable. Don't ever call me again. I'll tell you when my child is born, but leave me the fuck alone, or I may do something to you that I will not regret, Kendal, you muthafuckin' cheater!" Mattie hollered into the phone as she walked towards the revolving door.

The same people that had stared at her when she strutted in were now looking at her for a vastly different reason. Mattie knew she was uncontrollable with hatred and inconsolable now. She headed for the revolving door to leave, and as her feet hit the sidewalk she nearly passed out. Kendal was standing motionless outside, staring down at his phone with bewilderment.

The momentary shock passed when Kendal saw Mattie. He had no idea what to think as his mind raced back and forth. The attendant was attempting to hand Kendal the valet ticket, but Kendal was too far gone to think of anything other than the explosion directed at him.

. . .

"Hey" was all Kendal could muster up to say to Mattie, who was realizing that she made a grievous mistake as she tried back tracking in her mind as to what had just happened.

"I... I thought, there were noises... from the room... and... Shit, I'm sorry, baby! I'm so sorry!"

She was crying with her hair covering her face. Her hesitancy to take another step was warranted, so she waited as her heart raced, her chest tightened.

Kendal put his cell phone in the front pocket of his jeans and slowly approached Mattie without taking his eyes off her. There was a look of exasperation.

Oh God, what have I done? Please... please let him forgive me... She saw the pain in his eyes as she stood with her broken shoes in her hand and purse across her shoulder. She saw the confusing emotion on his face and pulled her shoes into her chest. She began to tremble.

"Baby, I..." her words were cut short as Kendal had closed the distance between them to simply wrap his arms around her, kissing her on the cheek to force the words into her ear.

"So, we're having a baby?"

The question should have been light, however, the flat tone of his words indicated Mattie had cut him deeply.

"Yes, we are."

Mattie tried to hug him tighter and repeat how she shouldn't have jumped to a conclusion and given him the benefit of the doubt. His embrace was rigid. Mattie had never felt. any type of distance when holding him. She broke down and began to cry harder. Unsure whether she was being forgiven or without any idea of what was to happen next, she would allow his lead.

LET THE WORLD SEE
CHAPTER 3

I'm sorry ... that I could… could ever doubt you. I said some fucked up things to you, but I thought, because there were loud moans and wild noises… people having sex…"

Although Kendal knew it boiled down to miscommunication, his heart was torn. In his mind, every moment since they had met at the spoken word event, he had been completely transparent. He had left nothing up to ambiguity. Kendal was a complete open book for her to read. He exposed himself intimately with emotion when speaking of how lost and unworthy he felt after losing Janine. Every hurdle Mattie had thrown at him, he stepped over with clear understanding that she had no competition. He loved her unquestionably, and she was having his baby, but her words cut him deeply.

They needed privacy to speak freely, without the eyes of New York city staring at them.

"Please, forgive me for ever doubting you as a man… my man. You didn't deserve that… my emotions are all over the place right now. Baby, I'm so sorry that I treated you with disrespect and went off on you, I'd be pissed too." Mattie held onto him as if she would never be able to put her arms around him again.

"Madison Imani Parks. Let's go sit down and talk. It's been a very weird night, and my mind can't stop spinning."

When she heard her full name roll off his lips, her heart sank. She steadied herself because passing out on a sidewalk in front of the hotel would only compound matters.

Kendal forced a smile on his face as he pulled away. He then tossed her shoes into the trash by the entrance.

As they walked back through the hotel's revolving glass door, Mattie knew that some of the conversations were being held about her, but she didn't care. She held onto Kendal's hand and gripped it harder than usual.

The front desk attendant looked up from his computer as his manager approached. The attendant was explaining something to the effect that other guests had complained about Mattie's disturbance with a quick glance towards them as they approached the counter.

The middle-aged woman dressed in a form-fitting, navy-blue skirt and blazer looked perturbed before excusing the front desk worker from his station. She then waved Kendal over to the counter.

Mattie noticed the ombré pixie cut hair before the woman's green eyes. Her almond complexion was nearly flawless and as she spoke with an island accent. Mattie expected that she would not be allowed to stay at the hotel.

"Mr. Scott, my husband, and I saw the show. It was amazing! I bought... well I have a magazine in my office that you are gracing the cover with the other artists. Would it be awkward to ask if you could sign it, and maybe a few more like Kwame?" she asked in earnest while nodding to acknowledge Mattie.

"Of course," Kendal paused and stepped closer to be discreet.

"I apologize in advance for any extra attention brought to you because of a misunderstanding. I honestly thought you were going to ask me to leave," he laughed but had really thought that would be the outcome after being asked to approach the front counter.

Mattie kept her head low. She felt so embarrassed. She experienced a small bit of jealousy and admiration when the manager asked for an autograph but suppressed the emotion.

The manager was dismissive. "This is New York City; most of the people have seen worse. I do ask though, if there are any additional… 'misunderstandings'…," she paused, "… they are not loud enough to disturb our other valued guests."

The front desk attendant returned with small pieces of paper.

"Please, don't forget these" he offered.

The manager glanced at the written messages before handing them to Kendal.

"I know it has been a long day, so I won't hold you." She nodded at Kendal and glanced at Mattie, who for the first time made eye contact with her.

"Thank you," Mattie mouthed to the manager for her kindness, the short-haired woman simply nodded with one eyebrow raised.

Kendal pivoted away from the counter with Mattie still gripping his hand. She held her gaze lowered into his shoulder area, not wanting to make eye contact with anyone she had passed before. Kendal held his head high, smiling and making eye contact with those still nosey enough to be paying attention. His shoulders could carry the weight even if his heart was bruised.

The elevator door opened as they neared, an elderly couple walked out and smiled. Kendal smiled and nodded at the two before Mattie followed onto the elevator.

When the door closed behind them, Mattie stared into the mirrored reflection of the elevator while he pressed the number 34 on the pad.

Kendal's expression couldn't be read; she had pushed them into the deep end. Now she was uncertain how long she would have to tread water.

"I fucked up... and I..."

"Don't, just don't right now. I can't process another 'I'm sorry.' I should be happy to see you, elated to know that you are pregnant ... that we are having a baby. But after everything, what fucks me up the most, is that you don't know me as a man... that you would ever think... that you don't trust me." Kendal's voice was tense and before he could continue, the elevator stopped at an intermittent floor where two more occupants entered.

No more words were spoken as they waited to exit on their designated floor.

While they walked the dark wood hallway towards his room, silence was golden.

Kendal scanned his keycard for entrance.

The room was much larger than Mattie imagined. It was a suite, built with a wet bar, kitchen area and dining space. There was a Rock and Roll Hall of Fame in Cleveland she had visited, but this Hard Rock Hotel was an experience all to its own.

Kendal had released her hand as they walked in. He dropped his backpack onto the counter and opened the refrigerator. He held onto the top of the door as he stared at the options.

They were in a room remodeled and upgraded. The natural lighting shined through the large glass window, nearly spanning an entire wall. The city that never slept was alive as Mattie walked to stare out the window to gather her thoughts. She could make out the shapes and bodies of people walking in groups, or others navigating traffic.

An office light being turned off in an adjacent building only traced the silhouette of the people behind. Mattie was grateful Kendal had not turned on any lights yet, she was a mess and was afraid to see a clearer vision of the hurt in his eyes.

Kendal walked into the living space and offered Mattie a bottled water. She accepted. He walked to stare out the window as the billboard lights flashed on various building tops and structures designed to support advertisements.

"I probably should've told you my room number changed, but I didn't think… well, you know, that you would be coming to surprise me."

Kendal walked to the desk adjacent to the television and emptied his pockets before turning around to face her.

"Baby…" the tears flowed as she took small steps forward. Her purse still hung from her shoulders and the water bottle in her hand. Placing them on the table next to his, Mattie tried pushing her hair back from her face before she started speaking again.

"I thought it was you, and I just jumped from zero to 100, and I shouldn't have. Please forgive me. I know you're a better man than that. It's just, Aunt Penny said that surprises… surprises…" Mattie was unable to control her tears in between her words as she tried formulating one complete thought.

Kendal reached his hands out, extending his arms motioning her forward. His facial expression was blank as she took his hand. He searched for the right words to say. He was hurt, more shocked than anything, but as he had learned a long time ago, he had to forget his ego when love was involved. But this unexpected range of emotions was difficult. He had not put a lid on his anger, but he was trying.

Kendal held her again before responding.

"Listen, part of it is my fault. I shoulda told you about the room change, and honestly, it's no big deal; if had I thought you were with someone else, I…" he paused because he didn't want to imagine what he was speaking on.

Kendal wiped her face as he still attempted to swallow his pride before touching her stomach to change the subject.

"We have a child," he said it with affirmation and kissed her fully on the mouth with passionate force.

She would forever remember not to jump to conclusions again. As she wrapped her arms around his neck, her only thought was submitting to him. She felt the tension in her body releasing and the butterflies return as his hand slid up her body to the back of her neck, where he held onto and began kissing her more deeply.

She noticed his hands gripped her tighter, so she pulled him closer until there was no separation. With no warning, his hands traveled to her blouse, and he ripped her shirt off until only the straps hung to her frame. It shocked her. She accepted it.

Kendal didn't know why he felt more advancing than normal but each time their lips kissed, inside, he felt emotions of joy and pain. So, when he ripped her shirt, he was aware of his hand, and the gulf, the separation of his heart and mind emotionally.

"How could you ever think I would disrespect you, our union?" He whispered into her ear before pushing her back into the large glass pane with passion.

Kendal undressed without a care that the curtains were wide open. The red hoodie he wore with the tour dates on the back was thrown onto the bed. Even from this height, those in adjacent buildings could see them, and at the proper distance from the street below, their silhouettes were visible.

"The world will know that we belong together."

He closed the small distance and pulled Mattie's jeans and French-cut panties down to her ankles before sliding each one off. As Kendal stood back up to face her, she felt the intensity in his eyes. As the next seven words fell from his lips, she heard the tone of his conviction.

"Everybody will know that you are mine."

Mattie couldn't ascertain the display of energy from Kendal. There was more aggression in his touch, but it wasn't disrespectful. She allowed his control over her.

Kendal held no greater love in his heart for anyone than Mattie, and he felt torn. He had no other revelations hidden; perhaps this is what made him feel even more strange energy racing through his veins.

He kissed Matte with one hand gripping the side of her face. Her hair wildly placed was being pulled back with the other hand as he bit her neck.

"I belong to you, Madison, whatever it is. I am only yours…" his words lingered as he tightened the grip in her hair, making her stare into his eyes.

"…and you're mine. Let everyone know it, let everyone see us."

Mattie had never seen this deep intensity in his eyes, and as the billboard lights flickered, she felt overwhelmed. The world could see them, the outlines of their bodies were on display high in the skyline. She found herself being lifted to straddle him. His shaft was full, and even without foreplay, she was wet enough to welcome his fullness. She gasped as he pushed deeper inside. She held onto his shoulders, the only aspect that she was in control of. Mattie realized she was holding her breath to not scream because the pain was pleasure.

Kendal could feel the tightness even as Mattie's wetness flowed down his legs, and it stirred something basic in his nature. As Mattie dug her nails into his shoulder blades from pleasure, he pushed her back into the glass pane.

Mattie's eyes widened to look at him, she trusted him and would allow herself to be what he needed; whatever lust was in between them was superficial in this moment. It was more primordial than even basic human physical desire.

"I can feel you in my stomach!" Mattie had attempted to control her signs of pleasure, but the way she was pinned against the glass pane, the curve of his shaft hit something deep inside the upper wall of her cavity. She poured wetness down his legs as she squirted everywhere.

He forced himself back inside.

"You will feel me for the rest of your life. Don't you ever question my commitment to you!" Kendal pulled her away from the glass and used only the leverage of their bodies to keep pulling her into him. Her ass cheeks slammed against his upper thighs, each time she braced for the deep penetration. Each time he thrust and rotated his hips, she struggled to catch her breath.

Mattie found it hard to think as she fought off her second orgasm.

"I won't... won't doubt you... ever..."

"No, you won't ever doubt me again!" Kendal put her legs solidly onto the floor before spinning her around to press her breasts up against the clear glass pane for the world to see while pulling her hips backward into him.

"I have nothing to hide from you." Kendal grabbed Mattie by her hair and pulled it tightly again until her back arched. With his other hand he pressed her face into the glass pane and thrust himself inside of her.

Mattie's juices couldn't be contained. Her heightened sexual energy met Kendal's head on. She would be whatever he needed her to be, his woman, his friend, his slut. The pleasure was overwhelming, so she closed her eyes to maintain herself in the sporadic rhythm of their passion.

"Open your eyes and stare out into the world, let the world see us, let them all know since you doubted the man I have shown you to be. I keep nothing from you and now you're going to take ALL of me. I take ALL of you. All of you, until there is nothing left, and then I'm going to let the universe know that you belong to me!" Kendal's voice was just as firm as his member forcibly stroking deeply inside Mattie.

Mattie felt herself orgasming. She could feel her cavity begin convulsing and attempting to push him out of her, but Kendal wouldn't let her. He pushed his face into hers so that they were cheek to cheek. His hand grasped a full grip of hair as he kept forcing himself. The wetness poured out. Mattie was shaking. Overwhelmed, she pushed away from the window, causing him to momentarily remove his shaft, but he gripped her harder and reached his hand around to hold her neck as he forced her back into the glass pane.

"You're not going anywhere, until I say you can and that you know what I say is true down to your core, Madison Imani Parks!" He said each portion of her name succinctly.

Kendal became more assertive, and she desired every pulsating inch of his rod.

She had never been dominated like this.

"I believe you ... I be..." Mattie's words stuck in her throat as she had a third orgasm, more intense than ever, feeling his hardened shaft stretching the inside of her wet pussy.

"I am yours!" Mattie struggled to speak, and it came out more like a forced scream.

"... mind and body... Oh God, not again!" she exclaimed as she convulsed.

"...this puss..." Mattie held her words on her tongue because she lost her ability to breathe, she felt as if she was going to faint.

"This pussy is mine for the rest of your life. You are mine for the rest of your life, and this is yours!" Kendal bit his bottom lip and thrust his hips as Mattie stuck her backside into him. She would take all his sexual release even if it hurt; she was already pregnant, and even if she wasn't, she still would've welcomed every drop of his seed into her garden.

COULD IT BE
Chapter 4

Mattie didn't want to leave but she had to fly back four days after arriving. The nights and days seemed to blend in when she was in New York.

Kendal took her shopping, sightseeing, and to dinner before each show. They never spoke of her tirade again. He had been caught off guard by Mattie's emotions and the knowledge that she was pregnant, but he accepted her emotions and marveled that he was going to be a father.

They decided to tell Kendal's parents about the pregnancy after the first ultrasound, so he would wait to fly back in a few weeks to go to her doctor's appointment and then drive to Cleveland with a photograph of the baby.

Mattie had learned a valuable lesson about jumping to conclusions and doubting Kendal's love. She also learned another lesson: that he wasn't afraid to push her boundaries. Honestly, she enjoyed being dominated because she trusted him.

She was lying in bed, rubbing her stomach, and enjoying the solitary moment between herself and the life growing in her belly, when the first bang on her door startled her. The second knock brought her quickly into her present.

"Madison are you up, child? You can't sleep the whole day away. Sheila's here to see you." Aunt Penny knocked repeatedly on her bedroom door.

Ugh, that woman...what time is it? Mattie looked over to her alarm clock as it flashed 6:58pm, indicating the power had gone out due to a heavy thunderstorm and downpour that she slept through. She reached for her cell phone and saw that Sheila had called four times and then saw it was nearly 11:30 a.m.

"Ok Auntie, she knows! Just tell her to come..." Mattie attempted to respond but Aunt Penny had already opened her door before stepping to the side to let Sheila into her room.

"Hey girl," Mattie said with little energy to greet Sheila who was still wearing her nurse's uniform as she walked past the older woman.

"Hey, how do you feel? You're sleeping longer than usual. When you go back to work, you are going to be hurting as your body shifts," Sheila stated, slowly waiting for Aunt Penny to close the door behind her.

"I do feel sick to my stomach." Mattie sat up, adjusting the pillows by her headboard to sit back with a tad bit more comfort and hoping the nauseous feeling would pass.

"Well, you gotta eat something. You want me to grab some orange juice out of the fridge? Have you taken your vitamins today yet?" Sheila whispered. She knew how important prenatal vitamins were during the first trimester of pregnancy.

"Orange juice… ugh, the thought makes me wanna throw up." Mattie's squished her face together before getting out the bed to use the toilet. Her taste buds were changing, and OJ had grown disgusting. After washing her hands, she climbed back into bed.

"Well, you need to eat something for…" Sheila hesitated knowing Mattie's aunt could still be listening.

"…well, I'm gon' get you some water while you get your pills," she said in more hushed voice. Sheila left the room to get something other than orange juice out of the kitchen and returned with two bottles of water, an apple, and a strawberry Pop Tart.

Mattie was forced to prove to herself that it was mind over matter. She hated taking prenatal vitamins or any pills because they felt like they would get stuck going down her throat.

Mattie ignored her friend, rolled out the bed, and threw her dirty clothes lying on the floor into a basket. She was still catching up on rest since her return and had let some things fall to the side.

"Here." Sheila handed her a bottle of water.

Mattie put the pills in her mouth, took a swig of water, and swallowed.

"Damn, I hate the way pills feel going down, they always feel like they're gonna get stuck in my throat or something. I don't want this apple," Mattie replied petulantly, pausing wondering why her friend was there. She redirected her attention to Sheila while taking hold of the silver Pop Tart package.

"What's up? Is everything ok?" She knew that her friend had something on her mind just by the energy surrounding her. Sheila tried keeping her personal business secret even though she would occasionally spill the business of her friends, but right now she needed Mattie's opinion.

Sheila took the apple back from Mattie and bit into it slowly to gather herself.

Mattie surmised it had to be something heavy if Sheila hadn't picked her children up from their grandmother's house after the morning shift. She hated asking people for favors, especially on their father's side. Mattie sat back on the bed, crossing her legs in front of her to wait for Sheila's response.

"James wants to get back together. He's been keeping the kids; they're with him right now and he's been so different with me. We ain't been arguing, he's listening to me now... and trying to date me. Seriously, take me out and dates... but I'm scared." Sheila took another bite of the apple.

Mattie was taken off guard; this was the *last* thing she expected to hear. James and Sheila's divorce had been bad to say the least. He fought her on everything—everything that is, but the children. That fact alone had created major animosity. Even the funeral services for Grandma Redd had been escalated because James had abandoned his children one day earlier than the agreement. After the divorce, Sheila had to seek therapy to prevent a deeper depression; something she couldn't afford to slip into because she had custody of the children.

Mattie was going to take her time in responding because this was a serious matter. Not only for Sheila and James but the children and family. Sheila's brothers had threatened James on more than one occasion and had pulled a gun on him.

"Well... I think you have to use all the factors and plug them into the equation. Your mind and heart will be the biggest influence," she paused watching Sheila's eyebrows move closer together. Mattie readjusted the pillow she was propped on and decided to continue.

"...but you gotta think about how things were in the past and where they could possibly be in the future. For a person to change, it takes life-altering experiences. For James to be changing, something..." Mattie paused as her phone vibrated, indicating a text message had been received from Cindy, but she continued speaking with Sheila about her predicament.

"...something has had to have happened to him," Mattie finished and realized that her mother, while she waited to stand trial, had also changed after shooting her father and as she did time in prison. Only Grandma Redd had been allowed to visit her in person. The wound of the ordeal had calloused, but on occasion the scab was pulled open by an unsuspecting memory.

Sheila's phone chimed and flashed as a text message shown.

"Cindy?" Mattie asked as Sheila threw her phone onto the bed.

"Yeah," Sheila paused after confirming. The weight of the topic about James and her marriage to him was heavy.

"I don't know what's going on with James. Honestly, I'd say a midlife crisis but he's only 36." Sheila forced a smile, attempting to joke.

"Well, has he stopped seeing that girl? Tasha? Maybe he's realizing what he had in you?" Mattie ate a corner of the Pop Tart. She didn't intend to dive into the affair James had with his assistant. Sheila had walked in on them while she rubbed his shoulders with her bare breasts pressed against his back.

Sheila sat back on Mattie's bed next to her friend after kicking her running shoes off.

"That tramp been gone, back to Louisiana, I think." Sheila paused, noticing her tone was changing. She wouldn't let the past be a trigger.

"I don't know. I married him because I loved him. Then I divorced him because I hated him."

Mattie bit her bottom lip because that wasn't actually true. The hate part.

"Well, I hated what he did to me and the children when he walked out because he needed time... time for what, I don't know... I just don't know." Sheila had grown wiser over the years and more self-sufficient. Financially, she didn't need James or any other man, but she loved him. She took another bite of the apple.

Mattie hesitated because she really didn't know what other advice to give her friend. A family unit was good when children were involved. She knew that 63% of suicides were from single mothers, while 90% of homelessness and runaway children were from single mothers. But James had scarred Sheila with his infidelity, not to mention missing child support payments on purpose simply to make her life more difficult. James was a good earner but had issues in the past of being a good man. There was no indication now of why he had changed.

"Well, whatever you do, take your time… it's no rush. You want to make sure that he ain't trying to play games. Just be patient is the best advice I can give." Mattie leaned over to give her a friendly shoulder bump. Mattie's phone vibrated again at nearly the same time Sheila's phone chimed.

CINDY: I said call me, damnnit.

Sheila dialed Cindy's number, and when she answered the phone, her personality came blaring through.

"Look I don't know why you are taking all day to call me back. I'm all out of my element!" Her voice seemed to amplify before she was interrupted.

"What Cindy, you ain't closed on that house yet, or you don't know what shoes to wear to set your outfit off… or…" Sheila was responding in the same over dramatic tone Cindy had taken, but silenced her words after Cindy stated her next five words.

"I think I've fallen in love."

Sheila didn't say another word; instead, she passed the phone to Mattie. She wasn't equipped to respond.

"Here, you gotta hear this for yourself."

"Hey girl what's up?" she asked instead.

"Oh, y'all two been sitting around bumping y'all gums and can't call me back. Bogus, both of y'all, just bogus. Listen, I don't know what to do. I'm confused, and I don't like being confused." Cindy's voice slightly hesitant, which was very much unlike her.

"Confused about what, will you just spit it?" Mattie put the phone call on speaker just as Cindy blurted out, "I think I'm in love, Mattie."

Mattie looked over at Sheila, who in turn raised her eyebrows and shook her head back and forth. She still didn't know what to say.

"Uh, with who, Cynthia?"

"With Peter Hanford, the general manager from the dealership. What the hell am I supposed to do? I've been taking him lunch and moving my schedule around to spend time with him. I'm losing control... I'm... I'm... I'm on my way over. Y'all not doing anything are you?" Cindy paused.

"Hold on. Is Aunt Penny there?" Cindy asked flatly.

"Where else she gon' be?" Mattie answered just as flatly.

"To hell with that. Can y'all meet me at the house? We can talk over margaritas... well Sheila and I can drink but come over."

Sheila nodded her head in agreement before responding.

"I can go for a minute, not long. I told James that I would pick the kids up by 2, and I plan on doing exactly that." Her voice was steadfast.

"Ok, we'll be over. I just need to take a quick shower. I'm gon' ride with Sheila, so you'll have to bring me back later." Mattie made sure everyone was on the same page for their afternoon. Her affinity for public transportation was waning as her pregnancy progressed.

"Ok... ok, just hurry up because I don't know what to do and I ain't feeling like myself." Cindy hung up without saying goodbye.

"Damn, we all got some shit going on." Sheila blurted out before finishing off the apple.

Mattie shook her head in agreement before getting out the bed to take a shower.

Mattie didn't have any issues for herself; she was in love and pregnant with the man she would share the rest of her life with. Well, if he asked; but her friend's concerns were hers too.

They left shortly after Mattie dressed as Aunt Penny prepped dinner.

As Sheila and Mattie drove up the long, semi-circle driveway to Cindy's house, a basketball came flying over the hedges. The landscape between Cindy's and her neighbor's home almost blocked the view of each other's property, but with two teenage boys next door, basketballs and frisbees were retrieved periodically. The only reason Cindy had not complained in her usual fashion was due to the fact she received a nice discount on her landscaping because these same neighbors owned one of the better landscaping companies in Central Ohio.

Sheila's quick reaction to slam on her brakes was the only reason she didn't end up with a dent in the hood of her car.

"Damn, damn." Sheila watched the ball bounce past her car to slowly stop in the grass.

Two boys pushed through a thin portion of the hedges and waved as if to apologize.

Cindy's home sat back from the road on a slight descending grade. It was large when looking at it from the outside. Built of brick, she had two enormous front windows equidistant from the front door and foyer. Her decision to have multicolored plants and shrubs decorating her lawn added to the beauty of her home. A small center piece of a unicorn surrounded by a water fountain in the front yard fit the home and landscaping perfectly.

Mattie told her years ago to get the driveway paved, but Cindy loved the white pebbles lining her entrance. The dust of the gravel was one reason she made sure she got free car washes with her most recent car purchase.

With one large oval window above the front door entrance, the staircase leading to the second floor could be seen from the outside.

Cindy opened her front door before Mattie and Sheila exited the minivan. She had a margarita glass in her hand filled to the top with an excessive amount of salt on the rim.

"It took y'all long enough. I'm in a crisis, heifers." Cindy walked to greet her friends wearing khaki shorts, a white tank top, and pink slides.

As she hugged Mattie, one of the teenage boys from next door was entering her yard to retrieve the basketball again.

"We're sorry Ms. Champion," he called out politely.

Cindy simply waved her hand and smiled at the young man before returning her attention to Sheila, who had her hand on Cindy's shoulder.

"They almost put a dent in my van," Sheila added with a smirk on his face.

"Girl, if I had a quarter for every time I almost fell victim to their escapades, I'd own their house by now," she paused.

"Come on, I got margaritas, and I made some wings 'cause I know yo' ass ain't ate yet." The last part was meant exclusively to Mattie.

The house was always impeccable. Her marble tiling and Venetian theme decorations complemented each other. She chose Old Victorian style furniture in most rooms to give it an old money feel, but her kitchen was modern with all the amenities. The smell of food brought Mattie's appetite to the forefront, so as Cindy poured Sheila's glass of drink, Mattie made her a plate with wings, carrots, and ranch dressing. Even with Cindy's house being immaculate, she had them eating off blue plastic plates.

"Y'all want to sit on the patio?" Cindy headed for the French doors, assuming they'd follow.

The cultivated backyard was more spectacular than her front.

Cindy's pride and joy was the gazebo that overlooked a medium-sized manmade pond. The distance between her back patio and the gazebo was nearly 30 yards and the walkway, like the front, was paved with white pebbles and solid stones for good footing and surrounded by various plants. On the opposite side of the gazebo was a clear picturesque view of the Scioto River.

The sun had beams of rays beating down, so Cindy extended the umbrella cover on the square patio table.

"What am I gon' do?" Cindy moved her chair to face both of her friends.

Mattie had been thinking about Cindy saying she thought she was falling in love from the moment Cindy had said it on the phone. Truth was Mattie knew her friend was in love just by acknowledging it. Cindy juggled men; for her, men came a dime a dozen, with insecurity issues and just plain scandalous behavior.

"What's wrong with being in love?" Sheila asked no one in particular while sipping on her margarita.

"I ain't saying nothing was wrong with being in love. I asked what am *I* gon' do?" Cindy paused, taking her hand to shoo a fly away.

"He's a good man for the most part, and I can't help thinking about his ass constantly. I've been giving him so much of my time that I'm losing control of things that I should not lose control of. He works like 12 to 13 hours a day in that dealership, but he wants to own one, so he works hard for it. I take him lunch or send him dinner. I been texting him more than I do y'all and…" Cindy hesitated again.

"He be putting it on a sista." She finished with a smile on her face.

"So, he's whipping you, is what you're saying. You're whooped," Mattie added as her and Sheila laughed. Mattie dipped a carrot into her ranch dressing and waited for a reply.

"Whipping it ain't the word, but it's more than that. He's got ambition and drive. Ain't never been married… no kids… it just seems too perfect to be true." Cindy responded.

The sprinkler system coming on turned Mattie's head to the lawn.

"Maybe it's your time, Cindy. Think about it! All the guys you meet and drop because they don't meet your criteria: too short… wrong smell… can't kiss. Whatever the reason, they just weren't your match! You gotta have someone that fits and has a life of their own, so they don't crowd you." Sheila's assessment contained much truth to it.

Cindy agreed. She had already decided that she would let things run their natural course, but it felt good having company and some positive reinforcement.

"What does he say though?" Mattie was learning that love and emotions were a two-way street that you didn't want to be on alone.

Cindy was hesitant before answering.

"Well to be honest, he says he enjoys my company and loves spending time with me. He hasn't really got all... you know... *open* about stuff. But he's sent flowers and cards to the office," Cindy replied, waving her hand across her face again because the insect was still flying close.

"I think you should take your time and feel it out, no need to rush. I mean a man's gotta earn what he's gotta earn," Sheila added as if she were answering her own question.

"That's damn good advice for the both of y'all," Mattie blurted out realizing that Sheila may not have wanted to share her story about James yet.

"Yeah... yeah... we all can't have the perfect man like you got, Pocahontas." Cindy joked before reaching over to eat one of Mattie's wings.

"And what's up with you? Something going on with you too huh? Spit that shit out," Cindy began addressing Sheila.

Mattie took that as a cue to get more carrots and chicken wings. As she excused herself, Sheila began to tell Cindy about James. When Mattie returned, Cindy was finishing telling Sheila what she thought and from the looks of it, Sheila wasn't necessarily agreeing.

"His punk ass plays too many games! You a good woman and mother. Your problem is you don't date anybody. I don't know why you haven't called the bodyguard who shielded you the night Mattie went all Kill Bill at event night. You gotta put yourself in the game if you gonna play. It's like someone always wanting to hit the lottery, but they never buy a ticket. You're too good of a woman for his sorry ass," Cindy paused as Mattie sat back down shaking her head in disagreement.

"What? I'm just keeping it real." Cindy finished off her drink.

"The bodyguard? I forgot he slid his business card to me. I'll find those jeans and get it for you, my bad." Mattie had completely forgotten about that. He was Sheila's type, but she knew her friend had been embarrassed a little.

Sheila smirked at her friends before scooting her chair back.

"You want another one?" Sheila asked Cindy as she stood up to refill her glass. She wasn't ready to hear any more of her friend's opinion.

"Oh yeah, thank you. I didn't mean it all funky, you know that." Cindy handed her the glass making sure the two made eye contact before turning her attention to Mattie.

"And what the hell? You eating chicken with mustard and relish, mixing carrots with ranch dressing, and topping it off with cranberry juice? Girl, there's Pepsi in there for you." Cindy reached over for a carrot before trying to eat a wing from Mattie's plate with mustard.

"I know. I've had some strange cravings, and Pepsi... I don't want to drink Pepsi anymore." Mattie shook her head while rubbing her stomach.

"Well, this is good; you keep reminding me not to get pregnant. I should just go get my tubes tied. I don't want no ragamuffins... no offense," Cindy finished as she put the wing with mustard back on Mattie's plate.

"Ugh... just nasty." Cindy frowned in reference to trying the mustard on the chicken wing.

Sheila returned with both glasses full of liquid and rejoined the conversation.

"After this I gotta pick the kids up. I ain't giving James nothing to complain about." Sheila sat back down as Cindy belched.

"What, y'all hookers do the same damn thing!" Cindy hesitated as her neighbors walked hand in hand down at the edge of the property, taking in the view of the river. The couple, in their early sixties, had born children late but looked to be enjoying life. They waved at the group on the deck and Cindy waved back.

"They seem happy." Mattie watched them make their way past Cindy's home.

"They cool as long as they keep my landscaping bill down," Cindy laughed out loud.

Both Mattie and Sheila shook their heads. Cindy was holding true to form.

Mattie had Cindy drive her home shortly after Sheila left. Aunt Penny texted Mattie that she would be waiting to be taken to the store because she was in the mood to cook and needed a couple more items. Throughout the entire conversation with her friends, Aunt Penny had called Mattie several times, but Mattie let it go to voicemail. Her aunt could wait for a change.

When they pulled up to Mattie's home, she saw Geri's SUV parked on the street, and Geri and Aunt Penny were getting out with bags. Aunt Penny scowled at Mattie, shook her head, and began walking up the steps to the house.

A horn blowing from a car running the light at an intersection drew their attention away momentarily.

Aunt Penny went inside the house, Geri reached into her back seat and handed Mattie two plastic bags with grocery items in them.

"People in Columbus just can't drive," Geri exclaimed before walking over to Cindy's car.

"What's up, mama?" She made sure she wasn't in direct line with oncoming traffic.

"Shit… what's up is you and Aunt Penny being BFFs? I don't know how you do it 'cause she damn near be cursing me out all the time." Cindy sat back in her car seat and exhaled.

"It ain't easy, but that old lady really got a heart of gold, and she loves Mattie for real. I just don't say much and put the radio on a gospel channel to let her sing while I drive," Geri paused as her text alert sounded.

MATTIE: HELP!!

"Oh God, I think Aunt Penny dun started in on our girl. You sure you don't want to come eat? She bought catfish, okra, and a bunch of sides?" Geri asked, looking back again at traffic.

Cindy put her left index finger up to her lips as if she truly debated the answer.

"Well… uh ... no," she decided, as both women laughed.

"That's cool. I'm going to church this Sunday, and you should come. There's a guest speaker coming from Arkansas, and they say she's pretty good. If not, we can do happy hour early next week, just not on Monday." Geri finished by tapping the top of Cindy's car.

"Yeah, that sounds good." Cindy pulled off while turning her radio up to Kendrick Lamar's newest release.

Geri shook her head to the beat as she walked up the stairs to Mattie's place to lend her friend some support.

MORE TO LIFE

CHAPTER 5

"**S**o how have you been, Madison?" Dr. Stevens asked as he sat back in his black leather chair. His office had still been the same over the years. Two windows were opened; one was overlooking a ravine on one side with benches surrounding it, and out of the other window only trees could be seen. A bathroom sat off to the right-hand side of the office with a small silver and black refrigerator situated outside its door.

Mattie, who sat on the white loveseat across from him, was second-guessing herself on why she had even come to her psychologist appointment. Part of the reason was that she promised Kendal she would; the other part she was still unsure on. She had been anxious a lot lately, but she attributed that in fact to the chemistry changing inside her body.

"I couldn't be better, honestly," she answered as her eyes focused in on a few picture frames on the wall with his accreditations. He was much older than she remembered when she first saw him with much more gray in his hair than black.

"Sounds like life has been treating you well. And you've met someone substantial?" Dr. Stevens asked, not taking his eyes from Madison.

"Oh well yeah, I did. I did."

"Well, I bet he is a wonderful man. How did the two of you meet?" The doctor asked casually but Mattie knew there was always something methodical behind his questions.

Mattie told him the story of the poetry night and joy was heard coming out of her voice as she described the poem that Kendal had impulsively made for her.

"Wow, that's a great story! Maybe he will write it down. It could be the beginning of a wonderful book," he paused. "Would you like some water?"

"No… no thank you."

She was thirsty, but she had to pee and didn't want to use the restroom right now. Water would only make matters worse.

"I'm amazed at your progress, Madison; it's been a long journey for you," he simply stated followed by silence.

"I guess… I guess it has been, you're right." Mattie could feel him probing. While she had promised Kendal that she would come to the appointment, that didn't mean she had to engage in much conversation.

"Is there anything else you want to tell me, besides you met someone?" he asked exploring deeper.

Mattie thought about telling him that she was pregnant but decided against it. Her childhood had been spent in and out of this office, and she wasn't going to allow her child to be tainted by her past.

"No… not really. I thought I needed some guidance after my grandma passed away, but I think I've been dealing with it in a healthy manner." She felt the answer sufficient.

"How so?" He sat back, crossing his legs over one another.

"What do you mean how so?"

She knew Dr. Stephens was a tricky one.

"What does 'dealing with it in a healthy manner' mean?" He pushed her a little further with a gentle nudge.

"Well, for one, I have accepted that she's no longer here and has moved on to heaven. Acceptance, as you've always told me, is a positive tool," she responded by giving him his own words, so that he didn't have much of anywhere else to go.

"Absolutely, it is a positive tool. Your grandmother was a great influence on your life," he paused to ask the real question he needed to know the answer to. "Are you upset at the person responsible for inflicting her injuries?" He adjusted his glasses up onto his nose as he met her eyes and waited.

Mattie sat back on the loveseat and sighed before answering.

"Of course I'm upset. Wouldn't you be upset? Honestly, who wouldn't be pissed-the-fuck off. I wish I would've locked the patio door, but I didn't!" She felt agitated.

"So, do you think you're partly to blame? Have you fought yourself on that issue at all?" he asked in a monotone voice.

Mattie had not thought about that aspect in such a long time. She pushed those thoughts into a compartment of her mind that she was willing to leave sealed, but now within 20 minutes of this session, she was being asked to face it head on.

"Maybe I do feel somewhat responsible. Maybe I should have called her to remind her to lock the patio door. Maybe, but I am in a place that I can't go back and change anything about that night now, can I?" She was becoming defensive. Her tone had changed, and she crossed her arms.

Dr. Stevens shook his head in agreement before uncrossing his legs to lean forward.

"Well, I agree with you, Madison. We can only be responsible for our actions," he paused again jotting something into his notepad.

Mattie always hated it when she said something that he would scribble down.

"So, Kendal… it is Kendal, right?"

Mattie nodded her head.

"Does he know much about your past? Have you felt comfortable sharing the early portion of your life with him? I ask because so much of the future is influenced by the past," he concluded as he picked up his coffee mug to take a sip from.

Mattie had shared bits and pieces of her past with Kendal. He knew Mattie's mom shot her father and was locked up, refusing her visits and letters for over 18 years. He knew her grandmother was awarded custody and that her father died but not before leaving her an insurance policy that would take care of her financially for the rest of her life. But the complete truth of the matter was, she had not told Kendal the "exact" cause of it all.

"He knows enough. I'm sure there are minor points of his life that he may not have told me yet, but he knows enough," she answered straightforwardly and without emotion. She tugged on the strings to Kendal's red hoodie before biting the end of the string.

"So, when you say 'yet,' you do plan on telling him one day... perhaps?" He wasn't pressing her as directly as he wanted. He knew he needed to back off a little; fidgeting with the string was a sign that his client was a tad bit uncomfortable.

Mattie began thinking deeper about the question. Did he have a right to know that her father was high on drugs and tried to rape her? Did he have a right to know that, in some sick way, she felt guilty for that night? That maybe it was her fault that her family had been torn apart. It took a while for Mattie to respond, but Dr. Stevens simply waited.

"Perhaps one day I'll tell him, but no time soon." She sat back up on the white loveseat and crossed her legs. She began feeling the barriers she had set up on her past loosening and felt uncomfortable. Dr. Stevens seemed to know what stirred her mentally and what made her think outside of her comfort zone. In her early years, she resisted his questions as rebellion. It had taken Mattie some time to be brave enough to admit that her therapy over the years had made her stronger in the end.

"Well, if he's the man you believe him to be, I'm sure he'll be supportive and understand," he paused again to change the subject.

"How are your friends doing? Do you still see them regularly? I think the last time we talked, Cindy was growing her real estate business, and Geri was close to a breakthrough with her publication. I'm sure they're happy for you," he said lightheartedly.

Either he's got an excellent memory or just keeps good notes. Mattie had once wondered if he had a photographic memory like her mom.

"They're doing good. Cindy is still doing real estate, and she's very successful. Geri's magazine may be going nationwide if this partnership pans out. You've got a good memory, Doc." Mattie wanted to acknowledge him.

"Well, it's not what it used to be, but I'm trying to maintain as I 'mature,'" he laughed slightly.

"And are you still working for that communications company?"

"Yeah, I'm still there." Her tone carried a little more negativity than she intended.

"Do you still like working there? I remember one of your main reasons for accepting the position was for healthcare and benefits for your grandmother and yourself. Does it still fulfill your needs?" He asked casually and placed his ink pen into his shirt pocket.

"Actually, I went back to work for one day after the funeral services, but I've been on disability ever since. I've gotta go back tomorrow though."

"Are you ready?" Dr. Stevens probed.

"As ready as I'll ever be I guess." Mattie saw the expression on his face shift.

"Hmm…" he leaned forward.

"Here's just a thought for you. If those same reasons no longer exist when you took the position, have you considered doing something different at this stage in your life? Something you enjoy doing. So much of your life has been doing what others needed you to do. You went to college because you wanted to make your grandma proud. You accepted the job for the health benefits, but what do you want to do, Madison? That's the question." He stood up and walked towards his desk.

Mattie just realized that the 50-minute session was over.

"Would you like me to pencil you in on the schedule?"

Mattie was thinking about everything he asked.

What did she actually enjoy? What did she want for the rest of her life, besides being with Kendal?

"I can get you in here in two weeks from today at the same time." Dr. Stevens affirmed without being pushy.

"That's fine, Doc." She waited until he handed her the reminder card for the next appointment.

I'll cancel it more than likely, she thought, walking out of the office and seeing the little boy in the waiting room chair, nervous for his turn with Dr. Stevens.

MASCULINE ENERGY
CHAPTER 6

The next morning came a lot sooner than Mattie had anticipated. She stayed up Tuesday night speaking with Kendal on the phone about dates for them to take their first planned vacation together before she got too big.

Taking the escalator up to her department felt weird. Three months of being away from her place of employment wasn't long enough, but as her paperwork indicated, today was the day of return.

"Your badge please." A security guard she wasn't familiar with asked for her credentials.

Mattie forgot to attach her badge to her pants; luckily, she carried the same backpack and knew both her id and swipe card were in the bottom somewhere.

"How long you been here?" Mattie asked as she showed him her badge, knowing she had never seen him before.

"Two months... well three, but out on the floor for two months," he answered dryly, handing her identification card back.

After showing her badge and using her swipe card, she proceeded through the double doors into her department. The office had changed. There were no more partitions separating the desk. Grace told her that other offices in the region had gone through the same change and had increased productivity. Mattie shook her head, thinking the company was always shifting away from its people and towards their bottom line—profit. That's why the company had been having a higher turnover rate lately.

She walked to where her desk had been when she left, but someone was sitting there taking calls on the phone already.

"This is Vincent, how may I make sure you are satisfied with this call today?" he spoke to a client through his headset. He was new to her department, but she had seen him the day she went out on disability.

God I'm not ready for this, she thought as she walked the floor of her department and passed a few empty desks.

"Hey Madison, welcome back!" An older man named Bob greeted her as he carried an enormous container of ice water and bag of potato chips in his hands.

"Hey Bob, it's good to be back... kinda, I guess." The two of them laughed.

"So, where's Ms. Grace sitting now?" Mattie looked around for her older counterpart.

"Oh well, just follow me. They have us sitting by productivity and not seniority anymore." He led the way to the other end of the floor.

Bob had been with the company for 22 years and only had six months left until retirement. Grace was only one year from retiring, but each employee who had gotten close to their end date knew the company would make things difficult for them.

"Yeah, this new girl is from San Antonio, Texas, and she only looks at the numbers. So, *you* really don't have anything to worry about, but old Bob is holding on by the seat of his pants. I remember when I first started here, life was good. Now we got quotas on quotas," he finished as he pointed at Grace sitting at her desk staring down at her checkbook.

"Hey Mrs. Grace." Mattie walked up behind her.

Grace stood up and gave Mattie a hug.

"Grace, you look like you're figuring some stuff out," she paused to scan the area again. "Things look so different around here," she concluded.

"*Look* so different? Things are *very* different, and this new broad don't be playing. Ain't no more putting the customer on hold or taking a few extra minutes for lunches or breaks. They monitor everything. There she goes right now," Grace huffed and pointed at a black woman with micro braids walking down an aisle leading to her manager's office. She wore a navy-blue pant suit with a white blouse. Her cell phone was plastered to her ear, and she was holding papers in her hand. From the looks of it, she wasn't very pleased.

"Mrs. Pamela Stover from San Antonio. She's the one the company sends in to either increase productivity or close the center. Her turnaround time for us was six months, and I've got less than one year, one measly year before I can retire," Grace said with a little concern in her voice.

"We gon' be fine Mrs. Grace. It can't be that bad," Mattie tried reassuring her friend.

"I don't know. Whenever we have morning meetings, she gives us our percent to goal, or some metric with something negative to say," Grace sighed. "You know, what this isn't how you're going to start your first day back at work. They put your stuff over here." Grace pivoted and led Mattie to a desk that was right next to the restrooms.

"Are you serious?" Why was her desk, of all people, stationed outside the employee restrooms on this floor?

With no response from her older counterpart, Mattie knew she was dead serious.

"This is not going to work. I'm not sitting outside of the bathrooms so that every time that door opens, I get a whiff of ungodly smells." Mattie's voice carried further than she would've liked.

"Girl, you do what you gotta do, but I have to make a phone call to the bank because they put two charges on my account, making me overdrawn, and I only have ten minutes. I'll come back on break," Grace said taking her cell phone out to dial the number to the bank.

There is no way in hell I'm going to be sitting here, Mattie thought, opening the top of her filing cabinet. The menus of nearby restaurants were scattered. There were packets of sugar and other condiments on top of pictures that she had of her grandmother. An open pack of ketchup had stained one of her pictures.

"Fuck!" Mattie said without disregard to anyone in earshot.

"Excuse me!" A woman's voice said sharply.

As Mattie turned around Pamela Stover, the manager, was standing behind her.

"Oh, my file cabinet is a mess! Someone ruined a picture of my grandmother and just ransacked my stuff." Mattie turned to face the new manager with her desk drawer still opened as evidence.

"We don't use profanity on the work floor. I take it then that you are Ms. Parks," the manager spoke in a superior tone, and it rubbed Mattie the wrong way.

"I am Madison, yes," Mattie responded, already seeing this had got off on the wrong foot. She wasn't sure if it was the chemicals changing her body or if the distaste was genuine.

"If you will meet me in my office, we can discuss your success plan before you get back on the phone. Bring a union steward if you like." Without waiting for a reply, she walked into the women's bathroom.

Mattie had no doubt that she didn't like this woman. She sought the help of a union steward and stood outside Mrs. Stover's office waiting for her to return.

"Ok, come in," she said after returning from the rest room.

Mattie sat in one of the two chairs on the opposite side of the desk. and the male union steward, Kevin, sat down next to her.

"Do you have everything you need?" Mrs. Stover asked Kevin.

"Yes," he answered.

"Ok, first things first: the language you used on the floor was not appropriate. At this time, I am informing you that you will receive a verbal warning. Any additional warnings for language will result in a suspension, and any subsequent will result in a suspension pending termination," she said in a matter-of-fact voice.

Mattie looked at the union steward, who was writing down what was being said, but did not look up or verbally respond.

"Hold on a sec. I wasn't even logged in or on the phone when I said that. You saw the condition of my filing cabinet and personal items, and no one was even around me!" Mattie wasn't going to let her say just anything, even though she understood that the manager's concern had merit.

"So, you just admitted that you did use inappropriate language in the workplace?" Mrs. Stover quickly interjected.

The union steward shook his head and kept writing.

Mattie felt ambushed and decided to stay quiet. She would ask Kevin why he hadn't spoken up in her defense and remind him that it was his duty to protect her as an employee.

"Now that we have that minor stuff out of the way, the second item of business is quite simple. We are here to service the customers and collect monies from them. We are scheduled for two 15-minute breaks and one 30-minute lunch. These times have been calculated to maximize productivity. You are not here to socialize. You can do that on your own time, not company time. We have goals to meet: hourly, daily, weekly, and monthly. My job is to ensure that we hit those goals. I always expect professionalism. If you fail to be professional in my work environment, then expect to be terminated. You've been gone three months on disability Ms. Parks, but the ship has sailed so you will either row or sink." She paused to look at the time on her computer screen.

"It is ten minutes after 8. I believe you can get situated by 8:30 and have your line open ready to receive calls. Do you have anything to add?"

"I have been gone three months. Company policy states that I must be updated on systems and changes, and that normally takes…" Mattie tried saying before she was rudely interrupted by her new manager.

"No system or policy changes have taken place since you have been gone. We're here to work, Ms. Parks. It's now 12 minutes after 8 and you have until 8:30 to be logged on. Thank you," she ended abruptly, looking at both Mattie and Kevin as if they overstayed their welcome.

Mattie was seconds away from cussing her out but instead she found herself asking the union steward why he said nothing as they exited her office.

"We're filing grievances against her on all levels, but it takes time. Trust me, nobody likes that bitch," he replied to her look, watching over his shoulder to make sure no one heard him.

"That shit was ridiculous! I'm telling you now if she says anything else to me today, you gon' need more than a grievance to take my foot out her ass." Mattie stormed back towards her desk. She turned her computer on to let it boot up and then snatched her headset out of her drawer.

Walking to Grace's desk, she started calming down. She sat on the edge of Grace's desk, but Grace looked up and at once wrote on a memo pad: "We can't have visitors at our desk."

Mattie shook her head and walked back to her desk, wondering why she had even bothered to come back to work. Back at her own desk, she arranged a few pictures and items to feel more comfortable. She looked at the time and still had five minutes to text Kendal good morning.

MATTIE: I work under the wicked witch :(

"We can't have cell phones on the floor," Bob said as he walked by going into the bathroom.

Mattie shook her head in disbelief.

"Yeah, I know… things have changed. Just fly under the radar," he said before disappearing into the restroom.

The smell coming out from behind the door nearly made Mattie throw up. As Mattie put her headset on and opened her line, a male's voice was beeping in, so she read the new greeting posted on her monitor.

"This is Madison! How may I make sure you are satisfied with this call today?" she asked, waiting for a response.

"Uh, yeah, I got my cell phone, house phone, television, and internet with y'all, and I just wanna get all that shit turned off. I keep getting charged for 900 numbers each month and adult movies and don't nobody here watch that shit or call those numbers," the man said, clearly offended.

Mattie scanned the past four monthly invoices and saw a pattern of movie rentals and 900 numbers. Each month, the man called threatening to turn his services off; each month, he received a credit to retain him as a customer.

"I understand, and I'll be glad to take a look at it for you. Now, I do see that we've credited the past few months for those charges, and we've asked if you wanted us to block them, which we did. But later, the block was removed. I can put a passcode on your account and then issue you a credit for half the charges for you," Mattie said, knowing that all the charges were valid, but she was willing to have the company eat half the charges.

"Half… half, just turn all my shit off. I can go somewhere else; don't nobody here be watching no adult flicks. I'm a grown ass man, so cut my shit off if you're not going to give me a full credit," he escalated his tone.

Something clicked in Mattie. She thought about what Dr. Stevens had asked her, if she enjoyed what she did for a living. The answer was a pure and simple NO.

Mattie looked down at Grace and wondered how much pressure she faced, knowing in three months she could be out of a job without a retirement package. She heard the bathroom door opening and Bob coming out. She saw the new manager pacing the floor with her headset on, monitoring calls, and then she heard the customers' voice again.

"Did you hear me; don't nobody call 900 numbers or buy adult videos! Either take all the charges off or just turn all my services off today, and I'll go somewhere else," the man demanded with the same superior tone Pamela Stover had taken.

Mattie knew that this was going to be the final call she ever would take for the company as escalation specialist or

employee of any kind. She adjusted her headset and then
responded.

"I hear what you keep saying over and over again, but
the fact of the matter is this. I can tell by the tone of your
voice that you be in the house late at night calling the 900
numbers and then ordering videos. Every muthafuckin'
month, you call up to get a credit. Over $300 worth of
credits per month. You can go out and buy some shit for
that amount. Don't be calling here asking for credits. You
spend 20 to 40 minutes on the damn phone, and less than
two minutes later you're ordering videos with yo' lame ass.
Be a man and go speak with a real woman instead of all
these fake scammers on the phone. All they're doing is
taking your money." Mattie took a deep breath and kept
going.

"You shouldn't have got credit for one single 900
number or adult flick. Somebody should have stepped up
and told you hell to the no. No credit, but they didn't, so
I'm going to do it now. Hell no… no credit, and because
we value you, we're going to accept your request and
disconnect all yo' shit. Right now, your television should
be off… your house phone and internet should be off, and
when you hear dead silence on your cell phone, you know
we have accommodated your wishes. We valued you as
a…" and then the line went dead, due to the fact Mattie had
placed each order to turn his services off with an override
code to make it immediate.

Mattie disconnected her end of the call and removed her headset. She felt nothing but empowered. Mattie looked at her computer screen, took the pictures of her grandmother out of her filing cabinet, and rolled her chair away from the desk. As she looked up, those people already on the phone were staring at her, while those just coming in stood in the aisles looking at her.

Pamela Stover was standing behind her as she turned around with the most amazed look on her face.

Mattie didn't give her time to say one word.

"Let me tell you something, so you understand me clearly. You can't just speak to anyone the way you want. Success ain't usurping authority like you think, you Ms. Thing. You're the person this company uses to do their dirty work—their rat face. And you walk around like you the shit because you've been getting' away with talking to people any old way. Well, I ain't the one, not today… not tomorrow… not ever.

"You're the worst kind of woman: taking on a man's characteristics, but you're not a man. Somebody, somewhere, hurt you and all you got left is your weak-ass ambition and masculine energy. The only reason I don't slap the shit out of you right now is because you're not worth my time. But I swear to you, if you even look like you're going to do or say something before I walk out those doors, you're going to wish you stayed in San

Antonio! And I dare you to try me!" Mattie finished her final speech by picking her army green book bag up, before throwing her badge and swipe card on the floor at Pamela's feet. As she prepared to leave, she waved to Grace and motioned for her to call her later.

Mattie flinched at Pamela, who covered her face like she was about to get hit.

"That's exactly what I thought," Mattie snorted, as she walked through the double doors.

Mattie took the escalator down, feeling relieved that she left the company in a way she could be proud of. She got bottled water and a fiber bar from the store and decided to walk to Geri's office nearly a mile and a half away.

. . .

"You did WHAT?" Geri exclaimed to Mattie after she sat down behind her desk. Geri's office was modernized with electric blinds to give her privacy; otherwise, it was surrounded with glass. The furniture in her office was a combination of black and white colors, and she accented it with red accessories.

"I quit in the most dramatic way. I kinda felt like Cindy would've done it the same way," Mattie laughed, feeling like a weight had been lifted off her shoulders as she drained the contents of her water bottle.

"Oh my God, I wish I could have been there! So you got bout it with the customer and the manager. They must have pushed you something fierce." Geri waved an assistant with a stack of papers in her hand through the door.

"Mondays are always busy. Artists and writers submit their work; advertisers try to get more space for their money. We're doing well. I'd give you a job but you ain't cussing me out," Geri grinned as her phone rang.

"Yes?" she answered. "Ok, send it through." She held up one finger to tell Mattie to give her a minute to take the call.

Mattie stood up and walked around the office. She noticed the pictures Geri had up of her parents' thirtieth wedding anniversary party. They still looked happy to be together after three decades. To the right of that picture was another one of the four friends; it was no mistake that all four of them were drunk.

But that night was a blast, Mattie thought.

Geri had a few more pictures that she had taken with national recording artists and athletes. As Mattie walked behind Geri's desk, she saw a photo from college of the group of friends when they went white water rafting in West Virginia for college credits. Halfway down the rapids, Cindy fell out of the raft and almost drowned. It was an experience that they had learned to laugh about over the years.

"They presented a good offer, all things considered. It would add a good deal of money into our financial statement so we could reach beyond the Midwest. But at the rate where growing… we're already getting subscribers from the West Coast and down south. Sure," Geri said as she listened to the voice on the other end.

"We just have to crunch all the numbers, and that's your job. How soon can you have a projection for one and two years, with and without the investment?" Geri asked. Another pause for a response from the other end.

"Two weeks?" she asked, sounding annoyed and then outraged.

"We need it done by the end of the week, Simon. Why do I feel like I'm doing all the work myself? I'm on my job, get on yours. Friday—*this* Friday, Simon," Geri hung up the phone as Mattie lifted the picture off her desk.

"Things just ain't as simple as they used to be," Mattie sighed, raising her eyebrows as she addressed her friend.

"Girl you ain't never lied. We're sitting on a huge decision: take the money and expand immediately or let it grow naturally. Our readers have increased by 18% in the last six months. If we take the money, our reach will take us national, but we gotta weigh the good with the bad. Our online presence has jumped too." Geri's phone rang again.

"Yes?" Geri answered with her standard greeting.

"Ok, set that appointment for this Wednesday. What times do I have available?" she asked, waiting for a response.

"Set it for 10:15 in the morning and contact Lewis to make sure his sketches are completed." She dropped the phone back in the cradle.

"Hey, I'm gon' take off, you all busy right now." Mattie placed the picture back onto the desk.

"I'm sorry, but people forget their job descriptions sometimes, and today I'm gonna have to lay the law down," Geri paused as Mattie raised her eyebrows, "and it won't be nearly as assholish as your new manager tried, but I'm gon' get it done." Geri stood up and adjusted her long sleeve wrap blouse as it cinched at her waist. Geri loved showcasing her femininity.

"Hey, you wanna take my truck and just come back around fivish?" Geri had no doubt that her friend had taken the bus to work before she arrived at her office.

"Actually... yeah, I do want to take your truck," Mattie replied to Geri's surprise. "Where did you park?" Mattie gathered her book bag.

"It's in the garage next to the sign that says G. Marcum," Geri smiled at Mattie who simply shook her head.

Mattie's phone vibrated as one of Geri's associates knocked on her office door frame.

Mattie read the incoming text as Geri spoke with the associate.

KENDAL: The wicked witch, huh… well, call me when you get a chance.

"."

"I gotta go." Geri paused to hand Mattie her spare keys out of her desk drawer. "Fivish, Mattie," she reiterated before walking out her office to attend her staff meeting.

Mattie sat down behind the desk and called Kendal.

"Hello baby…" Kendal answered while trying to clear his throat.

"Ooh, you sound like you're just waking up." Mattie swiveled around in Geri's chair to stare out the window.

"Yeah, I am just rolling over. Kwame took me out to an after hours joint last night and fed me something called Crown Hooters. I won't be drinking for another 20 years…" he paused to clear his throat again.

"So, the new manager is a jewel huh…Yoda got fired? Even though he was struggling to get the attendance numbers up, he paid attention. I thought you guys were number one though."

"Yeah, we are number one, in every metric, including lack of attendance. Yoda is gone, but the new one was just an asshole…" she paused, hoping Kendal would understand the next four words out of her mouth. "…so, I quit today."

"Well good!" Kendal exclaimed. "No need being somewhere you don't want to be," he spoke firmly without hesitation. Whatever she decided, he would support her.

Mattie told him how it all went down.

Kendal began laughing and couldn't stop, which became infectious as Mattie started laughing with him.

"That… that is too funny; you gave 'em the business, baby. What I woulda gave to have been there." He tried to curtail his chuckling, but in between clearing his throat and laughing, it was a futile attempt.

"Yeah, I guess I did what other people wished they could do. They had the *nerve* to stick my desk next to the restrooms!" Mattie added while laughing with her man.

"Oh God, that is too funny, baby," he chuckled as Mattie heard him get out of the bed.

"Hey, has Geri decided yet about the investors?"

"No not yet, she's getting some final numbers worked this week. The magazine has grown 18% in six months, so it's a tough one for her. But she'll know by the end of the

111

week." Mattie stopped spinning in Geri's chair and reclined back in it.

"That's great. Maybe she doesn't need the investment, but I'm glad she's got the option," his words were cut short as Mattie heard pounding on his hotel door.

"Wake yo' ass up!" Kwame's voice could be heard through the phone. A second set of knocks had Kendal walking to open the door.

"Stop banging on my door... I gotta headache." Mattie could hear Kendal speaking with Kwame.

"Ain't no rest for the weary! We've got an appointment today in less than an hour. Pat has some people from a network she wants us to meet. They're talking about a special broadcast of the tour. We goin' ta Hollywood, son." The excitement in his voice came through loud and clear.

"Hold on man, I got Mattie on the phone... just give me 30 minutes and I'll come up to your room." Kendal replied.

"Tell the soon-to-be..." Kwame words were cut off, from the sound of it, as someone hit the other person.

"...tell her I said hi and in thirty minutes, son." She heard Kendal closed the door to his hotel room as Kwame left.

"Baby..." Kendal said.

"Yeah, I heard! That's wonderful news! To think, months ago we sat in your office at the center, debating on whether or not you should take Kwame up on his offer. Get ready! You don't have much time. Call me later and tell me how everything went. I love you." Mattie was bursting with pride.

"I love you too." he replied as the call ended.

Just the sound of his voice made her happy. She picked up a pen from Geri's desk and wrote a note on the memo pad.

Thank you, I'm heading to the condo and then to the center. Just hit me if the plans change. She signed it 'M'.

Mattie walked out of Geri's office, passing the conference room to go to the elevators. She saw Geri standing in a conference room, addressing her staff. It looked like she had everyone's attention.

I've got great friends, she thought as she stepped off the elevator. She walked into the parking garage and shook her head at Geri's parking spot—two spots away from the door.

Rockstar parking, Mattie thought, pressing the key fob to unlock the doors of the SUV. She adjusted the seat and mirrors before backing out. As she hit the main street, her phone was ringing.

"What's up, Mrs. Grace?" Mattie asked.

"What's up? Girl, you know what's up! That was AWESOME! The office hasn't been the same since you left. That asshole been in her office for the past hour and a half, and the rumor mill is already buzzing. I couldn't even focus for 30 minutes. When I grow up, I wanna be just like you," Mrs. Grace giggled through the phone.

"She was tripping! You shoulda heard the way she was speaking to me in her office, and then Kevin didn't even speak up!? What's the union good for anyways?" Mattie asked, turning Geri's radio down.

"You're my hero! Listen, I only have two more minutes before I have to log in. Call me later. I just love you, girl." The older woman hung up.

Mattie turned the radio back up before she noticed she was running through a red light.

"Fuck."

A police siren was sounding and as Mattie looked up the cop car was right behind her with the lights flashing.

She pulled over and took her driver's license out. As the police officer approached, she rolled the window down.

"Ma'am, that light was clearly red, are you in a hurry?" he asked.

"No... no hurry officer." She responded with humility. She was in the wrong.

"License and registration please."

She was grateful the officer didn't press her harder than necessary.

Mattie handed him her license and proof of insurance card before reaching into Geri's glove box for the registration. She suddenly remembered she had Henry's business card in her wallet.

"I'm so sorry, officer! I just quit my job, so my mind was thinking about that," she said as she handed him the additional card from Henry that read "a friend" on the back of it.

The officer took the card and then looked at Mattie before telling her to hold on while he went to his cruiser to run the license and registration. It took longer than she imagined, and she figured he was back there writing her a citation. She looked down and realized she hadn't been wearing her seatbelt.

"Oh God." Mattie knew on top of the red-light infraction, there would be a second as the officer made his journey back to the SUV.

"Ok, Ms. Parks." He handed Mattie back everything, including Henry's card.

"I'm sorry about your job. I'm gonna let you off with a warning. We appreciate your generosity to our organization. You buckle up, now; it's a state law." He finished by nodding his head.

"Thank you... thank you so much," Mattie responded gratefully, strapping her seatbelt in before placing her license and insurance back in her bag. She opened the glovebox to put the registration back, and Henry's card fell out.

"You're welcome. Drive safe and have a good day." He walked away.

Mattie knew she had just dodged a bullet.

Henry, you are the man, she thought, as she merged into traffic and headed to Kendal's condo.

…THOUGHTS LEAD TO …
CHAPTER 7

The young boy was sitting at a desk barely able to put his elbows on the classroom table. There were crayons and a Black Panther coloring book lying in front of him, but he wasn't using the crayons yet; he was staring straight forward at Madison, waving. She stood in the doorway of the classroom with a smile on her face. Pride couldn't accurately describe the emotion she was feeling. She was proud of course, but there was another connection, deeper than any love she had felt for anyone else in her life.

The boy had her eyes and cheeks but everything else was the spitting image of his father as a boy. Mattie couldn't fathom why there were no other children sitting in the classroom but that faded away as soon as the boy picked up the crayon box to select the purple before opening his coloring book.

He put his head down to concentrate, flipping through the pages until he found a picture he would color.

Mattie's thoughts were on him.

Just color inside the lines, baby. she thought as if it were something she had told him over and over again.

So, this is our son. Mattie knew for certain all her worries about delivering a healthy child had been erased.

He's so beautiful, the perfect combination between us. She knew she had stayed much longer outside the classroom door looking in than she intended, but moments like this wouldn't always come, and she didn't feel like being in any other place than here watching her son on the first day of school.

The sun was shining through one of the classroom windows, but one window, situated on its own wall, had nothing but pitch-black darkness in it. Like two entirely different parts of the day existed in one place.

Strange… Mattie thought. She began wondering again why there were no other children present.

"Something is not right." Mattie didn't see a teacher present. She tried to remember who his teacher was. How had she and her son gotten here?

Her son was still coloring but wasn't doing so inside the lines of the coloring book. He was taking the crayon and scribbling on the desk for no apparent reason.

Mattie attempted to turn the door handle to the classroom to see what was going on, but the knob didn't budge. She tried again and again but each attempt was futile.

What the hell... She began to feel slightly worried. There had to be an explanation.

My baby, she tried saying, but the sound was muffled in her throat. She searched around the hallway and lifted the red fire extinguisher from its hinges and tried breaking the glass window portion of the door, but the fire extinguisher simply deteriorated in her hand before she could use it. She looked back inside the room and the rays of sunlight that had been coming through the first window were gone, there was nothing but blackness instead. Mattie felt panic setting in.

The little boy kept his head down, but the coloring book and the box of crayons was gone from his desk. On his hands. the purple color had somehow turned red, and it appeared to be liquid pouring down onto the desk and floor around him.

Mattie threw her entire body against the door repeatedly, banging her shoulders to bust it down, but everything felt heavier and now she was moving in slow motion… panicking… feeling so afraid.

The bright lighting in the room dimmed from the back of the classroom and in that darkness a silhouette was pacing back and forth… seemingly waiting and moving towards the young boy as darkness advanced the room.

She did everything she could to break in the door with the imminent threat and danger to her son, but she was helpless as angry tears streamed down her face. She hoped that the boy would look up and see her and run towards the door, praying he could unlock it from the inside. Instead, the young boy began running his hands back and forth in the red liquid surrounding him.

The outline of the body was taking form into the shape of a man. Mattie's mind was racing as she looked inside the glass window with her eyes pinned open.

"Let me in!" she yelled, slamming herself into the door again, over and over.

As the solid form extended the darkness that had now enveloped the room, it began moving out of the shadows. The face took form and Mattie's heart ached as Jimmie Frederick walked up behind her son, placing his hands upon the young boy's shoulders.

"That's good, Jr," he complimented the child.

Jimmie stared at Madison with an evil smile before rubbing her child on the head to indicate that he was proud.

As Mattie pounded the door, tears kept flowing out her eyes and she felt anger that she was helpless. Anger that the bastard she had killed was this close to her son and she couldn't protect him.

Jimmie smiled with a look of satisfaction.

"He belongs to me."

The red color no longer only extended the young boy's hands, but now, as Mattie slammed her fist into the glass of the door… her hands began bleeding and dripping with blood.

"You are a murderer, Madison from Columbus." The figure of Jimmie exuded sound as the darkness invaded all areas of the classroom.

Jimmie removed his hands from the little boy's shoulders and walked towards Madison, who simply stared at him through the glass pane as hatred extended from her being, but she was afraid too. Afraid for her child.

As their eyes met, she screamed out with purpose.

"I'll kill you! I'll kill you again if you touch my son!" She took both arms and began banging on the door again as tears flowed down her cheeks. She saw the reflection in the glass pane, and her tears were the color of blood.

Jimmie laughed at her and pulled the door shade down, covering the inside of the classroom.

"He's mine Madison from Columbus ... all mine."

"No!" Mattie yelled, jarring her from her deep sleep. She woke up panting, drenched in sweat, lying in only her panties and Kendal's college T-shirt.

She cradled her stomach as she sat up in the bed.

It felt so real, she thought, closing her eyes to get a sense of balance.

"Oh God…" she whispered as her heart rate slowed.

It was just a dream… a fucking dream.

The feeling of helplessness wasn't easy to shake as she rolled over to sit up on the other side of the bed, placing her feet onto the floor. She looked at the picture of her and Kendal at Cedar Point taken months ago before standing and walking into the bathroom to pee and wipe the sweat off her face.

Dawn was slowly forcing its way into the day. Even had she tried, there was no way she could return to sleep. The dream embedded in her recent memory was hard to get rid of, so she put her sweatpants on, changed shirts, and went downstairs to retrieve her jogging shoes. Out the front door she went.

Hopefully, I'll run this shit outta my mind, she thought before taking off without stretching or loosening her limbs.

Today was Sunday, "the Day of Praise" as Grandma Redd had called it. Mattie had not attended Sunday Service with regularity since her grandma had passed. As she ran, Mattie tried forcing good thoughts and memories into her mind, but the vision of Jimmie smiling and touching her child kept resurfacing. So, instead of forcing them out, she invited them in.

Mattie thought about the night Jimmie Frederick was killed and slowed down to walk on the sidewalk that had recently been cemented.

I'd do it again, she rationalized. *If I hadn't, I woulda been raped and left for dead.* Her body was not accustomed to exercise and with the baby inside her abdomen she thought it best to walk the rest of the way. Entering Kendal's condo, she sat on his couch, looked at the time, and decided that today was the best day to go to church and praise the Lord.

She drove home and found Aunt Penny nearly dressed, waiting on Geri to pick her up.

"I'm coming too," she told her aunt before texting Geri to just meet them at church.

. . . .

The cat sat patiently staring at the door as it slowly opened. It had done so each morning for the past few months, waiting to see its owner who had been bed-ridden after knee replacement. The cat licked the fur on its right paw before meowing to stare at another walking towards them down the hallway.

"Mom, why are you up already?" Her daughter's voice held concern as she approached the door, the cat rubbing up against her leg.

"Mr. Whiskers even knows you shouldn't be out of bed without help the first thing in the morning! I'm sure you and I both heard your orthopedic doctor say the same thing to you, Mom." Their deep mahogany skin was nearly flawless, and they looked identical besides being 32 years apart in age.

"Good morning to both of you, but my bladder said to get up." The mother hugged her daughter.

The daughter took that moment to mimic what the orthopedic surgeon had advised.

"Ms. Charlotte, I know you want to do things your way sometimes but…"

"Brittany, I know what she said, but move out the way or help me to the bathroom, child, because my bladder ain't waiting one more minute." She laughed but was dead serious.

Brittany helped her mother to the restroom and was waiting for her when she was finished.

"I know you said you wanted to go to service today, and we can use the old wheelchair that Ms. Penny gave you or the cane you don't like using, but it's one or the other." Brittany was ready for more pushback from her mother, but it never came. She headed into the kitchen to start the coffee maker to make a carafe of hot breakfast liquid.

"Baby, I'm laying my clothes out and then going to lay down for another hour. I'll be ready by 6:30." Charlotte kissed her daughter's cheek and slowly made her way back into her bedroom where Mr. Whiskers had positioned himself on top of her queen-sized bed.

After an hour, Ms. Charlotte was ready for church. On the ride to the sanctuary, she hummed each gospel song playing on the radio.

Brittany pushed her mother's wheelchair down the aisle of the church to sit in the front row. They had arrived early for this very reason. Brittany knew her mother would want to be seen today in her fashionable outfit and hat. It wasn't that she was fishing for compliments, but she sure liked receiving them.

Ms. Charlotte saw Cindy and Geri walking with Aunt Penny towards the first few rows and waved at them to get their attention.

"Brittany, will you tell Sister Parks that I need to speak with her after service? We need to get that box of letters to her," Ms. Charlotte advised her daughter.

Brittany excused herself to do as her mother asked.

"Aunt Penny good morning, it's good to see you." Brittany bent down to hug Aunt Penny.

"What's up Cindy... Geri?" She acknowledged them.

"My mother wanted to speak with you about some items that Grandma Redd had delivered to a P.O. Box. We just picked up the last of it over three months ago. To be honest, with mom's hip surgery we haven't had time for much. I doubt we'd be here today, but she's been dying to wear that hat," Brittany motioned towards her mom who was greeting folks who approached her to say hi and check on her since her surgery.

"Your Momma got some good taste." Aunt Penny smiled, advising the younger woman that they would speak after service as the band struck up the first note to praise and worship.

"We will catch you outside." Cindy finished as Geri secured seats and waved them over.

...

Evangelist India Monroe had come from Arkansas to share her life story with the congregation. The sanctuary was filled with more people still flowing in 30 minutes after she began. Pastor Morris sat on the pulpit in a chair as the evangelist began coming to her conclusion, speaking on the topic of the Path Chosen by God for individuals.

"You can fight the Lord, but He's already won. Go ahead and say what you gon' do... tell the Lord you ain't ready to do what He wants, be disobedient! All you gon' do is struggle... all you gon' do is fail and keep failing." She addressed the congregation but intently kept staring up at those in the balcony by pointing at them with her index finger.

"Be strong in the Lord! Be glad that the Lord's mercy woke you up today! Be grateful that He finds favor in you to get you safely to church to glorify His name today. Some people went to sleep last night and didn't wake up. It's the truth. But He's a good God... all the time..." she continued as Aunt Penny let out a loud, boisterous "Amen."

"He's a healer, your provider... and sometimes we treat Him like the enemy. Well, I know, as God is my witness that without Him, it be the end of me. I don't need validation from my friends... you don't need validation from your family. The path God has chosen for you has already been paved with everything you need. All you gotta do is walk it... praise Him!" Evangelist Monroe heard the Hallelujah's from the congregation and saw people in the balcony with their hands raised in jubilation.

127

"All you gotta do is submit to His will. Amen. I know people struggle with internal conflict. I know people second guess themselves to follow the path He's set before them. We want to follow somebody else's path, walk in somebody else's footsteps on their journey because there is safety in numbers." Evangelist Monroe paused as she lifted the microphone from the cradle to stand down onto the floor of the sanctuary.

"But God and one man make a majority," she spoke loudly as she stomped her feet against the carpet.

"Y'all didn't hear me! God and one man make a majority!" Hallelujahs and amens echoed throughout the church.

"I'm gon' tell you saints, ain't nothing safer than the haven of the Lord. You lettin' somebody else lead you when they lost. Can't nobody lead when they lost. How somebody who don't know their origin... their starting point... gonna lead anybody. You can't get somewhere not knowing where you come from. He is the Alpha and Omega. Some of us struggle to let go, to let go of our insecurities, of our fears, and that's what keeps us stationary," she hesitated again, standing perfectly still to make her point.

"That's what makes the day shorter and the nights longer. But if we believe and profess with our hearts and souls that God's will be done, if we just stand up and straighten out… the power of the Lord will fill you and erase all doubt. There is nothing mightier or more powerful than the greatness of the Lord. Shout out to Him… tell Him you love him. Lift your voices and tell Him… hallelujah… tell Him that you will obey! Amen!" She pointed towards the area where Cindy was standing. Cindy felt the Spirit moving in her, and she began rocking side to side. She was energized and began shouting out "Hallelujah" repeatedly.

Sheila was clapping her hands as she stood up to join in the worshipping of the Creator.

"With your heart open, tell Him that you're ready to take that step to righteousness. Back in Arkansas, we praise the Lord like you do, we serve the same God that you do. I was lost, broken down, struggling to get off drugs and get ahead, trying to rob Peter to pay Paul. I was on a dirt path filled with doubt and nonbelievers. A nonbeliever can't help you believe. A nonbeliever only intensifies doubt so all I did was travel in circles, repeating the same actions expecting a different result." She made her way back to the pulpit, looking at Pastor Morris before turning around to face the congregation. Nearly all in attendance were standing waiting to hear what was next.

"Y'all know what they call doing the same thing over and over expecting a different result…" she paused as she jumped up and down.

"They call that insanity! So yes… I was insane. Losing my mind, until I gave in to the Lord. I gave up my doubts and fears and said, 'God your will be done.' I kept falling short until I said, 'I am your servant, and I won't be disobedient.' I'm here today with you because I fell down and got up trusting the Lord. Hallelujah! I'm here today serving the Lord boldly because that's what I do. I'm here not just believing but knowing his power is the highest." She pointed upwards above her head.

People were shouting, some people were in the aisles stomping their feet.

"Knowing my path that I walk now is the same one that I coulda, shoulda been walking. But that don't matter, saints, because God is the Master of my soul and the Orchestrator of my spirit. Don't be afraid to kick off those old shoes and put on new ones. You're a new man," she said, pointing to one side of the floor.

"You're a new woman. Who you were yesterday is not nearly important as who you are now." She moved back down to the floor again.

"I don't think y'all heard me! Who you were yesterday is not nearly as important as you are right now. So, stand up… stand up and take the shackles off and walk the path He has set before you. Stand up and give Him praise because He is worthy of praise. He knows your heart and all the secrets in your closet, and He still loves you. All you gotta do is take a step… and then another and another… before long you gon' be running… running with the Lord. I ran up to Columbus, and next week I'm running to Pittsburgh and then Philadelphia, I'm gonna be running for the Lord all the rest of the days of my life. It's my path. What's your path?" Evangelist Monroe began jumping up and down on the stage.

"Praise Him!" She exclaimed.

Pastor Morris stood up, clapping his hands and yelling.

"Praise the Lord!"

Mattie was up and out of her seat with her arms spread wide and stomping her feet. The Spirit of the Lord had engulfed her. She asked for forgiveness for killing a man, she begged to be forgiven for hating her parents and hating herself. She was humbled when Aunt Penny reached over and took her hand.

"God loves you, Madison… I love you."

Mattie was so overwhelmed that tears poured from her eyes.

"I love you, Auntie, I've been so disobedient. I haven't lived the way I should." Her firm grasp pulled holding her aunt closely. She wanted to admit to killing a man. She needed the weight of that burden off her soul, but she couldn't mutter the words.

"It's ok, baby… He has mercy." Aunt Penny held her tightly as the choir began singing.

MORE THAN A MEAL
CHAPTER 8

After service Aunt Penny invited Mattie's three friends over for a fish fry. She cornered Detective Jenkins and his wife, extremely adamant that they should come over too with their son Jay.

The energy Mattie had exhausted in church prevented her from putting up a fight against having so many people in her house when she was dealing with internal issues. If it would not have been so blatantly disrespectful, she wouldn't have even gone home at all.

"Mattie, you should just rest. We can handle this. It looks like you got some stuff on yo' mind, I see it," Sheila started to speak when Cindy chimed in.

"Shit, we all see it…"

Sheila looked at Cindy with widened eyes while interrupting.

"You just got out of church and cussing already? Girl, I just can't." She directed the conversation back to Mattie. "You worried about the baby?" Sheila asked lightheartedly, as she shucked the corn on Mattie's kitchen counter.

Cindy reluctantly was making the salad, slicing tomatoes and cucumbers to add to the large bowl already with mixed greens in it. Aunt Penny had delegated each task for a specific person, knowing Cindy was going to complain about anything she was asked to do.

Geri was outside keeping an eye on the deep fryer burner as Aunt Penny sat down with her, drinking iced tea, giving her advice and instruction on life while frying Lake Erie perch and walleye.

"Make the grease too hot and the fish cook too fast. Just like life, you can't speed through your life without getting burned. That magazine of yours is yo' baby right now, but it is not your life Geraldine." The elder woman rocked forward, standing up from her chair. Her silver hair held volume still. In fairness, Aunt Penny did not look her age.

"Will you get Auntie some more drink?" She took a spatula to move the fish around in the pot.

"Yes ma'am. Do you want anything else?" Geri asked.

"If you can get me some new knees and take this arthritis away, yes Lord, bring them back with you when you bring that tea." Aunt Penny smiled. She had grown less rigid with Mattie and her friends as the time had passed after her sister was laid to rest.

Geri opened up the glass pane behind the sliding screen door and walked through the dining room.

"Oh, wow Cindy that salad looks good." Geri joked as she walked behind the counter where Cindy was now slicing eggs and layering the tossed salad.

"Whateva' SpongeBob. You smell like fish. She knew not to ask me to fry the fish, or we woulda had problems up in here" Cindy replied in a matter-of-fact tone.

"You woulda took yo' butt out there and fried that fish, Anna Mae," Sheila told her, as everyone laughed along with her.

"Have you eaten anything at all today, Mattie?" Geri saw Mattie sitting on the stool with a look on her face that couldn't be discerned.

"Ugh… no… not yet." She was finding herself more exhausted. The mental and spiritual gymnastics were getting more difficult to balance. In the end, she would carry the secret to the grave.

Sheila threw her knife into the sink, opened the bread box and took two slices of bread out and began making her toast.

"I don't want no…" Mattie began but got interrupted.

"Who cares what you want? This is for the baby. Don't eat, and I swear I'll walk out there and tell her you're pregnant," Sheila threatened. Mattie wasn't sure if her friend's tone was genuine, but she wouldn't press the issue.

"You wouldn't…" Mattie started, but from the look on her friend's face, she backed off.

"So go get your prenatal vitamins, Madison," Cindy added, taking a shot at her friend.

There was no need to fight a battle she would lose. Mattie got up and walked down the hallway, wondering if last night's dream was a once in a lifetime occurrence. She didn't want to have it resurface ever again. Her protectiveness of the baby had grown, and she knew it. She was his or her protector and hoped her fears weren't somehow being transferred into the baby.

And I do need to take these for you. She rubbed her stomach as she retrieved the vitamins from her purse. She picked up her phone and called Kendal, but there was no answer. Mattie had not talked to him since yesterday before his last show.

"He's probably taking a nap." She was done jumping to conclusions; there was no way she would ever doubt him again after she blew up at him in New York. She was making her way back to the kitchen when the doorbell rang.

"I got it!" She hit the talk button on the intercom. "Who is it?"

"It's the Jenkins family, Ms. Madison," young Jay answered.

Mattie buzzed them in and opened the door, allowing them entry. Michelle was wearing a blue jean jumper with a t-shirt and wedged flip flops.

Henry was carrying a bag with snacks and more drinks, still wearing his church clothes.

"Welcome to the fish fry." Mattie hugged Michelle and rubbed Jay on the top of his head.

"It smells really good in here ladies," Henry declared, and then asked where to place the bag he was carrying.

Sheila handed Mattie the toast before taking the bag, making room on the counter.

"Service was off the Richter today," Henry paused. "I almost took off in a praise run up in there." Michelle and Mattie laughed with him.

"It was awesome! I bought one of her books and two CDs," Cindy added.

"Y'all can make yourself comfortable and lil' man you can change the channel to cartoons if you want. Geri and Auntie are outside with more chairs if y'all wanna go outside. They're still frying fish though." Mattie walked to the coffee table, grabbed the remote, and handed it to Jay.

"Thanks for the invite! Luckily, we hadn't made plans because I don't think your aunt was taking 'no' for an answer." Michelle reached out to take Mattie's hand with a smirk on her face before Mattie walked her to the patio.

After eating, Cindy and Geri watched cartoons with Jay on Mattie's couch while the rest of the group sat at the dining room table drinking coffee. Michelle had just sat back down from pouring herself a second cup when her husband began talking about a case he was working on.

"It's difficult work sometimes, especially when you have no leads. For all intents and purpose the case is going cold." His voice carried a frustrated tone.

"One of my recent cases as detective and I have nothing substantial to follow up on." He shook his head as he told them that his captain had been riding him and his partner hard on this particular case.

"Honey, I'm sure no one wants to hear about cops and robbers after a marvelous meal like that. Thanks again for inviting us over today," Michelle said as she sat back down while adding two spoons of sugar to her coffee.

"I don't mind listening! If your husband can help rid the community of scum, I am grateful. That's means there will be less negative stuff going on around my kids and Jay."

Sheila loosened the drawstring around her waist because the second round of food had stuffed her.

"And you have to feel protected having a dicktective in the house," Aunt Penny chimed in.

Sheila looked at Mattie who had already started laughing.

"It's detective auntie, not dicktective," she said as the table burst out in laughter. Even Aunt Penny had to chuckle about it.

"Yeah... yeah child, I'm sure she's glad she got both," the older woman blurted out, adding to the giggles.

Henry smiled and shook his head waiting for the chuckling to cease.

"Take for example, the body of the victim. It had one fatal puncture wound and what we've surmised is that it was given by a metal rod from one of the fire escapes that broke down, but it rained hard that weekend, so the lab hasn't been able to narrow the actual weapon down. The victim's working girls," he cleared his throat. "The victim was a pimp by profession and his working girls said he had walked out the back to chase a woman he had bought drinks for and was talking to at the bar. This man was over 6'3" tall and from the description of the woman she was about..." he hesitated again. "About Madison's build, I'd say. I highly doubt that this woman killed him. If his brother didn't have City Hall in his pockets, I don't think I'd be catching all the flack over it. For me though, I wanna catch the offender because everyone needs justice." Henry concluded with a matter-of-fact statement.

Mattie sat listening to every word he said. She felt anxious. Not only had she dreamt about the night of the murder, but she also sat across from the man responsible for solving the case.

If he only knew... if they only knew.

It ate away at her, but she knew it was up to God to forgive her.

"You're gonna catch a break on it, Henry. I just feel it. People can't just get away with murder." Sheila's words hung in Mattie's ears as Henry added more information.

"Well, I hope so; forensics did find some material in his hands. Some type of man-made fiber typically found in women's wigs. Over the next week or so, they should have a strong determination of the manufacturer and then I'll have to canvass any local stores that may have carried it." Henry reached over to take a sip of his wife's coffee.

Mattie couldn't help thinking back to the moment Jimmie Frederick had grabbed her by the head. Had it not been for her wearing the wig, things would've turned out differently. It was that brief moment which had saved her and now she was praying she left no other clues behind.

"Wow, technology can do that, narrow the fiber down to its end use? NCIS huh?" Mattie attempted to add humor to the moment. She felt sick to the stomach, uncertain whether it was from the conversation or the baby. She didn't excuse herself, hoping the feeling would pass.

"The labs we use in Columbus are good, but we had to send the sample to the Federal Bureau of Investigation. Their funding for forensic science is unmatched. At least I'll have more to go on when it comes back than I do now," Henry answered as the front door opened. Standing there was Kendal, pulling his luggage in.

"I hope y'all saved me some fish!" His voice carried and he was happy to be home.

Mattie's eyes widened as she pushed her chair back from the table and ran to jump in his arms.

"Baby!" she exclaimed.

"Hey honey… I missed you too." He hugged and kissed her.

"Get a room… we have a kid in here" Cindy called out before walking to the door to slide his bags out of the way.

"Why didn't you tell me? You knew you would be coming home?" Mattie paused.

"This is the absolute best surprise!" They kissed again before she walked him into the dining room to say hi to everyone else.

Aunt Penny along with Sheila sat with smirks on their faces.

"Hey Kendal." Henry stood up to shake hands.

"Hey sergeant... or should I say detective?" Kendal hesitated as Michelle and Sheila laughed aloud.

"What? What did I say?" Kendal asked, completely dumbfounded.

"Nothing baby, I'll tell you later." Mattie interjected.

"Your plate's is in the microwave, Mr. Broadway." Cindy called out abruptly in her usual manner.

"What? You knew he was coming in today too?" Mattie asked.

"Everyone knew but you! I'm surprised Sheila didn't let the cat out the bag." Geri walked into the dining room to sit down. She was a little tired.

"Oh my God... I *am* surprised. I wasn't expecting you for another two weeks." Mattie added as Kendal removed his plate from the microwave. She was truly surprised to have her man home.

"What do we have to drink? Any Pepsi?"

"Pepsi is in the bottom drawer. I see some of Mattie has rubbed off on you." Geri slapped him on the shoulder.

"I'm famished. I haven't anything to eat except the small packages of Biscotti crackers on the plane." Kendal sat down at the table and began eating.

The questions didn't stop, so Kendal answered questions about the tour after eating before asking Mattie to show him the blanket she had begun crocheting.

Aunt Penny's eyes showed pride when Mattie brought her unfinished work out.

"I like the colors, baby! It's gonna be gorgeous when it's done." There was pride in his voice.

"Maybe Susie Homemaker can make me one when she's done with that one." Cindy fired off in an amusing tone giggling by herself.

"Maybe you can make yo' own..." Aunt Penny paused.

"...in fact, I'm gon' teach you too."

Mattie looked around the table as it became silent. She burst out laughing as her eyes met Cindy.

Cindy went to respond, but Mattie spoke up first, cutting off any response her friend was about to say.

"When do you have to go back on your tour?" She was beyond ecstatic to have him home; a day that started out in turmoil had turned completely around just by him walking through the door.

"I only have two days, but it's two days more than we had. The only thing I've got to do besides spending time with you is visit the center. I brought the kids back mega souvenirs. I hope they'll be happy to see me."

Kendal turned to redirect towards Henry. "And I definitely have to thank you for helping with the mentoring program; it's good for the kids to get as much positive reinforcement and feedback as they can. My peers say that the kids have a different outlook on law enforcement, so thank you and your partners." Kendal took Mattie by the hand, leaning over to kiss her.

"No problem," Henry said. "If we had more men involved in the lives of these children, it would make a world of a difference, so you keep up the good work." Henry reached for his wife's coffee mug to take another sip.

Aunt Penny felt a certain joy in seeing what amounted to those who were bonded because of her niece.

"This coffee is good, but do we have something a little stronger since Kendal came in today?" Aunt Penny asked suddenly.

Mattie hadn't thought her Auntie drank anything a "little stronger."

Sheila was quick to respond that there was both wine and liquor and that she would grab it.

"Yeah, I think so. But Auntie? You don't drink?" Mattie became confused, watching Sheila walk out of the room.

"Here, I'll help you." Kendal excused himself from the table followed by Geri and Cindy.

Henry and Michelle held hands as they sat waiting at the table. They looked to be holding some emotion in, but Mattie couldn't tell if it was a secret shared between lovers. The unfinished blanket lay in her lap and when Aunt Penny told her to pass it to her so she could take a closer look, Mattie simply extended it to Michelle who gave it to the elder woman.

Geri, Sheila, and Cindy were in the kitchen huddled around Kendal.

Mattie couldn't see what was going on, but she felt like she was being left out of something and as she stood up, her aunt told her to sit back down.

"They know how to get drinks, don't you think, Madison?"

Without hesitation, Mattie sat back down and when Kendal returned surrounded by her three friends, Aunt Penny, Michelle, and Henry stood up as Kendal dropped to one knee in front of Madison.

"I have felt the pulse of the Universe and learned the ways of love. The Creators' secret resides in my ears, the Creators rhythms pound in my soul. If I have become what God has intended me to become it is because His mercy knows no depth, His love has no boundaries, and His power has no limits. It has always been you, my soul mate… my spirit has no other choice but to love you and thus my heart must follow suit. You are my intangible healer; you are the tree that grows in the forest, silently awaiting the whisper of the wind to set it free. You are the waters that wipe away the depths of my sorrow, the fire that cleared the doubts that began to erase me.

I know of no greater triumph than loving you. I know of no greater purpose than in protecting you like God protects His Chosen. I choose you to forget my ego; I choose you to open my soul and heart to all the possibilities of tomorrow and this lifetime. I have searched both heaven and earth for you, and I want no other step to be taken, thought to be made, breath to be inhaled. You are the air I breathe; you are the gift sent by God as promised, and you are the very reason I exist in the being I am today. I will love you and cherish you, respect you and protect you. I will honor you and our love in each breath the Creator allows me to take, no matter how deep or shallow. My breath is your breath, my heart is your heart, and my love is your love. My life, my soul, and spirit belong to you. Matthew 16:18 says, "Upon this rock I will build my church; and the gates of hell shall not prevail against it." So, I say, upon this rock, I will build a home that you will always know love and will never be alone. Will you marry me, Madison?" Kendal's question held meaning as his eyes stared up at her. He was completely exposed.

Mattie's heart overflowed as she sat in her chair looking down at Kendal. No one else existed in this moment; she only knew that this man was the man that God created for her, that his words matched his actions, and that like him, her soul knew no boundaries. In this moment, Mattie was free of doubt and fear.

"I will."

Kendal slid the engagement ring on her finger. The sexy 3.0 carat, radiant cut, three stone engagement ring with platinum band sparkled from any angle.

Mattie's tears came from emotions that ran so deep she couldn't recognize it at first. She felt worthy of being loved.

The whole room shed tears for nearly ten minutes between enormous smiles and laughter. As the elation died down, Mattie excused herself to the bathroom because she was getting sick in her stomach and needed to evacuate something she had ingested.

Kendal and Geri spoke a little longer together as the rest of the small party filtered out. Geri had decided not to take the help of investors. The growth of the magazine had been enough that they would let it grow naturally.

"Yeah, I think that's a good idea," Kendal affirmed. He had witnessed grassroots growth firsthand by being on tour as the word of mouth spread and created new opportunities.

"I thought what they presented was a great offer, but we want to keep control of what we can. We're just minimizing the hands in the pot, but it was a hard decision to pass up on all that money." Geris rubbed her fingers across her eyebrow.

"Rumor has it that there's a network interested in the tour. Maybe when y'all come to Columbus, you can get me some tickets man." Geri yawned; it had been a long day.

"Come on, you know I've got y'all covered already. Plus, my boy Kwame keeps asking about you," Kendal responded, passing along information.

Geri smiled before replying. What woman didn't like getting attention? But Kwame had women from coast to coast.

"He's a great talker and performer, but he is a little too fly for me," Geri responded in earnest.

Mattie was still up but had excused herself to take a shower; her day had brightened after such a terrible start.

Aunt Penny had retired to bed, and Sheila and Cindy left shortly after Henry and his family.

"Do you think we could get an exclusive interview with Kwame though?" Geri was always thinking about her business and growing her publication.

"Well for you Geri, you'd get the interview, but knowing how he works you're going to owe him something. At the very least a dinner date," Kendal laughed aloud shaking his head, knowing all and well Kwame would try to get into her panties.

"The interview may not be worth it." Kendal chuckled trying to do his small part in protecting Geri by being honest.

"Put me in touch with him, and I can handle the rest. I'm sure his ego is ridiculous, but the buzz spreading about what you guys are accomplishing will definitely boost our sales. I'm gonna get going, I know tomorrow is the big day and you look tired." Geri stood up from the dining room table before snatching her purse off of the kitchen counter.

"Alright man, tell Mattie to call me after the appointment and before y'all hit the road." Kendal walked her to the door.

"You got it, and I'll have Kwame get at you." He locked the door behind.

Kendal picked up the last of the glasses left on the table, putting them in the dishwasher before turning off the lights. He walked back to Mattie's room and closed her bedroom door behind.

DOUBLE ENTENDRE

CHAPTER 9

In the morning, they woke up running late. Mattie showered and put baby powder on before dressing. She was tired after last night's sex session and sore on the inside of her walls, but the pain was welcomed after taking their bodies and minds to a higher level than ever before.

Kendal had already cleaned up and in the kitchen making her toast and boiled eggs with relish on the side. He was exhausted too, but more ecstatic about seeing their baby for the first time.

"Baby, we gotta hurry up! Junior is waiting to say hi." Mattie took the saucer of food before he could finish.

"Can you get me some juice for my vitamins? And what if she is a girl?" she asked, standing up to throw a t-shirt on that was identical to the one he was wearing, featuring the tour and dates.

"Ok, but we gotta go, and all that extra you put on me was bomb. We gon' have to try some new thangs. And if she's a girl... she's still Jr." Kendal laughed while smacking her on the ass playfully before going back into the kitchen.

Mattie put her tennis shoes on and laid back on the bed. She was anxious about the visit to the obstetrician.

The doctor's appointment was in 45 minutes, and it would take 30 minutes to get there in normal traffic. Kendal seemed more excited than she was. Today was a big day, the ultrasound and then the drive to Cleveland to tell his parents and show off her ring.

"Here, sweetie." Kendal handed her the glass of apple juice helping her stand back up.

"We can rest afterwards. I'm tired too, but you're gonna have to eat the rest of this in the car. Baby, grab your purse and let's go... gotta go, gotta go." He shook his head watching her walk back into the bathroom to brush her teeth.

"Baby!" He exclaimed, pleading with her to hurry up.

"Jus' hold on... I'm coming! Pull the car out, and I'll meet you outside," she responded, looking back at him through the mirror.

"Ok, just hurry up please." He left.

Mattie was waiting for him when he pulled up front.

"Give me your keys, honey, you took mine." She ran back up the stairs to lock the door.

As they drove to the appointment, she put the Watercolors station on from Sirius Satellite and held onto his hand. He was pushing the limits of driving safe when he normally took his time. He had just run through a light turning red.

"Baby, we're going to get there in time, we still have 30 minutes."

Kendal sensed her concern and slowed before he would have accidentally run his second consecutive red light. The car to his right sped up to make it through instead, and a police siren was heard.

"See?! That could've been us, and we would've been late," Mattie offered.

"I'm just excited ever since you told me… in your own special way." He paused as she hit him on the shoulder as they both thought back to the first night in New York City.

"Alright, I know I said I wouldn't bring it back up, but we're having a baby."

Mattie listened to Kendal and felt joy. She had thought about children but was afraid; afraid that she would be like her mother… absent.

As Kendal pulled into the parking space, he leaned over and kissed her cheek. He sensed her anxiousness, and this was his way of saying everything would be ok.

"Are you ready to see junior, Mrs. Scott?" She gripped his hand as he opened the door to the medical building.

Mattie expected more out of the office. It had the usual chairs and receptionist desk, but it did not look kid friendly at all. She expected to see parents with children running around, but there was only one other woman sitting down, and she looked nearly ready to give birth. Then she realized that they were one of the first appointments of the day.

"Madison Parks to see Dr. Hinoway." Kendal greeted the receptionist.

The office assistant gave him a clip board to fill out the usual first visit paperwork.

"Your insurance card and driver's license; I just need to make a copy of both. I'll bring it right back, Ms. Parks." She spoke to Madison before looking at Kendal with more than a glance.

Yeah, he fine, Mattie thought as she waited to make eye contact with her to let her know she saw her staring at her man. She knew women found her man attractive, but the young Asian woman could've used more tact.

"You still have insurance?' Kendal asked as he watched her fill out the paperwork unaware of Mattie's unspoken dialogue with the receptionist.

"Yeah, until the end of next month, then I think I'll have to get Cobra." Mattie crossed her legs to get a better base to write on.

"I looked into some insurance a while ago, but it was so damn expensive. Maybe we can get some good coverage because we'll need it as a family." In Kendal's eyes they were already joined whether they had gone through a matrimony ceremony or not.

Mattie finished the three pages of paperwork and returned it to the receptionist, who handed back her cards.

Two more women came into the office shortly thereafter. One woman carried a newborn, looking less than four months old. She had a Winnie the Pooh diaper bag strapped across her shoulder. Her dark skin was flawless and as she smiled at her baby, her brilliant white teeth showed. Mattie could tell that she was happy to be a mom because after she checked in, she spent time holding and talking in baby talk to her daughter.

The other mom came in with what appeared to be a three-year old along with another child about the age of five. She seemed to be in her mid-twenties. Her nails and hair were done properly.

The five-year boy immediately went to the kids play area as his mother signed in. She was holding the younger female child on her hip, carrying a large designer Coach bag.

"Oh God. Why didn't you tell me you had to pottie?" she asked, clearly upset that the diaper leaked and now she had urine on her clothes. The look she gave the young girl wasn't a look of patience.

"Come on," she said frustrated pulling a diaper out of her purse before changing the girl.

"Mommy look…" the five-year old said excitedly because he had finished one of the small puzzles. He had pieced it together in a short time. He was standing off to the side of his mother.

His mom was putting the new diaper on, and Kendal noticed her disposition was nasty as she mumbled under her breath.

"I'm going to pop you if you do that again," she snapped, with a hint of resentment in her voice. She still had not looked up to see her son's finished project.

"Mommy…" the boy called out again, but she ignored him, instead checking her cell phone after sitting the young girl firmly in the seat next to her.

Kendal couldn't help but believe that was why so many kids ended up being lost, searching for love. Why so many kids in his program had to be shown what unconditional love is. Many people wanted to be friends to their children instead of parents; others felt their children were a burden. This mother seemed to fall into this category.

"That's a good job young man," Kendal decided to speak up, letting the small boy realize someone was paying attention to him.

Mattie had been resting her head on his shoulder and sat up taking notice of the puzzle.

"Thank you!" he said with a huge smile on his face.

The mom finally put her phone down and responded.

"Yeah, that's nice, now throw this diaper in that garbage," was all she could muster before her phone rang.

"Hello?" she answered.

"Yeah, I'm here now and afterwards I'm dropping them off at Neese's house and then we can go shopping," she paused.

"Hell, yeah, they both just paid child support. Ok, I'll call you later, baby." She finished the conversation before the little girl tried getting out of her seat to go play with her brother.

"Sit down!" she said, positioning the girl firmly into the back of the chair.

Kendal wished he could have mentored the children to show them a better way. He was two seconds off from telling her his mind, but he decided today wasn't going to be ruined by a selfish parent.

I'm going to be involved in all aspects of my child, he thought as a question formed. *How can I help kids like that?*

We need to get them before they're teenagers. He answered in silence.

"Baby, what do you think about opening a child-care facility in the center?"

"Sounds good, but there's a lot of certifications to go through. My friend owned a daycare center but went bankrupt." She was thinking the same thing.

The little boy was playing with a small foam basketball, trying to shoot it in a small hoop when the medical assistant called for Mattie.

"Ms. Parks." She held a file in one hand while holding the door open with the other.

As Mattie stood up, the boy had hit his mom accidentally with the foam basketball.

"Come here!" she stared at him with anger.

Mattie heard the anger in the voice and was saddened that a parent could be that way with their child.

"Sit yo' ass down, you son of a bitch and don't move," she said quietly, but both Kendal and Mattie heard it. Mattie felt the resistance in Kendal's movement, and she tightened her grip on his hand, knowing he was going to say something.

"I hope you see the irony in what you just said." Simple and to the point.

The mom was trying to figure out what Kendal meant but clearly hadn't realized she was the brunt of her own tirade.

"That went over her head." Mattie followed the medical assistant into a room to get her weight and vitals. This room was friendlier than the waiting room. White, pink, and blue walls made it warmer. The pictures of flowers and children playing in a sandbox gave the room character.

"The doctor will be in shortly to see you. Please remove your shirt and put this on." The assistant smiled and walked out of the patients' room.

"We're going to see Junior today, honey." Kendal's elation could be seen in his cheek-to-cheek smile.

"You keep saying Junior, but what if it's a girl?" Mattie asked.

"Again, she'll still be named J.R. too." he laughed.

"You're sick, Kendal Abraham…" she paused to kiss him.

"Can you believe she called him that?" Mattie asked still with the family from the lobby still on her mind.

"Now *she* was sick. She's so far gone; those kids need better. I think we should start a day care center for kids like that, don't you?" He answered Mattie's question with one of his own.

"Yeah, I do, we'd have to get certified teachers." Mattie understood that Kendal wanted to make a difference in any way he was able.

She could see his mind working. He was a quick thinker, but he would take his time on formulating the plan, but his mind was made up to move forward.

"I'm gonna call the county and see what criteria has to be met," he asserted as a knock was heard on the door.

"Come in!" They replied in unison.

"Hi, I'm Dr. Hinoway." She shook Mattie's hand and then Kendal's. She looked to be of Indian descent with jet black hair and naturally tan skin. She wore designer glasses with a charm around her neck.

"So, you're having a baby." She smiled at Mattie as another light tap was heard on the door.

Dr. Hinoway opened the door allowing her assistant into the room. She was carrying a bottle of liquid gel.

"Well what questions have you had so far?" She directed her questions towards Mattie.

Mattie had not thought of too many questions, largely due to Sheila always giving her tidbits of information on having a baby; like what to expect in each trimester, how eating and sleeping affects the child.

"Actually, my best friend is a nurse, so she's been drilling me on the do's and don'ts." Mattie answered.

Kendal nodded his head, because Sheila had been doing the same to him, informing him by email about pregnancy and different forms of childbirth.

"Yeah, she's sending all types of birthing methods. I didn't know having a child born in water was safe," he added in amazement.

Dr. Hinoway just laughed.

"Yes, there are some great alternative methods we can discuss." She continued to smile showing her amusement. Her accent frequented her words the more she talked.

"Well, today we get to see the little one! Are you guys excited?"

"Oh yeah, we get to see our baby! That's all I've been thinking about for the past few weeks." Kendal excitedly squeezed Mattie's hand as he had remained standing the whole entire time.

Mattie was happy too, but she was still just as nervous with her palms sweating.

Dr. Hinoway put on latex gloves while her assistant moved the ultrasound equipment closer to Mattie. The doctor lifted the gown and spread the gel onto Mattie's stomach.

Mattie flinched because the gel was colder than expected.

Kendal was still standing up on the opposite side of the doctor and machine, with his eyes glued on the screen.

It seemed to last a long time before Dr. Hinoway was able to locate the baby, but when she pointed out features, clicking on the apparatus to take snap shots, Kendal could not have been prouder.

"Here's the head…. and here is the heartbeat." Dr. Hinoway clicked the mouse to take a few more pictures. She advised it was too early to do a gender scan.

"We have a baby… we have a baby," Kendal sang while Mattie just smiled.

"They will set your next visit up front. If you have any questions about anything, just call, but it sounds like your friend is a walking encyclopedia! Congratulations again," Dr. Hinoway said before exiting the room. The assistant wiped most of the gel from Mattie's belly and congratulated them both again before reaffirming they would set the next appointment when they met her at the counter to check out of the office.

Mattie made sure to wipe the remaining gel off her stomach and put her t-shirt back on as Kendal stared at the pictures. They set the next appointment and decided on the way back home to take Aunt Penny to breakfast and give her the news before driving up to Cleveland.

DISSONANCE

CHAPTER 10

Henry sat at his desk in the police station. The results had come back from the FBI lab; as he cross-referenced the number of stores that carried the wig, he believed he was no further along in the investigation than he was yesterday.

"Jenkins, in my office." His captain appeared and called out to him standing while in the doorway of his office. He had been pressing Henry and his partner.

It had been like this for the past six weeks; every week he was summoned to get an update on the case because the mayor's office wanted results.

Bob Fredericks was not only a big-time developer and one of the mayor's political allies, but he also had a long reach in the streets. The pressure was being extended from city hall to solve the case.

"Sit down, detective." The captain took the opposite chair.

"So, you got the information back from the FBI yesterday." He was an older white man with thinning red hair who had been on the force for nearly 20 years and captain of this precinct for the past nine years. The station had been involved in scandals, but each time the officers had been acquitted.

"I've just completed a list of local hair shops to canvass today with Roberts." Henry was quick to respond.

This case was burdensome as Jimmie Fredericks, the deceased, was the youngest brother of Bob Fredericks.

Henry had other cases he was working but nothing in his workload had taken on more importance than the Jimmie Fredericks file. The mayor was riding the chief of police, and it was all trickling down.

"I'm getting my ass chewed out over this, and the shit is going to roll down hill," the captain complained as he stood up to sit on the corner of his desk. "We need something, Detective, regardless of how many run-ins with the law he had. Maybe you should interview the bartender again." His voice was strained as he shook his head.

The way he said it made Henry think that he was missing something in the statement just made. The captain knew Henry had interviewed the bartender twice thus far and her story had not changed. In fact, Henry and his partner had interviewed thoroughly every person in the bar that night that could be identified.

"Sir, she's given the same account: cash was paid, and she had never seen the woman. The victim had never spoken with the suspect before that night," Henry countered.

"Perhaps she remembers more today, Detective. Make it a point to visit the bar!"

Henry had no doubt that it wasn't a request but an order.

"I'll expect to be briefed no later than six o'clock. You are dismissed, Jenkins." The captain moved from his desk back to open the door, excusing Henry.

Henry walked out of the office feeling at odds; he didn't like being reprimanded for how he was handling the case.

"Jenkins, you ready?" A new detective named Roberts called out across the floor.

Detective John Roberts was nearly nine years younger than Henry but had already had his detective shield for two years. His ambition drove him and only two years out of the academy, he had done undercover work resulting in the bust of a major narcotic ring that traveled I-70, covering three states.

"Let me grab the list, and I'll meet you downstairs," Henry responded. The list contained over 30 stores and they both knew it was a long shot, but it was the only viable lead they had.

"Why am I going to waste time with the bartender again?" He took the elevator down. He felt at odds with the captain, but he would oblige him because following the chain of command was part of his job.

"Let's hit the west side first and work our way back," Detective Roberts said as Henry closed the door to the passenger side of the unmarked car.

"Yeah, that's fine." Henry had been extremely skeptical about partnering up with the younger man, but the truth was he was a good detective. With his older partner still recuperating from surgery, Roberts was about as good as any partner he could get in the interim.

After visiting half of the stores on the list with no results, they decided to pay the night spot a visit and interview the bartender again.

The bar wasn't going to be opened until later but as Detective Roberts exited the Impala, the bar door opened and Ruby the bartender stood there, as if she was wiping the glass portion as they walked in.

"Looks like she's expecting us," John whispered, curious about the timing.

"Yeah, it looks that way," Henry affirmed.

After taking seats at the bar, Ruby turned the juke box on and asked if they wanted something to drink.

"Sprite," John responded, and Henry took a simple water with lemon in it.

"You know I had forgotten something from that night, and I wanted to make sure you had it for your records," Ruby said before lighting up a cigarette.

"So, you have something else to add, is what you're telling us?" John asked as Ruby nodded her head.

Henry took out a memo pad so he could write down the new information.

"Well... one of his girlfriends... you know Jimmie's workers had taken a man outside that night... and uh... I think him, and Jimmie had a few words about paying for her services." The bartender finished by taking a long drag on the cigarette.

"Does this man have a name, Ruby?" Henry felt like Ruby was struggling giving this new account of what happened that night.

"Uh, yeah his name is Mark... Mark Floyd," she stuttered as she answered.

"Out of curiosity Ruby, the other two times we have seen you, why didn't you tell us this?" John probed.

"We asked a good number of questions. Just seems convenient for you to remember now," Henry added before he drank down the rest of his water. Ruby took another drag on her cigarette before putting it out on a wet bar napkin.

"I... I don't know you guys kept asking about the woman at the bar, so I guess it slipped my mind," she answered as she filled Henry's glass with more water.

"People get nervous around the boys in blue, and I mean Jimmie... Jimmie didn't deserve to be murdered like that." She extended the refilled glass of water.

"I'm fine, thanks." Henry closed his memo pad.

"Is there anything else you can remember or want to tell us Ruby, anything at all?" Henry attempted to hide his frustration. He did not believe her new account of what happened.

Ruby looked afraid when she shook her head.

"Well enjoy your day." John made pleasantries before he and Henry stood up from the bar and headed out the door.

"I don't believe one word she just said." The younger detective wasn't impressed.

"Well, that makes two of us," Henry agreed.

"Somebody had been talking to her; we've got to be very careful moving forward, partner." John pulled the keys out to the car.

"Let's grab a bite to eat before we finish with the last few places on the list, and we'll look up Mark Floyd first thing when we get back." John started the engine, pulling the car out of the parking lot.

Henry was already thinking the same thing, but he also had an indication that the captain was involved in misdirection at best and a possible cover-up at worst.

NO MORE SURPRISES
CHAPTER 11

"**I** don't know what to think about dinner and some music," Geri told Kwame over the phone.

He was trying to corner her into agreeing to have a late dinner that also would serve as a date.

"How about a business lunch and I'll buy?" Geri tried to control the flow of the conversation. She had men of power assume that she would do anything for an interview before, but she never let it go beyond professionalism.

"Now Geraldine, you know I'm going to have to say yes to your offer. Are you flying to Boston?" Geri was well aware that the next leg of the tour was scheduled to begin there in a few days.

"It would be in your best interest. In fact, I'll give you the first exclusive interview after we sign the deal with the network. If you play nice, I'll plug the edition for you on air," Kwame concluded with certainty that she would accept his offer.

"I'll have to see what my schedule looks like for the week—prior obligations. But if I can make it out this week, I'll be in Boston. I've got a couple of friends I haven't seen since college," she paused to make sure Kwame was listening. "This is purely business, Kwame." Geri reiterated her stance. It wasn't that she didn't find him attractive and charming, but she had no intention of falling for a player who had scores of women across the globe.

"Of course, Geri, I wouldn't have it any other way."

Geri could hear the confidence and smile on his face through the phone. He knew he had gotten as far as he could until he saw her in person again. She was challenging him.

"Well, I'll speak with you soon to finalize the interview." Geri ended the call.

Mattie, who had been in her office for this call, just shook her head as she addressed her friend.

"You gotta be careful with that one; he's polished."

"I know," Geri sighed. "I'm gonna keep my guard up, you don't have to worry about that. I've got one more housekeeping item to handle and then we can pick Auntie up." Geri stood from her seat behind the desk and walked out of her office. She was wearing a canary yellow pant suit with a pair of Mattie's shoes to match.

Mattie texted her aunt to tell her they would be there shortly, and Aunt Penny responded with "k." The older women had learned to use that cell phone and could text and go online to check information she needed for just about anything. The few days while Mattie was in Cleveland were enough to give her aunt ample time to hone her skills with the device.

Cleveland had been more refreshing than she thought. Kendal's mom picked out not only the crib and changing table but the dresser and chest too. She was more excited about shopping than Mattie had been. After their shopping spree, they had dinner where Mattie met Kendal's sister and two more cousins.

"Ok, now that I got that over with, you ready?" Geri was standing in the doorway of her office, looking back at her workers who were whispering about something.

"Damn, that was quick! What you do, fire somebody?" Mattie asked as a passing thought.

"How did you know... I hated letting him go. He was a good writer when he showed up, which was two to three days per week. He had more excuses than Brian," Geri said comparing him to one of Mattie's ex boyfriends.

"Then you should have fired him a long time ago." Mattie laughed as she stood up without taking offense to the reference.

Geri and Mattie were going out on a limb by taking Aunt Penny to a Japanese steakhouse where they cooked the food right in front of the customers. They both agreed rice, steak, and chicken were staples among the older woman's food list, but they had no idea how she would react to the atmosphere.

Traffic was moderate from Geri's office to Mattie's home. When they arrived and walked in, Aunt Penny was sitting in the recliner in the living room speaking with a woman.

"Ah, here she is now," she said as they walked through the front door.

"Madison, this is Stephanie Nixon. It seems you had an appointment with her today about the vacant unit."

Mattie looked on with a puzzled look on her face before it dawned on her.

"You have to excuse me, I completely forgot honestly. Did you print the application off from online?" Mattie walked towards the sofa and shook the woman's hand.

Stephanie reached down to the coffee table and handed Mattie a manila folder that contained the application. Aunt

Penny and Geri excused themselves to the dining room to let Mattie finish the interview.

"Ok, so you've been employed at the same place for six years and the same residence for that amount of time." Mattie scanned through the application.

She saw that Stephanie had no kids but had a pet.

"What type of pet do you have?"

Small dogs less than 25 pounds would be allowed, but Mattie had a preference to have no pets inside her building.

"I have a British shorthair, declawed and spayed," Stephanie answered politely with her legs crossed.

Mattie had a good feeling about her, unlike some of the other applicants she had interviewed. There was a woman who came with her children to the interview who said she was homeschooling her kids, but the woman kept using incorrect grammar.

There was another couple she had interviewed who showed up 30 minutes late because the husband lost track of time. Mattie smelled the marijuana on him when they walked through the door. She didn't mind people who smoked, but when it interfered with daily activities like being on time, she drew the line.

"Stephanie, you are a breath of fresh air… trust me." Mattie paused.

"I'll have to run a credit and background check. How soon were you trying to move in?" Mattie asked as she glanced her over again. Stephanie's nails were done and hair in place, something that spoke volumes.

"Within three to four weeks I would say, but I can pay any deposits required if things work out," Stephanie answered.

Mattie hoped her background and credit information was solid. Having tenants was one thing but having "good tenants" was another. Mattie's was sad to see her previous tenant leave but after the minor stroke she needed 24-hour care.

"Is this the best number to reach you?" Mattie slowly stood up from the sofa.

"Yes, it is. If I don't answer, please leave a message letting me know your determination. I have one more place to look at but honestly, I love the layout of the space. I'll be looking forward to hearing from you soon." Stephanie also stood up.

Mattie walked her to the door with the folder in hand.

"Thanks for coming and being patient." Mattie closed the door behind her and walked into the dining room to see if Geri and Aunt Penny were ready.

"Yes, I'm starving," Aunt Penny replied as Geri helped her up. "I think she's the one, Madison. I just got a good vibe from talking to her," the older woman added.

"So did I, I just gotta run a couple of checks and then I'll call her."

"We are going to Golden Corral?" Aunt Penny said it as more of a statement than question.

"No ma'am, they already know you by name there. We're going to try something different." Mattie was interrupted by the older woman.

"Just like I told Geri when she wanted to surprise me; I eat my food cooked." The older woman quickly reminisced to when Sheila and Geri took her to try sushi.

"But I did like that cheesecake place you took me, but that menu was too damn big." She nodded towards Geri.

"Well good Auntie, because I didn't want to be fussed out." Geri led the way out of the home. There wasn't too much talking in the SUV, the drive to the restaurant was a short distance so as the second song on the radio ended, they pulled up to the Japanese steakhouse with excitement carried across the older woman's face.

"I saw the commercial for this! They cook it right in front of us, right?" she asked expectantly.

"Yes, they sure do." Geri pulled into a parking space.

Mattie was relieved that Aunt Penny seemed to be enjoying herself. It had taken months after Grandma Redd's death for them to find a common ground, and now they were cramming in moments before the older woman flew back home to check on her property and a few more family members.

The restaurant was filling their tables quickly since it was lunch time, and their party was the last to be seated, so they didn't have to wait long before their orders were taken.

As they ate, Aunt Penny tried using chopsticks but gave up on that notion because her arthritis prevented her from gripping them properly.

"Whoa!" a man's voice yelled out and as the patrons looked towards the sound, they saw a man falling slowly backwards out of his chair due to the unsuspecting flame surprising him when the chef prepared the hibachi grill for another table.

"I'm ok... I'm ok." He stood up before taking a bow and sitting back down.

"He's a good sport to laugh at himself." Aunt Penny giggled.

"I can't eat all of this." Mattie stared over at Geri, who had devoured her plate already.

"Box it up, I'll take it back to the office and eat later. I need to finish this project tonight if I'm going to fly to Boston for Kwame's interview at the end of the week." Geri extended her chopsticks to Mattie's plate, picking a piece of steak up to dip in the yum yum sauce.

"So, you decided to go?" Mattie asked as a server boxed her remaining food.

"Are you kidding? Of course I'm going! An exclusive with Kwame Hill on the brink of a network sponsorship, and he's going to plug the edition on television." For Geri it was a no brainer.

"Maybe you should fly out with her honey." Aunt Penny motioned to the waitress to add her left over food to the box of food Geri was taking.

Mattie thought about it, she had work to do at the center as she was gathering information on how to become certified to offer childcare. She also had moved her appointment with Dr. Stevens to Thursday morning.

"I've got a doctor's appointment on Thursday early." Mattie was going to do everything to have a healthy baby, including ensuring her mental compartments remained strong.

"Well, we can fly out Thursday evening, go to the show. I'll have the interview Friday afternoon. I wanted to visit Tasha McIntyre and J.J when we get there. We haven't seen them in forever… and I'll put the tickets on my business account." Geri already knew, without Mattie saying a word, she was going to Boston with her.

Mattie needed to make sure her older family member would be alright for a few days.

"Well, what are you going to do, Auntie. I feel like I've been stranding you by yourself lately." Mattie stood up from the table to scan for the restroom. She found herself needing to frequent it more the last few weeks. When she returned, Geri was waiting for her credit card receipt.

"I'll get Sheila to bring her children over and have Cindy take us to the movies. I have been promising them kids a movie for two weeks now." The older woman had slowly become a part of the bond.

"Well, I don't need much. We got food and I got this cell phone. If I need something, I know how to use it." Aunt Penny laughed out loud knowing she had texted Mattie and her friends at all hours of the day and night, sometimes just because.

"Yes, you do Auntie… yes you do." Mattie laughed with her as they walked out the door of the restaurant. It was final; Mattie was going to see her fiancé and this time she was calling him beforehand so there would be no more surprises.

WHO IS IT?
CHAPTER 12

As promised, Kwame gave Geri the interview and followed up by introducing her to one of the network agents. Geri had been elated just to get the exclusive, but meeting the agent took it to a whole new level. In fact, she was so thrilled that she even agreed to have a non-business-related dinner with him when the tour came to Columbus.

Mattie and Geri were leaving the office of their college friend July, an attorney in Boston. She was moderately successful as she chose to start her own practice instead of working for a large firm.

"Thanks for the tickets! Jamaal and I are going to enjoy them. Are you guys sure you won't stay a couple more days? I'd love you all to meet him. He'll be back from Portland tomorrow night." They waited for her car to be driven from the parking garage.

"We're flying out tomorrow, I need to get this interview to press." Geris stepped to the side to allow a couple to pass.

"Yeah, and my aunt is home by herself," Mattie added.

"Well look, I've got a briefing in 30 minutes, but if you aren't tied up later ... dinner?" July asked.

"Mad Mattie! Congratulations on the engagement and the baby," July said giving her friends hugs before sitting in her car.

Mattie hadn't heard her college nickname in years. She became "Mad Mattie" after several altercations about how loud her music was, cussing the dormitories hall monitors out. The name stuck for the rest of her years in college.

"Yeah, those were the good old days," Mattie replied as they waited for Kendal's rental car to be pulled around.

"So, what do you want to do?" Geri asked sitting down in the passenger seat of the import SUV.

"I'm tired and need to take a nap. Tasha still hasn't called back yet, so let's just head back to the hotel and later we can shop or something, grab a bite before their show begins." Mattie had been getting exhausted much quicker.

Geri decided she would begin editing the interview with Kwame to get a head start on it. It was a dynamic session; he had shared things about his personal life as a kid that helped shape him. Geri found it refreshing to see a whole different side to him.

When they arrived at the hotel, Mattie called Aunt Penny to make sure she was ok.

"Yes, I'm fine. I let Darrien and Samantha spend the night, and they slept in your room. I hope you don't mind," the older woman said.

"No, I don't mind," she answered, realizing her aunt was taking her feelings into consideration.

"You should've seen 'em last night. Samantha put your wigs on and started singing Beyonce and Rihanna songs. I tried taking pictures with this cell phone but think I got videos instead. I'll show you later." Aunt Penny paused as Darrien's voice was heard in the background.

"Auntie, can we have some more juice?"

"Yes, baby, have your sister pour it though," she answered.

"Children with manners make a world of difference... and I was thinking, what if you and Kendal have the wedding down south? It'd be so pretty. It'd be on your own property, and it wouldn't take much to get it ready. Your kin folks would love it," the elder woman said.

Mattie didn't put too much thought into it although she did want to see the land her grandmother had left for her.

185

"I don't know… it be a lot of money, and people would have to make traveling plans and such…" Mattie was saying when her aunt cut her off.

"It's just a suggestion. Just think about it before you say no. Don't rush to say no, baby."

"Excuse me, Auntie, Sam isn't pouring the juice! She won't get off the couch," Darrien interrupted her from the hallway.

"Yes, I am! He just wanted to take my spot on the couch and turn the channel from what I'm already watching! That's my spot." Samantha made sure she was loud enough that Aunt Penny heard her.

"I gotta go. These two argue like cats and dogs, but they love each other and that's what important…" Aunt Penny hesitated.

"Cindy got her first lesson yesterday," she stated before hanging up.

"She has patience with kids and none with adults," Mattie exclaimed to Geri as her phone rang.

"Yes ma'am?" she answered, thinking it was her aunt calling back.

"I'm going to kill y'all for leaving me with her!" Cindy's voice came through.

Mattie simply laughed, telling Geri it was Cindy on the phone. She placed the call on speaker.

"She has texted me a thousand times at least, made me... made me spend the whole day with her and the kids, and then had the *audacity* to sit me down next to Samantha to teach me how to crotchet like I was a kid. I'm less than 15 seconds away from slitting my wrists. I hate it with a passion when she calls me *child*." Cindy's voice held all the disgust she was feeling.

"Yeah, I know, but that just means she cares about you," Mattie reminded as Geri pressed the button up on the elevator.

"Well, I wish she would care less. You talk to Sheila?" Cindy asked.

The way it came out Mattie knew there was something else hidden behind the question.

"Not for a few days, what's up?" Mattie asked.

"Oh nothing ... nothing at all... ok I'm bullshitting. Sheila and James spent the whole day and night together... you hear me?"

"Yeah, I heard you, and we are going to stay out of it," Mattie responded with the emphasis on *we*.

"I ain't all up in their business." Cindy clearly felt a certain way.

"Kinda sounded like you were," Mattie replied.

"Whateva'." Cindy changed the subject. "I saved yesterday's paper for you. Henry arrested somebody from that case he was working on, you remember? That one he told us about the night you got engaged."

Mattie didn't quite understand what her friend had just said.

"What did you say?"

"That case he was working with the dude found dead behind the bar? You know, the one the mayor's office kept riding his ass about. They arrested somebody, and it was all in the paper. Aunt Penny said they mentioned it on the news too. So, I saved you the article," Cindy answered.

"Wow," was all Mattie could muster.

Somebody is taking the fall for what I did, she thought, not exactly knowing how to feel about it. Part of her was relieved but another part was apprehensive that someone else was being blamed for her actions.

They have the wrong person, she thought.

"Who is it?" Mattie asked.

"Hell, I don't know who it is, but Henry caught him." Cindy paused. "I gotta go. This is Peter calling." Cindy hung up.

"What's going on?" Geri asked.

"Uh, Sheila and James hooked up all day and night… Aunt Penny strong armed Cindy and…" Mattie hesitated over her words. "I guess Henry found the person responsible for that man's murder behind the bar he told us about at dinner." Mattie's mind was spinning.

"Your aunt is not so bad as y'all make her out to be and if Sheila is happy for right now, we just need to let her be," Geri responded, not saying anything at all about Henry's case.

"I'm going to lay down." Mattie opened the hotel door to Kendal's room. She went to the bathroom to wash her face off. Staring into the mirror at her reflection, she wondered how Henry could make such a huge mistake.

What if they find him guilty? Mattie silently questioned. If they found him guilty, that would be another burden for her to carry.

They won't find him guilty because there's no evidence… but what if they do. A tiny voice in her said as Kendal walked into the room.

"Hey baby." He kissed her on the lips.

"What's wrong you look like you just seen a ghost," he asked.

"I'm good honey, just tired." She went to lay on the bed. She hadn't seen a ghost, but she was thinking back to the day her mother was taken to jail and about the man falsely arrested. How could the legal system be so unjust?

GINGER ALE

CHAPTER 13

"Oh yes, it's ladies' night, and the feeling's right! Oh yes, it's ladies' night, oh, what a night." Cindy was bobbing her head as they walked into Second Saturdays at the Masonic Lodge. It was event night, and it was her turn to pick the event. She loved to dance so it was no secret this was where they would end up.

After she flew back from Boston nearly six days ago, the week had flown by for Mattie. She alternated spending time with Aunt Penny and helping out at the center.

"Damn, it's crowded up in here," Mattie said loudly sliding through groups of people talking, attempting to find an area where there were tables left unattended, but she didn't see any.

"Girl, you ain't think I'd have you on your feet all night, did you?" Cindy grabbed Mattie by the elbow, motioning towards the DJ's booth. She was acquainted with the DJ and had him save her the table closest to him. She had sold him his first property and saved him tons of money.

Sitting to the sides of the speakers wasn't as bad as they thought, since the sound was being pushed out towards the crowd. They would have their very own server so they wouldn't have to push and shove to get to the bar, which currently had two rows of people trying to order drinks.

Geri stood up and started dancing with Cindy next to the table. They were already having a good time without having drinks ordered yet. It had been a good work week, and they were letting off steam. The waitress came and Geri ordered six shots of "buckeyes" and three Corona.

"First rounds on me," she yelled as she kept bouncing to the music. Although Geri was white, she had hung around Mattie and the girls long enough for over 15 years that she could keep up with them. As she put her hands above her head, feeling the music, two men approached their table, waving at them to get their attention to ask them to dance. At first Geri and Cindy tried ignoring them to be polite, but the men did everything to make themselves noticed.

"Not yet." Cindy waved bye-bye to them and the look of rejection shown on their faces. One of the men motioned that he would be back, but Cindy waved him off again.

Mattie shook her head at her friends.

"That was cold," she yelled above the music as she looked up at them.

Neither Cindy nor Geri cared as they laughed it off. Sheila sat down with Mattie. She wasn't feeling the music quite like her friends were, but Mattie knew after they took shots, Sheila would be throwing her ass all over the place.

"We gon' drink for you too, momma." Geri bent down to say in Mattie's ear. This was the second event night she had gone to after finding out she was pregnant, so she had volunteered to be the designated driver.

Mattie smiled and nodded her head in agreement.

The hall was packed with people socializing and drinking. The way the lodge was set up only a few people were able to have tables, and the other folks stood elbow to elbow. The waitress came back with their shots and beer.

Mattie had ordered Sprite and a glass of water. She had been sweating before they had entered, and now it seemed like it poured out of her skin. Her metabolism had clearly changed.

Cindy grabbed Sheila by her arm and made her stand up to take the first shots.

"To event night, ladies!" Cindy yelled out before they clicked glasses together and tilted their drinks back.

Geri reached for the second shot and made her toast, "To event night, bitches!" she screamed before downing the second.

Mattie felt left out but knew why she was sipping on Sprite and chasing it with water. Her baby was her priority, and she wasn't an expectant mother who believed taking a sip of wine every now and then was acceptable. She had made an about face by taking her vitamins regularly and maintaining a proper diet. As Mattie looked out into the crowd, she saw a few women dancing energetically on the dance floor like they had done at that age when they were younger.

The DJ was spinning a variety of mixes that kept the party flowing without pause and with the liquor in their system Mattie's friends were ready to party.

Sheila asked Mattie if she would be ok as the trio made their way to the dance floor.

"I'll be fine, go on and shake that thing," Mattie responded, feeling a little better about getting out of the house.

The three women eased a few couples out the way to make room for them to dance. Each time a group of men approached, they turned their backs to them and danced together making sure the men got the point. As they loosened up, the DJ started mixing, "To the left, to the left, to the left to the left, to the left, now kick that…" and the hall erupted as people made their way to the dance floor with drinks in hand.

Even Mattie started to stand up, but remembered at the last second all their purses were sitting on the table. Mattie smiled, watching her friends have fun together and she thought to herself,

I can't wait 'til you're born, your mom ain't gon' be all nerdy and dull. Mommy is going to teach you how to get it.

She pulled out her cell phone to text Kendal.

MATTIE: I can't wait to see you next week. Isleofview.

The song skipped so Mattie looked over at the DJ station. He was waving for people to back away from the stage, but no one listened. Luckily, the song stayed on track. He then loaded Tamia's song, "Can't Get Enough," and the dance floor was packed. After nearly 20 minutes of line dancing, he began mixing danceable songs back into his set.

Her friends were walking back to the table, and they were drenched in sweat. Sheila picked up her beer and drank the whole thing down.

"Whew!" she yelled.

Geri and Cindy tried keeping pace with her but only got through half of their bottles.

"I need another shot," Sheila said looking for their waitress.

"Mattie, are you drinking this water?"

Mattie shook her head, and Sheila gulped it down.

"Take your purse with you when you gotta go pee 'cause if they play another line dancing song and be rocking it like he just was, then I'm on it. I ain't gon' sit here by myself all night." Mattie figured that a dance or two wouldn't hurt anything.

Geri was drinking her beer when a man approached the table. He was wearing a gray, short sleeve button down with nice fitting jeans and black leather shoes.

He looked vaguely familiar to Mattie and when Cindy gave him a big hug and kiss, she remembered it was Peter Hanford, the general manager of the dealership.

"Geri this is Peter, and you remember Madison." Cindy made introductions before pulling him to the dance floor.

"I can't even remember the last time I saw Cindy so happy," Geri yelled much louder than she intended.

"Those drinks must be all up in here," Mattie said loudly, rubbing her chest as Geri laughed.

Geri sat down and drank the rest of Mattie's soda. The temperature kept increasing inside the building and with people having a good time no one seemed to mind.

Yeah, she does seem happy, Mattie thought.

Sheila had come back to the table at the same moment as their waitress returned. "Bring the same as before with a whole pitcher of water." Sheila was shaking her body vigorously to the music, making her ass jiggle and attracting more attention to their table.

"Shake that ass, girl!" A man's voice called out, but no one saw who said it.

The waitress laughed.

"So, a whole pitcher of water." She repeated, to make sure she understood Sheila's request.

"Yes, a whole pitcher of that shit." Sheila was smiling. "I needed this," she said, as she sat down in between Geri and Mattie.

"This James shit has got me confused, but I am not gon' be talking about it tonight. This is our night!" Sheila declared before looking around. "Where's Cindy's ass?" she asked.

Geri pointed her out on the dance floor.

Cindy was letting it out, dancing and moving around Peter who had some moves. But with liquor in Cindy's system, there was no way he was going to be able to keep up with her.

"James can dance," Sheila belted out the blue.

Mattie looked over at Geri before looking at Sheila.

"My bad… my bad. These drinks just got me toasted… I'm done." Sheila quickly ended the subject.

Geri stood up as one of the men who first approached them came back, waving at her to dance. She obliged him, telling Mattie, "Sheila is all yours," as she followed behind the man to the dance floor.

The waitress had finally returned, followed by a man carrying a pitcher of water while she sat the drinks and beer onto the table.

"Thank you," Sheila said.

Mattie poured herself another glass of water because she was sweating as much as her friends were and hadn't even been dancing.

Sheila took another shot and sat back to sip on her beer.

Cindy and Peter were making their way back to the table.

"She was getting it in, wasn't she?" Peter said while motioning to the water.

Cindy poured him a glass and then took one of her shots.

"You wanna drink?" Sheila asked Peter.

Peter smiled and declined.

"No thanks, I don't drink."

Mattie wondered why. Was it his religion or he just didn't get into alcohol?

"Congratulations on the engagement, Madison! Maybe we can all hangout soon." He poured another glass of water.

Geri was walking back to the table slightly agitated.

"Motherfucker grabbed my ass," She blurted out.

Cindy handed Geri her other shot and Sheila picked her glass up.

"To getting that ass grabbed!" Cindy yelled out and downed her shot, followed by her girls.

Geri had gotten over being groped, but she was done dancing.

Cindy grabbed Peter and made their way back to the dance floor.

Geri stood back up and moved side to side. She was worn out and tipsy but wasn't going anywhere near the dance floor.

Cindy came back to the table and grabbed her purse. She told Mattie that Peter was taking her home, and she would catch up with her later.

Mattie checked her phone, but no reply had come from Kendal.

The show ain't over yet, she thought.

The waitress came back with the bill, and Mattie paid for it with cash.

"Y'all ready?" It was only one o'clock, but she was tired.

Both of her friends nodded. As they made their way to the exit, Mattie's phone was vibrating, but it wasn't Kendal. It was Aunt Penny texting her at this odd hour in the morning.

AUNTIE: Will you bring some ginger ale home? My stomach is all torn up.

Mattie shook her head.

"This woman is gonna be the end of me. She wants us to stop and get ginger ale."

Sheila started laughing uncontrollably.

"Woman, what's so damn funny?" Geri asked while joining in the laughter, unsure of why her friend was giggling.

"Grandma Redd, Aunt Penny, and now this child-carrying beautiful woman, love that ginger ale shit too. Pepsi is played out."

Mattie smiled because it was true. Ginger ale was her new drink.

As they pulled out of the parking lot of the Masonic Lodge, people were running out the door, scrambling over each other. Listening to the radio as they drove home, the radio announcer said there had been a shooting with one person confirmed dead.

"Damn, we just got out of there in the nick of time," Sheila slurred.

Before Mattie dropped her friends off, she went to a gas station still open late at night to get the ginger ale. She took the shooting as an omen and wasn't doing anything by herself. At this hour of the night, she was lucky to have found the filling station open or she would have had to go to a 24-hour grocery store, which would've been another 20 minutes out of her way.

Mattie hoped that by the time she got home her aunt would've been asleep in bed, but she wasn't. She was up watching reruns of Family Feud with a blanket and pillow on her lap.

"You stayin' up to make sure I make curfew and get home safe, Auntie?" Mattie joked closing the door to her home behind her before securing the locks.

"I wish it was that, baby. Please pour me some ginger ale? My stomach has been cramping. I drank one of those nasty Pepsis, and that will be the first and last time I do." She rocked forward from the sofa to sit up, placing the pillow off to her side.

Mattie could tell that her aunt was in discomfort but was trying to hide it.

"Here you go." Mattie gave her aunt a glass of ginger ale.

Aunt Penny took a sip and then another before belching loudly.

"Excuse me, but that feels so much better."

Mattie excused herself, saying she was going to take a shower because she felt sweaty and sticky. There was no way she would be hopping in her bed feeling so nasty. She thanked God for protecting her and her friends by making them leave when they had.

After the shower, she found herself sitting in her recliner in the living room watching Family Feud with Aunt Penny. She wasn't as tired as she thought.

Since leaving Global Communications, she had slept a little longer and on occasion took naps throughout the day. She pulled her cell phone out to see if any messages or calls had come from Kendal but nothing. She figured Kwame had him out again, a habit Mattie was gonna slow down when he got off tour.

"Name an item used regularly by couples living together," Richard Dawson asked the contestants on the show.

"Toothpaste!" Aunt Penny called out. When the answer was revealed on the board, she let out another burp.

"I'm glad to see the ginger ale is working," Mattie joked without regard to anything her aunt could respond to.

"That make two of us… y'all had a good time?" she asked as the show went to commercial.

"Yeah, Sheila and Geri definitely had a good time, Cindy left early with her boyfriend." Mattie left out the news of the shooting.

"That's good." Aunt Penny replied. "I think I'm going to be heading home soon," she said out of the blue.

Mattie heard what she had said but did not comprehend it.

"Say that again, Auntie."

"I think I'm going to be leaving Columbus. You're ready to stand on yo' own two feet. You have a fiancé and a baby on the way, a family, Madison Imani Parks." She belched one last time.

Mattie had dreamed of this day, every day since her aunt had arrived, but now hearing the words being spoken she didn't feel quite as relieved as she thought she would.

"Well, you can stay a little longer. I know I can be a pain in the a..." Mattie started to say before correcting her language. "...in the butt. But I'm not asking you to go, Auntie," Mattie exclaimed. The truth was Mattie felt nervous. Since coming home from college, she always had Grandma Redd there and Aunt Penny had replaced her in spirit.

"Well, I haven't picked a date yet, but you don't need me here any longer. I only stayed because you weren't ready... and I guess I wasn't either. But we both gon' be fine. God has been good to our family; most of our women live longer than their husbands. It's important to have family Madison, but more important to love family," she paused to pull out a book lying under her blanket.

"I've been working on a book of our lineage and I'm going to leave it with you," her aunt said.

Mattie realized that for the first time since arriving, her aunt was speaking to her as an equal. What prompted the change Mattie had no idea, but it felt good not being spoken down to.

"Oh, auntie thank you... thank you." Mattie sat up from her recliner to give her aunt a hug.

"I love you, child. Will you get me some more ginger ale?" Aunt Penny asked.

"Yes ma'am, I love you too."

Mattie picked up the glass and went to pour more. She felt thirsty so she pulled a second glass out to pour some Cran-Grape juice. She saw a bunch of celery on the shelf and decided she'd eat it with peanut butter while watching the rest of Family Feud with her aunt.

"Name something that people do when waking up in the morning," Richard Dawson's voice asked.

"Brush their teeth!" Mattie called out immediately.

"Use the bathroom," Aunt Penny gave her answer.

When "use the bathroom" came up as answer one; Mattie smiled. She realized she was going to miss her aunt much more than she expected whenever she decided to leave.

REPRESSED
CHAPTER 14

G randma Redd was looking down into the crib at the baby as Mattie carried a small tub of water back into the room to wash the baby boy off.

"He's so handsome! Reminds me of your cousin Matthew when he was a baby… head full of hair," Grandma Redd said, stepping to the head of the crib as Mattie took the cloth and wiped her child down.

Kendal was his name, but the nickname Junior had stuck after his father began calling him that. The baby's room lacked nothing. The changing table and chest matched the dresser. The carousel above the crib was specially designed with Disney characters, and Mickey Mouse was captured on the walls in picture frames.

Mattie was happy; the baby had brought more joy into her life. The baby was born healthy and happy, and she had no worries about being a mother. She welcomed it. Mattie turned away as she heard the door close. When she looked back, Grandma Redd was no longer standing at the head of the bed. When Mattie turned back and looked down in the crib, her baby had disappeared. She was no longer standing in a baby's room but outside in an alley as the rain began falling on her.

The environment looked vaguely familiar, but she couldn't put two plus two together.

"What the fuck?" She saw a figure standing above her on the landing between fire escapes.

"I killed you motherfucker... I killed you!" she screamed upwards as the shadow disappeared before her eyes.

"Am I dead then?" a voice asked from behind her.

She turned around and Jimmie Fredericks was standing there with the same washcloth Mattie had used to wipe Kendal Jr.

"Where's my baby?" she screamed, reaching out for Jimmie but she grabbed nothing but air.

"I'll kill you Jimmie... I'll kill you again!" she yelled as he reappeared on a lower landing of the fire escape holding a blanket-covered baby in his arms.

"You've already killed me... you've already killed me, haven't you?" The figure disappeared again and where he had stood, a tiny bundle remained.

Mattie tried running over to the landing, which seemed to be less than 20 feet away, but she had difficulty moving forward. The harder she tried, the slower she moved.

She heard a baby crying from the bundle and struggled to close the distance. Eventually she reached the lower landing. As she picked up the bundle, the blanket fell away, leaving nothing covered, but maggots and worms now crawling onto her hands and arms.

"NO...!" she yelled, waking herself up from the dream.

She sat there in the dark rubbing her stomach, realizing that she had had yet another nightmare. She peered over at her digital alarm clock, and it read 3:18 a.m. Mattie sat back up against her headboard and slowed her breathing. She was overwhelmed and tired of waking up in the middle of the night.

I won't feel guilty about killing Jimmie in self-defense, she thought, but she knew as soon as she thought those words, she was admitting to herself that she did have some sense of remorse stemming from her subconscious. It was a heavy weight to carry alone. But who could she tell? She kept asking this question, but the answer never changed; she could tell no one.

Mattie tried lying back down to sleep, but she kept thinking about that night. What if she had not gone to the bar or stalked him at his house after taking the call that day? Was it all premeditated? She tried changing the course of that night by sneaking out the back, but he followed her. So, what choice did she have?

I didn't have to... she began to think. "That girl could have chosen to leave but she stayed. She wasn't my responsibility," she whispered to herself.

Mattie's entire life had been marked by tragic violence. Why God had made her father such a sick individual, she never knew.

Mattie thought about the moment her mom had shot her father. She could still smell the gun residue and still see her father's naked body sprawled out on the floor of her bedroom, lying in a puddle of blood. The memories came crashing back, and she felt afraid and vulnerable. She remembered how she hated looking at the members of the jury after the verdict was read, finding her mother guilty to receive the maximum penalty allowed. It was all at the expense of saving her daughter's virtue.

She was drawn back into the now, after hearing footsteps walking down the hall. She needed to talk to someone about her dreams, her nightmares, not only for her sake but the sake of her child.

Aunt Penny said she was going to be leaving very soon, and Mattie had never been alone in her own home since graduating from college.

The television turning on in the front room forced Mattie out of her bed. Before she knew it, she was laying down on the couch with her head on Aunt Penny's lap, losing the battle to hold back the tears. She closed her eyes and thought about her appointment before dozing off.

CIRCLE OF LIFE
CHAPTER 15

Walking into the office didn't make her nervous. Mattie could think back to the first few times she had met Dr. Stevens after she had been sent to live with her grandmother. She had been so withdrawn from life that the sessions in the beginning made her numb. Over the years, a certain level of trust was established as they talked about the various pieces of her life. She had made her way back for appointments during her freshman year in college but didn't see the point after a while.

What made her nervous was she was debating telling him about Jimmie Fredericks. After all, he *was* her psychiatrist, and she believed anything that was discussed in session would remain confidential.

She checked in and sat in the lobby with other clients waiting for their own appointments. The office had four working psychiatrists and a social worker that managed the building. She had noticed a bit of change in Dr. Stevens the last time she sat across from him, besides the fact that he had aged. When she was younger, he would press the issue by asking questions. Now he probed and spent more time managing the session.

He had been with her for so long; he understood the depths of her personality. He was able to prescribe medications but unlike many of his colleagues he still took time to listen to his clients instead of simply writing scripts to be filled.

As the client walked out of his office, Dr. Stevens asked Madison to give him a moment as he explained to the receptionist what he needed her to do about cancelling the client's future appointments.

"Yes, cancel the next three but make a note to call each week offering more sessions." Dr. Stevens advised the receptionist.

"Ms. Parks," he said as he ushered Mattie into the office.

"That's the first time you've called me anything other than Madison."

"Well, you're all grown up now," he said, closing the office door behind them. He was dressed more casually in khaki pants and a polo type shirt.

After the usual offering of something to drink, Mattie began talking without being asked anything by him.

"I know the last time I was here you asked if there was something else. I wanted to share, and I said no, but that wasn't entirely true…" Mattie paused; she wasn't fully committed in disclosing Jimmie yet.

"I'm going to be having a baby," she told him, crossing her legs on the love seat.

Dr. Stevens looked up above the rim of his glasses at her.

"A baby, wow! Well congratulations are in order. I am happy for you, Madison, very happy," he said, reaching over to shake her hand, genuinely happy for her.

"I didn't want to tell you before, until after we had the ultrasound. I guess I felt like it would've been bad luck or something," she said, reaching into her purse to pull out a picture of the ultrasound to show him.

Dr. Stevens took a look at it and smiled.

"A baby," he replied before giving the picture back to her.

"I take it that Kendal's excited." He sat back in his chair.

"Possibly more than I am! He's already named the baby Junior," she laughed.

"Your grandmother would be very proud of you," he watched her expression. "So, no more fears of bad luck?" Dr. Stevens queried.

Mattie was trying to decide if she should share her concerns about the nightmares but then that would lead to a topic she wouldn't share with anyone—Jimmie Fredericks.

I'm not telling him, she thought.

"No, not bad luck, but I do have thoughts about my parents from time to time. My mother still refuses to have any real contact with me besides the few letters. Aunt Penny has taken Grandma's place to contact her. I thought she'd be out by now. I don't think she blames anyone but herself, but it would be nice if she knew she was gonna be having a grandchild."

Dr. Stevens sat back in his old black leather chair and didn't respond so Mattie kept talking.

"Don't you think she would want to know?" she asked him directly.

"I think your mother does what she does because she thinks it's in the best interest for you. A mother's love can be misunderstood sometimes," he answered matter of fact.

"Is it more important to you for her to know or you to tell her?" He followed up with a probing question.

"What do you mean?" Mattie didn't quite understand. She didn't want to get cornered and stuck dealing with additional emotions.

"Would it be more important, for example, if she heard it from a third party or you telling her? Is her knowing more important than you telling her?" he explained.

Mattie hadn't thought of it in that way, in those terms. But it was her personal business and no one else should pass the information along for her.

"I want to be the one to tell her," she replied bluntly.

"Well, why?" he asked.

"Because I want to let her know that I'm going to be a mother like…" Mattie stopped in mid-sentence.

"Like what Madison?" Dr. Stevens pried, pausing before he continued. "Like she was? You can't be a mother like she was because your circumstances are different, so don't compare yourself to her," he responded.

Mattie nodded her head in agreement, understanding his point completely.

"You are going to make a fine mother; I have no doubts about it. Your child will be given a lot that other moms can't."

"Thanks. My aunt is ecstatic, she is leaving soon and after all the conflicts of her invading my privacy and thinking of me as a child... I'm actually going to miss her." She purposefully changed the subject.

"Well in a sense she's an extension of your grandmother, thus an extension for you."

Mattie thought about his words. Indeed, Aunt Penny and Grandma Redd were cut from the same cloth. Mattie laughed out loud.

"Tell me." Dr. Stevens asked.

"They are cut from the same cloth, so I'm a piece of that fabric too. My aunt taught me how to crotchet, and it's ironic that grandma couldn't because I was too rebellious. I think it's funny that Auntie is more stubborn than I am," Mattie answered.

"Well, the apple doesn't fall far from the tree, but each apple is still individual and unique, just like your baby will be," Dr. Stevens responded by motioning towards her stomach. "So, what else is going on? You've got some pretty big life moments happening now."

"I quit my job," she said, feeling the relief of no longer working for Global Communications.

Dr. Stevens smiled.

"Was it anything that I said?" he asked her.

"Well, I guess… maybe." She went on to tell him about the events of that morning and how she left the company.

"It sounds like you did what made you happy! So, what's next?" he asked.

"I honestly don't know. I've been spending a lot of time at the center, getting all the ducks in order to set up a day care portion. I'll be flying out to Boston later today but beyond that I'm just taking it as it comes," she answered.

The thought of telling him about her nightmares resurfaced, but she wanted to ask him an indirect question.

"Can I ask you something?" she followed up before he responded.

"I'm having difficulty sleeping, dreams and stuff. Does that often happen with pregnant women with all the chemicals shifting in my body?" she finished.

Dr. Stevens wrote something in Mattie's file before answering.

"Well, I guess it depends. The chemicals could be playing a part but the subconscious Madison is far more likely the culprit. What kinds of dreams are you having?" he asked.

Mattie knew she had opened up a can of worms, but she wasn't prepared to put the worm on the hook.

"Just stuff in my past." She kept it simple.

The doctor shook his head.

"I won't pry, whenever you are ready. Remember nothing we speak about leaves this office," he reminded her.

That was the one thing that she had appreciated about him now. He didn't push quite as much as he used to.

"And remember your past is exactly that. What you do now for your life and the life of your child is what matters most. Remember that, Madison," he said before she responded.

"I think I'm done for today." She said with still ten minutes left in her session. She had nothing else to talk about.

"Well, this is your time and if you're done, then I'm done. I'll see you in...?" he said, leaving the decision up to her.

"Two weeks. You'll see me in two weeks and one of these days when Kendal is here, I want him to meet you. You've been the only man constant in my life," she said suddenly, not knowing where it had come from.

"I'm your psychiatrist and if you're comfortable having him sit in, then I don't mind… but do this. Really think about your request and what we talk about in here. This is your life," he said as he wrote down her next visit on the appointment card.

"Thank you," she spoke gratefully.

"As always my pleasure, Ms. Parks," he responded after opening his office door.

SQUARE ONE

CHAPTER 16

"How many times do I have to show you how to tie your shoes?" Samantha asked her younger brother as she bent down to show him again. "Crisscross and loop," she added.

Darren's fingers weren't as nimble and agile yet, but he kept trying until he got it right.

Sheila simply looked on. Samantha was taking her job seriously, and it was Sheila's way of adding responsibility while helping her son learn.

"I did it!" Darrien exclaimed with pride in his voice. "Mommy I did it!" He showed off his shoelaces tied but loosely tied.

Sheila smiled as she finished packing his Wakanda book bag. She had already done her daughters but both bags contained the same—an extra pair of clothes, juice boxes, and their iPads.

"Is Aunt Penny taking us to the movies or is Auntie Cindy?" Samantha asked.

"Both, sweetheart." Sheila was grateful to have a complete day to herself, away from work and the children. She and James made plans to shop and have lunch together, something they had not done in years. She didn't expect much but it was a starting point to a better friendship she believed with her ex-husband.

"Both of you go brush your teeth, and I don't want to hear any fussing over the toothpaste... actually Sam use my bathroom." She nipped any arguments in the bud.

Sheila threw the leftover food from breakfast into the trash before tying it up to take outside. She poured herself another cup of coffee before sitting down to read the morning paper. She saw Henry's name in a small article about apprehending the person suspected in a homicide months ago.

The article said a man had been identified as Mark Floyd was suspected of murdering James Fredericks behind a south side night spot.

Henry be on it, Sheila thought, happy that someone she knew was doing a great job in protecting her city.

"Hurry up!" Sheila yelled at her children, knowing that it didn't take that long to brush teeth and that the longer they took the more of a mess she would have to clean up.

Sheila kept her home pristine, something her mother had instilled in her.

Darrien was first to come back downstairs, leaping from the third step.

"Smell, Mommy," he said as he blew his breath. It smelled like mint mouthwash.

"Me too!" Samantha added.

"Smells minty fresh and clean," Sheila commented. She made Darrien grab a paper towel to wipe a bit of toothpaste residue out of the corner of his mouth as the doorbell rang. Sheila looked out the window and saw it was Cindy coming to pick the kids up.

"I need some coffee," Cindy said barging in heading straight to the kitchen. She poured a cup of coffee, black, before taking her sunglasses off.

"That woman sends me texts at 6 a.m. then 6:30…" Cindy paused as she sipped her coffee, "…every 30 minutes asking me if I'm up… if I'm ready… am I on the way. I don't know how Mattie can put up with all that," Cindy said frustrated.

"Well, it worked, you're up, and ready to get the day started," Sheila pointed out.

"Shit…" Cindy said before correcting herself in front of the kids. "…my night just ended. Peter had me up late last night," Cindy finished as another text message came through.

"Look at this," she said, showing Sheila the message.

AUNT PENNY: Have you picked the children up yet?

"I had to turn the sound off; I just couldn't take it," she replied, shaking her head.

"Aunt Cindy!" Samantha said, turning around to show off her new clothes before giving Cindy a hug.

"You look so pretty, Sam," She acknowledged.

Darrien stood off to the side looking disappointed about something.

"And what's with you little man?" Cindy asked him.

"I wanted to show you my new clothes first," he answered.

"Well, come here…" Cindy said looking him over.

"You look so handsome," she told him, giving him a hug and a kiss on his cheek.

"So… what's your plans for today. No work… no kids. You should pamper yourself; there's a new spa retreat out east," Cindy said, giving Sheila some options.

Sheila hesitated before responding because it was too early to have a discussion about her spending time with

James. Knowing Cindy had not completely approved, even though it was her choice to make.

"Uh, I'm going shopping at Polaris Mall and then grab something to eat, nothing big. Just kinda relax today," Sheila said before showing Cindy the article about Henry.

"Mom... dad said you guys were hanging out today when he picked us up yesterday," Samantha said.

Cindy didn't even look up from the paper, but she had a sly smile planted on her face.

"Henry is a modern-day Dick Tracy, I'm telling you." Cindy said, not commenting on what Sheila's daughter had just revealed. She took another sip of coffee and told the children to get their bags.

"Ok we're about to get out of here and go pick up her old as..." Cindy paused, realizing the children were likely to repeat what she said. "...old Aunt Penny up," she finished, standing from the table.

"Give me some kisses and hugs," Sheila said to her children. She followed behind Cindy and the kids with the trash bag in her hand.

"Hey Sheila, don't buy anything you ain't ready to pay for," Cindy yelled out before opening her car door.

"I hear ya," Sheila replied watching them drive off. She was excited about today. It was the first time that James and her spent time without the kids. She was skeptical because this was so unlike him, and she still doubted that he finally saw the error of his ways.

Sheila walked back inside and put the coffee mugs into the dishwasher before pouring out the rest of the coffee in the pot. She double checked her doors to make sure they were locked before going upstairs to run herself a bath and picking something cute out to wear.

BALANCE
CHAPTER 17

"That's so cute," Michelle said looking at the pictures off Aunt Penny's phone. Samantha had played dress up in Mattie's clothes and wigs to give an impromptu Beyoncé performance.

"Yeah, she had herself a good old time; she gave us a good laugh too." Aunt Penny asked Michelle how to play the video on her phone.

"Well let's see… ok here we go." Henry's wife shared her screen as the video started.

Samantha was finishing her second dance routine before Jay and Darion started rapping their own made-up song.

"That's good." Cindy's voice echoed in the background of the video.

"Let me send these pictures and video to my cell; Henry is going to love it," Michelle said before forwarding both pictures and video.

"Thank you again for watching him last night, he doesn't want to go. You said him and Darrien played good together?" Michelle asked, zipping up Jay's book bag.

"Lawd yes, they didn't stop with that shooting game... Duty Calling all night." Aunt Penny reached to give Jay a hug.

"Auntie, it's called Call of Duty and the parental controls are on. Can I come back later, Mommy?" He clearly was not ready to leave.

"No, not today. We're going to get some work done around the house, and dad said he was taking us for ice cream later," Michelle paused.

"Aunt Penny thanks again, we really needed it. Henry's been working so hard lately with these cases. I was amazed that he didn't fall asleep in the theatre, but that movie was so good. You need anything before we take off?"

"No, I'm ok, Mattie and Geri are coming back today. I'm jus' gon' rest up a bit," the older woman sighed slightly.

"Well, we're outta here, thanks again." Michelle said as she and Jay walked out the door.

Aunt Penny was tired although she would never admit it. Intentionally badgering Cindy early yesterday morning and then running around to the mall and movies with the children was taxing. However, the two hours spent sitting in the sun as the children played outside at the park drained her completely. Luckily, Cindy stayed and lent her a hand.

She gon' be alright too, Aunt Penny thought as she walked into Mattie's room to pull the sheets and covers off the bed. She was doing laundry today and knew her niece would have a fit if her room wasn't exactly as she left.

As Aunt Penny pulled off the pillowcases, a very old photograph fell onto the bed. It was a picture of Madison with her parents when she was about the age of eleven on a camping vacation. Everyone was smiling in the picture and in the background a large tent had been set up.

She's been through a lot, Aunt Penny thought placing the picture on Mattie's nightstand next to her alarm clock. She dragged the sheets and pillowcases into the laundry room and started the washing machine. She then walked back into the kitchen, cranked the dishwasher on before opening the window dressings in the front room.

Aunt Penny decided now was a good time to get cleaned up. Thankfully, the bathroom she used had a built-in seat that had been installed for Grandma Redd. Sitting in the chair letting the water engulf her, she thought about the past few months and how she had been given more vitality for life by being around the younger women.

She did miss her older friends back home, and she missed her house, even though it didn't have quite the same amenities as she had grown accustomed to while in Columbus.

Then the thought of her sister's death filled her mind. The events that led up to her taking her last breath; she wasn't there to support her, to comfort her. She envisioned her sister sitting in the same exact spot, doing what she was doing now and all the times she asked her sister to come back home to live with her, she always got the same answer: "Madison needs me."

Aunt Penny could see that her niece walked a fine line between life and death. She understood the sorrow Mattie felt with the loss of the only parents she could remember who played an active role. This was one of the main reasons Aunt Penny had not left after the funeral services. She felt herself on the verge of tears when the water temperature changed in the shower.

"Lord, have mercy!" She realized too late that the hot water was being used by both the washing machine and dishwasher. Aunt Penny turned the water off, dried off, and got dressed. She walked into the living room and turned the television on.

In a sense, she was missing her niece. She knew she had been difficult on purpose with Madison because she needed to know the younger woman could stand on her own two feet. The day Mattie gave in and agreed to learn crocheting, she knew she was ready.

Crocheting and sewing had been a craft passed down generation after generation in their family. Yes, it served as a means to clothe the family but more importantly, as their mother had told them, it taught patience and how to look at knots in life and how to detangle them and rebuild. It showed them that life had multiple loops in it and that each loop was both instrumental in connecting pieces of yarn and detrimental in constructing the whole piece.

Aunt Penny sat back on the couch and noticed that Cindy had left her knitting needles and yarn under the table.

"She did that on purpose." Aunt Penny reached for her cell phone to text Cindy.

AUNT PENNY: I ran out of washing detergent, call me.

Five minutes later she sent another message to Cindy.

AUNT PENNY: I need toilet paper too; I'm stuck in the bathroom now.

She counted down the next few minutes before sending another text. *Serves her right, discarding her work like that,* she thought before sending another message.

AUNT PENNY: I need some toilet paper, child!

ON THE MARKET
CHAPTER 18

"I told Sheila we'd meet her after I make sure these properties are ready to be shown. I had to get another crew to fix a couple of minor things but overall, they're ready to sell," Cindy told Mattie, pulling up to one of the two houses she would be showing to prospective buyers. She drove around to the back of the secluded house.

"Damn this is nice." Mattie scanned the 3,400 square foot single family home.

"They've got more privacy than I do but wait until you see the inside." Cindy motioned her to follow. The grass was freshly cut and the shrub manicured.

"It's been on the market for three months and the owners just asked me to list it, so I'm trying to get it done in the next couple of weeks. It's a buyer's market and it does not hurt that the mayor and a two congressman live in the neighborhood either." Cindy stepped around a small step ladder and toolbox to open the back door.

"How much is it going for?" Mattie was amazed at how nice the outside looked. It had a three-car garage, hot tub, and swimming pool.

"It's listed at $709,000. The owners said they'd take anything above $680,000. Even at that, I'd make a killing." Cindy waited for Mattie to enter before she closed the back door behind them.

Cindy walked from room to room shaking her head in approval.

"Now that's more like it. The last realtor just threw the rooms together. Presentation is the key." Cindy said.

"How many square feet?" Mattie asked again as she walked upstairs to see the whole layout.

"A little more than 3,400, but with the setup it feels much larger." Cindy answered as her cell phone rang.

"Hello… yeah…" was all Mattie heard before she reached the upper floor.

The master bedroom was larger than hers. It has a small balcony overlooking the hot tub and in-ground pool. The room itself contained mirrors on each wall and a fireplace situated beneath an area where a large flat screen television could be placed.

The master bedroom was all done in chrome with gold accents and the tiling on the floor had been done with alternating colors of white and gold.

That's too much, she thought before noticing the step-down tub which could fit two people comfortably. She left the master bedroom and walked through the other three bedrooms, all spacious with large windows.

Two of the bedrooms had standing showers and the third, simply a washbasin in the bathroom along with toilets.

"So, you like it?" Cindy asked as Mattie walked back down the stairs.

"It's nice, I can't even lie... it's got a basement too?" Mattie was curious.

"Follow me." Cindy led the way.

Walking down the stairs, Mattie wasn't prepared for what she saw. There was an entertainment room that had six stadium recliners, a bar area, and a projection screen. Next to this room was a gaming room with a nine-foot pool table, six full sized arcade video games, and a 180-gallon fish tank built into the wall.

"Damn..." was all Mattie could muster.

Further back was the laundry room with shelves on every wall and a huge folding table next to where the washer and dryer would go.

"They had it made, didn't they?" Mattie asked as Cindy turned off the lights.

"Yeah, they did and then they lost money in the stock market. Now they live in an apartment in Little Turtle." She opened another door to a different room.

There was a workbench with tools laying on it. Newspaper was scattered on the floor mixed in with saw dust. On a smaller table were beer bottles and paper bags.

"I told them to get all this shit out." Cindy shook her head at wine bottles on the floor beneath the table. "Fuck!" she said clearly, agitated that this room still looked a mess.

"Don't be yelling like that and have the neighbors calling the po…" Mattie tried saying.

"The neighbors can't hear shit down here… trust me. The entire basement is soundproof." Cindy interjected before pulling her cell phone out.

"No fucking signal down here… just meet me upstairs. Somebody decided to do a half ass job and that is completely unacceptable." Cindy walked back to go upstairs to be able to make the phone call.

"Is Marvin there?"

Mattie thought it was a little overboard that she had gotten so irate when the rest of the house was to her satisfaction. Mattie picked up some of the tools, trying to figure out what each one was for. She knew how the electric saw worked, and the caulking gun. There was a nail gun on the table too, but she had no clue as to the use of the other tools.

This would be a nice place to live, she thought before turning off the light and closing the door behind her. As she walked back upstairs, she could hear Cindy's conversation.

"You don't think I understand that it was a mistake... an oversight. I do understand but it would have taken less than ten minutes to finish one fucking room, Marvin. All they had to do was open the door and they would've seen it wasn't a utility closet. I have a client here right now and one little thing is the difference between buying and passing on a property. So next time send your best workers, those who don't overlook the small things please." Cindy paused as she listened.

"That's fine just have them back out today." She finished before hanging up.

"If you're going to say you have a professional fucking business, then act like it." Cindy put her cell phone into her purse.

Mattie thought she was a little ridiculous but realized in Cindy's business, it was only slight degrees to being successful or not.

"I feel ya…" Mattie responded.

"This house is nice as all get out. I can't believe no one has snatched it up and it's been on the market for as long as it has." Mattie said as they walked into the kitchen.

Cindy opened the refrigerator and took out a bottle of Sprite and asked Mattie what she wanted. She had orange juice, Sprite, and bottled water to choose from.

"Water."

"I keep this stuff in here just in case the prospect is thirsty. $10 worth of liquids can make a world of difference. We gotta run by the other property really quick. Just do a drive by because I need to make sure the lawn is cut. Text Sheila and tell her to meet us at CJ's Soulfood around 4:30."

Mattie sent the text as Cindy turned her car around to drive out forward.

A police officer cruiser drove by in the opposite direction as Cindy turned out into the street.

"One of the safest neighborhoods in the city," Mattie said as Cindy waved at the police officer.

"From the outside looking in; they play big boy politics over here," Cindy replied.

Mattie couldn't help but shake her head thinking about what role politics had played in the arrest of Mark Floyd and how Henry had made such a grievous mistake.

WIGS WIGS WIGS
CHAPTER 19

The list had been narrowed down with only three remaining hair shops to investigate. Mark Floyd had been arrested and was sitting behind bars in the county jail. He had quite an extensive criminal record: breaking and entering, grand theft auto along with multiple drug charges. But even as Henry and Detective Roberts made the arrest, they felt jumping to murder for the suspect was a far cry from his past criminal activities and behaviors.

"Captain is going to ream us if he finds out we're still following up on these leads," John reiterated.

"Well, he doesn't have to know. If we get through these last three shops with no more information than what we started with, I'll be more satisfied. But the perp just doesn't fit the crime," Henry replied.

The day was much hotter than a normal autumn day. The humidity made it feel over 90°. The air conditioning in the large room instantly made them feel better as they entered the beauty supply store.

"Hi, can I help you?" an older Asian woman asked as she sat on a stool behind the counter with a smile on her face.

Henry and John flashed their badges.

"I'm Detective Jenkins and this is my partner Detective Roberts." Henry was first to speak.

The smile on the woman's face was replaced with a look of bewilderment.

"We just have a few questions about some merchandise you carry, specifically wigs." Henry then showed the woman the information off the manufacturers list.

"Oh… we haven't carried that one in months; they keep sending us everything but that one. It's a nice wig," she said, looking relieved.

"Would you happen to have any records as to who you may have sold it to, credit cards or transaction receipts?" Detective Roberts asked.

"Oh, we keep impeccable records… hold on." She motioned to an older Asian man walking out from the back room.

The woman spoke in Mandarin before he spoke to the detectives. "Oh, we keep impeccable records, impeccable... hold on."

"May I...." he nodded towards the invoice number in Henry's possession.

"Oh, I know this... we sold out of it months ago. They won't send us anymore; we ask but they don't send... give me a minute to get you the information." He walked back into the storeroom as two women made their way to the counter to purchase for their merchandise.

"Ladies," Detective Roberts said in a flirtatious way.

"Hi." One of them smiled back.

Henry took that as a cue to walk away. John was a big flirt, and Henry didn't want any parts of it.

Henry was amazed at all the hair care products the store carried: wigs, weaves of human hair and synthetic, and even relaxers. He laughed because he remembered relaxing his hair as a teen to look like Prince.

The older Asian man made his way back to the front counter with a register roll.

"I remember now, we sold this wig and two others. The woman was very pretty," He acknowledged.

"Well, that's been over five months ago, how can you remember her?" John was curious.

"Because he tried to flirt with her in front of me, and I made him remember who the boss is." The wife balled her fist up at the old man in a joking manner, but she was serious.

"She had too nice of hair for wigs, she didn't need them!" the woman exclaimed.

"Do you think you can describe her?" Henry asked.

The woman shook her head and walked away leaving it up to her husband to give the description.

"About my height and a small build but, nice... nice body with muscles... uh sunglasses with a baseball cap... no basketball cap. I remember because I like basketball."

John wrote down the description.

"These cameras, how long do they hold a recording?" Henry pointed to the various cameras in the store.

"Oh those... those don't work, haven't worked in years..." the man paused, "...but these do." He said motioning to a shotgun and pistol off to the side on a shelf behind him.

"They are registered, and I have a permit for both," he finished with a smirk on his face.

"Can you show us the other two wigs that were purchased on this ticket?" Detective Roberts asked.

"Sure… sure," he said walking from behind the counter to pull two wigs down from the wall.

"Here… here you are." The older Asian man said.

Henry took one and John the other.

"You're buying." Henry tossed the wig to John.

John pulled out his credit card and handed it to Asian man.

"Oh, today's special buy two and you get one free." He smiled at Henry.

"These two will do," John said politely as Henry walked away to wait at the door.

"You know if you put the one on, you'd look like Rick James." John laughed aloud.

Before he signed the receipt and grabbed the bag.

"Funny… real funny John." He walked out the door behind his partner.

AN HONEST ANSWER
CHAPTER 20

The moonlight was shining through the window of her bedroom. Not able to gauge what the actual time was, Sheila rolled over and picked up her cell phone. It was 2:36 a.m.

James reached over and pulled her closer, wrapping one arm around her before laying his head back onto the pillow.

Sheila was exhausted. She had worked an entire shift and a half before having to draft a memo at work to make sure the nursing staff was made aware that tardiness and calling off could result in disciplinarian action leading to termination of employment.

The attendance rate had changed slightly since she had been promoted, enough for the hospital administrators to make her aware of the trend. Whether or not she had made bonds with a large portion of the staff before her promotion didn't matter now. Everyone would be held accountable.

James had picked her up from the hospital after dropping their kids off at his mother's house. Sheila did still not know what had changed in James' life to make him more attentive to his children and much more patient with her, but for now it didn't matter. What mattered now was the feeling of being wanted and loved by the man to whom she had once said "I do."

She backed up into him while spooning. She knew he hadn't fallen asleep yet because she didn't hear him snoring.

"She..." James said softly, "...do you think we could ever build a home together again?" he asked.

Sheila hadn't expected those words to ever come out of his mouth. She turned her body to face him, adjusting her pillows so she could look at him face to face.

"I... I don't know," she responded unsure of how to answer him. Part of her was still hurting from the fights and quarrels they had had towards the end of their marriage and from the long-drawn-out divorce. Part of her still loved the idea of being married, but she was afraid to take the chance of opening calloused wounds.

"I know I've said and done some fucked up things, and I know that I hurt you as a friend and a man, as your husband..." he paused as he took his hand and stroked her face, "...but I believe in soul that we deserve a second chance." He stared into her eyes.

There wasn't anywhere to run or hide lying next to him and Sheila felt vulnerable. This wasn't the same man she had known. He had been self-absorbed and selfish. He had put work and play over the life of his marriage, his responsibility as a father. Now he talked with maturity, and Sheila just couldn't understand why.

"I'm going to ask you a question and I want you to be honest with me." Sheila paused to make sure she had his full attention.

"Ok, just ask."

"What's happened to make you change, to say the things you're saying? You're so different now. Why?" Sheila asked, staring at him while reaching up to take hold of his hand.

James' seemed to be searching for the right words to say, but as he began to answer it was the truth that came out.

"The truth is this… almost nine months ago I noticed a lump under my armpit. At first, I thought my glands were swollen, but after two weeks it hadn't gone away instead it had grown…" he paused seeing the concern on her face.

"After a doctor's appointment that included major lab work, I began to reflect on what my life consisted of. What good had I done with my life? To be honest, the majority of my thoughts showed that I had been selfish, childish, and ignorant to those who mattered the most to me. For the next two weeks, every day, I would stare into the mirror while forcing honesty out of myself. Making myself deal with my shortcomings and how to live a better life," he paused again trying to contain his emotions, but Sheila saw the tears forming in his eyes.

"Each day that honesty came out, you were there. You, who I promised to love and protect, to provide for, were there. I failed so grossly, not because of any other reason than I was selfishly caught up in the world. I have been so disobedient to God. I've gotten the results back from the testing a few months ago, and it's not malignant. I know you deserved more than I ever gave you and the children."

Sheila could only stare at him. She was listening but she understood how fear of death could always focus someone on their life. She had seen it numerous times at the hospital. Even her run-in with the assassin that Henry shot and killed had changed her.

"I…" Sheila started to say, but James put two fingers over her lips to continue speaking.

"I know now that life is more than about me, it's about all of us—you… Darrion… Samantha. It's about the health and growth of our family, the one that you and I created, the unit we both said we would protect. With God as my witness, I am no longer 'that person.' I am a new man. I don't expect much, but I will be the best father for our children and, if you will have me, as your friend or your partner for life," he said as he wiped the tears away from Sheila's face.

Sheila couldn't respond, her emotions were too hard to control. She understood now why he was changed; she could hear it in his voice and see it in his actions over the past month or so, but she was still afraid.

"I don't expect any of this to be easy for you and I don't expect you to make any decisions soon. I wanted you to know about everything and know that I love you," James finished reaching over to kiss Sheila on the lips.

"Don't say anything. You're tired and so am I; let's get some sleep."

Sheila lay there silently, and she couldn't sleep if she wanted. She wasn't the same woman she had been while they were married. She had managed a life with her children without him. She would pray on it. It was a strange sensation hearing James begin snoring because it made her feel protected once again.

IN A ROW
CHAPTER 21

Henry was lying across the sectional watching a re-run of Jeopardy when he heard the garage door opening. His week had been exhausting being assigned two more homicide cases. The number of homicides was now increasing, something many people attributed to the economy still being bottomed out and people out of work.

One of the cases would be solved quickly as he waited for forensics on a possible murder weapon. A woman, presumably, shot her boyfriend of 12 years after learning he had infected her with the HIV virus. There was a confession, but they wanted to make sure all the loose ends were tied up, so they were patient, ensuring the gun found was the actual murder weapon.

The second case was a drive-by shooting, and they had two suspects in custody. They had no murder weapon, no confession and only one eyewitness who had come forward but now that witness was recanting her story.

"Daddy!" Jay exclaimed as he walked down the stairs of the split-level home.

"What's up my handsome man?" Henry stood up to give his son a hug before walking to his wife.

"Daddy, Mommy bought me a new PlayStation, so I can play with Darrion when he comes over this weekend, and she got me a game too!" Jay couldn't control his excitement.

"Did she now?" Henry asked as he gave Michelle a kiss on the lips as she walked in from the garage with bags in her hands. He retrieved the remaining sacks from the trunk.

"It's just a few more bags honey," Michelle mentioned.

"I'm making tacos tonight and chocolate chip cookie dough ice cream." She knew her husband had been putting in some serious hours, so she was going to make his favorite food.

"Somebody is getting some TLC later." Henry rubbed his hand across Michelle's backside as she smiled.

"Daddy, can you open this for me?" Jay extended the game box to his father.

Henry sat down at the kitchen table, to open the box.

"Well, well... Call of Duty?" He looked at his wife before plugging the game into the electrical outlet. They had discussed violent shooting games for their children over a year ago, but Michelle said the store clerk reassured her they could make sure the parental controls were active.

"Baby, we're going outside to shoot a little hoop before the kids get here. Call us when it's ready." Henry disappeared to slip his sneakers on.

Dribbling the basketball out from the garage and closing the door behind him, he told Jay that today he was shooting free throws.

"The same deal: if you hit five in a row, I'll give you $10 and if you hit ten in a row that's $20 for you." Henry pulled his wallet out to show Jay the cash money.

"What about I get a dollar for everyone I make?" Jay asked.

"Nope."

Jay would make three in a row and then miss and start over getting frustrated, but Henry would say the same thing.

"Start over and focus, son. You've got this."

Henry knew repetition and practice would make any task easier, something his high school coach had taught him to help him earn all-state honors. Henry was starting Jay off by teaching him the fundamentals of the game.

"Baby, John's on the phone!" Michelle called out through the front screen door holding Henry's cell phone in her hand.

"Keep practicing." He motioned to Jay before putting his phone to the ear.

"What's up partner?"

"The forensic report is back on the Tomlin case, if you come down and sign off on it, we can close it tonight and be done with it." John didn't have much of a life outside of work, so he worked a little longer than most.

"Ok, give me an hour, I'm finishing up with Jay."

"Ok, see you in an hour… and make sure Jay keeps that elbow in." John had played horse with both father and son. John had played Division II basketball in his past life.

Henry and John had played at the same high school, a decade apart. Taught by the same coach; it always came back to the fundamentals.

Henry put his cell phone down to the side of the garage to not have it accidentally destroyed by a random bounce of the basketball.

"Ok, keep that elbow in and let's get it."

Jay had made four in a row and needed to make this shot in order to earn $5.

"Elbow in and follow through," Henry said as Jay concentrated on his free throw.

The ball hit the rim before bouncing against the back board to only roll around the rim again to bounce through the net before landing on Henry's cell phone. It shattered his screen.

Jay's face was excited because he made the shot while Henry's face was disgusted because his phone was shattered. He hadn't moved it far enough away.

"Ok, I'll give you $5, plus another five for keeping your room clean and helping mom." He handed over two five-dollar bills to his son.

"Go put it in your bank." He watched his son disappear inside before picking up the two pieces of his cell phone.

"Shit." There was no way to fix it, and he hated dealing with his cell phone company.

After walking back in, Michelle was just finishing dicing the tomatoes.

"Honey, I've got to run to the station and sign off on a report." He washed his hands in the kitchen sink.

"Ok, I'll make you a couple for you to eat now and leave the rest out for you later." She paused as she took a look at his phone split in two.

"Another one babe? Really?"

"Yeah, another one... I'm going to grab yours when I leave and stop by the wireless store to get a replacement." He slammed down the tacos before going upstairs to wash up and change.

Henry felt tired but knew signing off on the report lessened their case load by one. With the captain breathing down his neck, he would take the win.

"Here," Michelle called out after he kissed her goodbye and headed out the door, handing him her cell phone.

"I'll be back, it shouldn't be long."

When he arrived at the police station, John was talking to the captain outside his office who motioned Henry to come over.

"Both of you get in here," he said closing the door to his office behind them before drawing the blinds.

"You two are going to stir up a hornet's nest. Why on the expense report is there monies for women's wigs... will one of you tell me?" The captain was agitated and waiting for an answer.

"No big reason, Cap... we just wanted to close out the list and..." Henry tried to respond.

"The case is closed, Jenkins. Mark Floyd is being arraigned. We have a confession from the prosecutor's office. Case closed!"

"All the evidence is circumstantial cap, to be honest," John spoke out when Henry wished he would've remained silent.

"What are you wet behind the ears? We have witnesses saying the victim and Floyd had words! We know that he was in the alley from the semen sample left in the condom. The woman said he followed Fredericks back outside. It's an open and shut case! Is that understood?" His voice was firm and authoritative.

Henry felt anger but now was not the time to show it. He was certain that there was a cover-up, misrepresentation of their findings so far.

"Gotcha, Cap." John realized the same thing his partner had without knowing.

"Understood," Henry added.

"Dismissed!" The captain excused both detectives by waving them off dismissively.

"You put the wigs on the expense account?" Henry shook his head at his younger counterpart. said shaking his head.

"I did because I wasn't going to use my money and wait for reimbursement. So, I don't need no shit from you right now partner, for real… there's the report." John sat down across from Henry and picked up his desk phone to make a call.

A funny noise sounded, and Henry was unsure what it was before realizing it was his wife's cell phone ringing. It was her mother calling so he let it go to voicemail.

Henry put the cell phone on the desk before reading the report and signing it.

Michelle's mother was calling a second time and the music playing began irritating him for some reason. He searched through her phone to find out how to turn the ringer off and accidentally hit the photo icon in the menu.

At first, he smiled going through the pictures of Jay and Darrion playing together, but the smile quickly faded to something else. His mind was trying to formulate beyond speculation as he saw Samantha dressed up wearing the two wigs that he had just got chewed out about purchasing.

His thoughts were racing, throwing out some ideas that didn't add up before putting those ideas back into the equation. Henry shook his head back and forth, realizing that this would be such a large coincidence.

"Here's the report back, John. It looks solid." Henry handed the younger man the signed report, the initial reason he came into work. However now, now he had to rationalize the new factors into who killed Jimmie Fredericks.

"I'll see you tomorrow." Henry needed to maintain his demeanor as he walked onto the elevator staring down at the cell phone studying the pictures again.

"It doesn't make sense." In his gut, he knew Mark Floyd was more than likely innocent. Now as he looked at the pictures with the wigs again, he understood he was about to go down the rabbit hole.

TECHNOLOGY
CHAPTER 22

"Oh, my goodness, Frances, it's wonderful. The kids are going to love it." Mattie stood amazed as Frances opened the door to the new computer room at the center. Brand new desks and computers sitting on top were the focal points, but the room was designed with a large mural on each wall of the Planet Earth and all its continents.

"Yeah, I think they will. We have one-hour sessions that kids can sign up for, two-hour daily maximum. The IT guy said each computer is networked with major security and already set up for restricted access to certain sites. The best part is, we are under budget with this still leaving a few thousand dollars for other projects." Frances replied.

The older woman had just celebrated her 55th birthday. She had once been a school administrator who lost her job when the city cut back the budget on education. She had a short salt and pepper afro and typically wore khaki pants with some sort of simple shirt. Still maintaining her youthful spirit, often listening and dancing to approved hip hop at the center. Her expertise in finance and building educational curriculum was by far her greatest assets. One of the reasons Kendal hired and trusted her with the facility.

"You know Kendal is just going to love this." Mattie had elation in her voice.

"I'm sure, his vision when we first opened is beginning to come into focus. He's a great visionary; I saw a commercial with him in it a few weeks back about the tour coming to Columbus. The kids brag about him all the time," Frances told Mattie as two teenage boys walked into the computer room behind them.

"No… no… no, it doesn't open until tomorrow," Frances said, showing her pride that students were already taking an interest in the computer room.

"Wow, it's nice, Mrs. Frances!" One of the teenage boys wearing his basketball cap tilted to the back of his head chimed in.

Mattie took the hat off and turned it around, brim facing forward.

"Oh, I'm sorry, Ms. Parks. I forgot."

Kendal didn't have many rules on appearance, except no sagging jeans, no shorts that showed "cheeks," and no hats worn backwards. He was also big on hygiene, so when a new student came into the program at the center, he furnished them with items and one book to read.

"That's fine Roger, we all forget sometimes. But you know Mr. Scott would've confiscated it and put it in lock up." Mattie nodded her head in agreement with Frances.

"Hi, Ms. Parks!" the other male said looking excited about the computer room.

"Hi Terry! Do you and Roger have your name on the list to use the computers tomorrow?" Frances waited for an answer.

"What list?" Roger asked.

"The list is by the front counter. You can sign up for two sessions daily," Mattie interjected.

"Ok, at the front counter?" Terry wanted to make sure he understood correctly.

"Yes, the front counter. Just ask Mr. Jackson, he'll show you." Frances walked to the door of the computer classroom and pointed towards the front desk.

"They're good kids," Mattie added. Many of the participants of the program came from single parent homes, and the majority of the homes were headed by their mothers.

"Yeah, they are but we have to keep an eye on Roger though. His older brother is a big influence on him, and he's still in the streets." Frances paused to change the subject. "How are you coming with the proposal for the childcare center?"

Mattie had been piecing together the items of consideration the state used when opening a day care facility.

"Frances, there are so many codes and regulations that have to be met. Food restrictions and the kitchen back there is adequate, but honestly, when was it inspected last? I'm working on it all but it's still going to take a while." Mattie grimaced when speaking about the kitchen because it would need an overhaul, which would cost more money. She had offered to extend money to Kendal for the center, but he declined.

"Are you ok?" Frances asked with concern in her voice.

"Yeah, it's my lower back that has been hurting off and on the past few days. I just need to sit down," Mattie answered attempting not to put more concern on the older woman's face.

"Four months and you still are not showing. You gon' end up being all belly, I'm telling you." They walked back towards the office so Mattie could sit in Kendal's chair.

"I've had a few cramps. Sheila says I need to slow down and take it easy, let my body adjust." Mattie opened the small refrigerator in Kendal's office to take out a bottle of apple juice.

"That should keep you cleaned out," Frances said jokingly.

Mattie smiled and took a sip before noticing Henry walking back to the office.

"Detective Jenkins," Mattie said lightheartedly as he walked into the office.

"Hey Henry," Frances said.

"Afternoon ladies, I see you two are still hard at work or hardly working…" he paused seemingly making a revelation.

"Your aunt told you I dropped the reward check off?" He sat down next to Frances.

"Yeah, she did and in the same breath told me she had invaded my privacy once again…" Mattie paused as she laughed.

"She's a hard egg to crack, but she means well."

"Henry, we didn't expect you until next week." Frances wondered why he had shown up today.

Henry leaned back in his chair throwing his hands behind his head, interlocking his fingers.

"Yeah, just working this case and was just in the neighborhood. Jackson said the computer room is finally finished. I'm telling you, any minute, this center is going to be bursting through the seams with parents signing their kids up for the program. Kendal said he's trying to open a daycare portion too." Henry watched as a small group of kids headed to the front desk and formed a line.

"Yeah, but it's tough, codes... regulations... more codes." Mattie took another sip of her apple juice.

"You alright?" Henry had concern in his voice for Mattie's health.

"Yeah, just been on my feet all day. I walked the park twice this morning and haven't slowed down since," she answered.

"I'm no expert, but you gotta take it slow." Henry didn't know what it was like to carry a child, but he understood the nine-and-a-half-month process could be taxing.

"And tell your aunt thanks again for watching Jay the other weekend. I'm amazed they didn't wear her out. I know Jay and Darrion were stuck on video games, but that Samantha has got some talent. You and Cindy must be teaching her some of y'all old moves," Henry asked for a bottled water from Kendal's small office refrigerator.

Mattie tossed him the water.

"Samantha watched too many videos. She has way better moves than me and Cin," Mattie said with a grin on her face.

"You ain't never lied. Her little Beyoncé and Rihanna skits are hilarious," Henry said.

"You seen them yet?" he asked both ladies.

"No." they replied in unison.

"Hold on, can I use this computer... Michelle emailed them to me."

Frances switched chairs with him giving him access to Kendal's computer.

Henry signed into his email account and then pulled up the videos that Aunt Penny had taken.

"Oh wow, she's getting it." Frances enjoyed seeing the video.

Mattie was smiling too but she felt odd. Samantha's renditions were nearly perfect, but she had on Mattie's clothes and was wearing the two remaining wigs Mattie had bought.

"She's got the moves and charisma," Henry added.

"Oh my God, look at those wigs," Frances said laughing out loud.

In that brief moment, Henry looked at Mattie and she in turn caught his gaze.

"Grandma Redd had wigs for days, I thought I threw all of them out and yeah that girl is getting it." Mattie finished trying to sound casual.

Fuck… fuck… fuck. Mattie knew the expression on her face had changed.

"Are you ok, Madison?" Henry asked using her formal name.

"Yeah, just these cramps again, I probably need to just go home and lay down. Make sure y'all log his computer off. I'll see you tomorrow, Frances. Henry, tell Michele I said hi and kiss Jay for me." Mattie hugged them both before walking out of the office.

Whether or not Henry suspected anything she couldn't know for sure.

His visit seemed normal; he said he was working a case. Mattie thought walking out the building feeling slightly paranoid.

She was going home to get the wigs before proceeding to Kendal's condo to cut them into tiny pieces as she had done with the others before discarding them.

"Fuck, how could I have slipped up like that?" she pulled out of the parking lot. She felt tension in her lower back but pushed it aside as she went over and over in her mind what other mistakes she needed to correct and fast.

IT'S ALL RELATIVE
CHAPTER 23

"Let me have the best margarita the bartender can make and a shot of Patron," Cindy told the server.

"Any appetizers?" she asked.

"No… not yet, I'm on an alcohol diet right now," Cindy grinned, and the server laughed out loud.

"For you ma'am?" she nodded at Geri who was still looking at the menu.

"I'll have a margarita too… the same as her and bring out some potato skins with extra cheese." Geri needed food with her liquor.

"I don't get a huge appetite after working out. I don't feel like eating shit," Cindy said as the waitress walked away.

"That's the one thing Mattie harps on; she says it's important to eat something and replenish your body. She used to give me protein shakes after working out, they weren't too bad…" Geri paused as the waitress brought back two glasses of water with lemon in them. "Thanks," Geri said before continuing her conversation.

"So, you and Peter… good?" she asked.

Cindy smiled slightly before she answered.

"Better than what I would've thought. His schedule keeps him in that dealership sometimes 16-hour days, but he makes good money… sometimes it stresses him and puts him in a funky mood," Cindy responded.

"I work 10, sometimes 12 hours per day so I can only imagine. If I worked 16-hour days consistently I'd be pissed all the time too," Geri replied.

"If we keep working out like this, by the time Mattie's baby is born we can be her trainer and I'm going to put a hurting on her. She used to kill me," Geri said.

"Mattie's a machine when it comes to physical shit like working out. I ain't messing with her, baby or not. I'll leave that all up to you," Cindy said giggling as the waitress brought back their drinks.

"I'll have your skins up shortly." She left two saucers and napkins before walking away from the table.

"To a good workout," Geri said lifting her shot of Patron with Cindy.

"No doubt, a good workout," Cindy said, downing the tequila. Cindy had been more consistent over the past month in her workout routine since Peter came into the picture. Even on days when Geri was stuck in the office, Cindy would go by herself. It gave her more energy and Peter was complimenting her on the definition of her muscles.

"I closed on one of those properties yesterday; the commission is going to be fat. I'm going to invest it in something, maybe Gamestop or AMC stock and become an ape." Cindy flailed her arms like she was a gorilla.

Geri almost choked on her margarita.

"I can't believe that you're not serious, are you?" Geri said with a frown on her face.

"Shiit, I'm dead serious. Right now, is the best time to jump on board... don't be hating," Cindy told Geri in a non-offensive tone.

"Girl, what am I going to do with you? Geri asked, taking another drink of her margarita before the potato skins were brought to the table.

"I'm just going to eat one," Cindy said while taking her hand sanitizer out from her purse, sharing it with Geri.

"Oh, did I tell you that Kwame keeps calling me at the office?" Geri asked in between chewing.

"He's a persistent dude, ain't he?" Cindy said smiling.

"When was the last time you been out on a date Geri… a real date? Not a business luncheon or dinner but an actual date?" Cindy asked as she started in on her second potato skin.

Geri didn't answer immediately because she had to think about it. Business had been the most important aspect of her life. She put so much time and energy into the magazine to success that she hadn't left much room for a personal life, besides spending time with her girlfriends.

"I don't have time for personal stuff like that, after we go nationwide, maybe… but not now. Benelle and I still hook up once in a while," she answered.

"Benelle is a fine brother, no doubt. But I think you should let Kwame wine and dine you…" Cindy paused as Geri began to say something. "… just hold on and hear me out. We all know that your mom and dad wanted you to be an attorney or doctor like they were, and that you work as hard as you do to show them, you're your own woman. You're very successful, Geri. How many people can say that they run a company that's growing in the midst of a recession? How many people could start a business from scratch their senior year in college and stayed with it as their profession?" Cindy sipped her drink and continued.

"Your dad respects you and so does your mom, she's just too stubborn to admit it. Go on the date with Kwame… a real date and still see Benelle. I ain't telling you to give him some ass but go out and enjoy yourself when the tour comes here." Cindy's eyebrows raised as if she had a revelation.

"If you want Peter and I can go with you," she offered as Geri spoke up.

"I don't know he's a player…"

"Like you ain't never dated a player before… come on girl," Cindy scoffed.

"I'll think about it…"

Cindy frowned, not believing her.

"I'm serious, I'll think about it," Geri insisted.

"You're the only one of us that got cobwebs on her…" Cindy was louder than intended as an older couple stared their way. She waved at them. "…your cat."

Cindy simply smiled at them before returning her attention back to her friend and took that as a cue to back off, so she switched the subject.

"I think Sheila is contemplating something with James again."

"Well, I'm happy for her; she's been through a lot. Sheila is not the same woman he dumped though," Geri said drinking down the rest of her margarita.

"Do you all want any more drinks, a second round? There's still ten minutes before happy hour ends," the waitress circled back around, checking on their progress.

"I'm good," Geri answered.

"Let me put an order in for buffalo wings, extra sauce, and another order of skins with extra ranch dressing." Cindy was taking Peter food.

"Ok, anything else to drink?" she asked Cindy who was still debating on another margarita.

"No... no I'm good too, and make that order to go," Cindy added as Geri checked her cell phone. Mattie had just texted her to see what her plans were for the evening.

GERI: At dinner with Cin, leaving in a few, what's up?

MATTIE: Nothing, seeing if you wanted to go to a movie, I wanna get out the house.

"You feel like catching a flick with Mattie tonight?" Geri asked Cindy.

"It will have to be the late show. I'm going to drop this food off to Peter first." Cindy was being more attentive than usual. "…and y'all pick me up for a change." She added.

GERI: Yeah, we can go, Cindy's coming too; we'll have to pick her up from the house.

MATTIE: The late show starts at 10:20.

Geri and Cindy talked about how happy they were that Mattie and Kendal were engaged.

"Here's your food to go and the check," The waitress said not splitting the orders.

"I got it," Cindy said pulling out her American Express card before grabbing Geri's attention.

"You interested in buying a house?"

"Nope," Geri answered.

"Now I'll just write it off," Cindy said laughing. As they left the restaurant, Geri told Cindy to be ready at 9 p.m., knowing Cindy would take more time than that.

"Ok, 9:30 and don't be late" Cindy laughed, and Geri shook her head as she got into her car.

Geri went home, looked over a few articles for an upcoming edition. She thought about what Cindy said at happy hour. Did she avoid real companionship and simply use her ambition as a shield? She changed into some blue jeans and a t-shirt before heading to pick up Mattie.

"I'm outside," Geri called when she pulled up to Mattie's place.

"Ok, just give me two minutes; Aunt Penny is a little under the weather so I'm giving her some medicine." Mattie and Aunt Penny had found a deeper bond over the past months. It wasn't that Aunt Penny didn't work her nerves still, but Mattie knew it came from a place of love.

As she waited for her friend to come out, Geri texted Cindy to tell her they were on the way and to be ready.

CINDY: Ok, the front door is open, I'm changing right now, and Peter may be here but just come in.

Just as Cindy's test dinged, Mattie walked out her house and down the stairs with a bottle of apple juice and dill pickle wrapped in a paper towel in her hand.

"Damn, what type of taste buds are you developing? That don't even sound good at all?" Geri asked as Mattie closed the door to her SUV behind her.

"I know, I don't even like apple juice or pickles, but my body is craving this shit... the salt." Mattie took a bite of the pickle.

"So, what are we going to see? I don't want to see any romance flicks. Cindy has already lectured me on dating, and I don't need any more reminders."

"I wanna see that new Will Smith movie..."

Geri interrupted. "I don't know how I feel about that still, after he slapped the shit outta one of my favorite comedians! And plus, I haven't even seen the new Denzel movie yet."

Mattie hadn't thought that deeply about the altercation at the Oscars.

"Oh yeah that's cool. Either is fine with me. Let me check to see what time the next showing starts." Mattie pulled out her cell phone as they merged into traffic.

"Mattie, can you text her again and make sure she's ready? Peter may be over there too so make it clear to her that no dudes are allowed to come with us." Mattie sent the text but didn't get a reply.

"If she's getting her funky on, we're just leaving her." Mattie said with a little agitation that Cindy might be making them run late. Mattie had already been dealing with spasms in her back for the past few days along with minor cramps. She wasn't sleeping well with her dreams waking her throughout the night. But the idea that she had made mistakes in covering up her crime and Henry had pictures of the wigs was the most prominent thought she had resurfacing.

From the outside looking in, everything was normal but inside she was struggling with all types of internal conflicts that she could not resolve.

As Geri pulled up the gravel driveway, they saw a Corvette with dealer plates on it.

"He can drive anything he wants," Mattie said as they stepped out the truck.

Peter could be seen from the driveway through Cindy's front window. He looked to be yelling with his fingers pointing across the room, but they couldn't be sure.

Mattie took another drink from her bottle of apple juice, trying to figure out what was happening inside. She knew her friend couple push anyone's buttons.

"If she's not ready we're leaving her Geri, I'm serious. I don't want to be drawn into their lovers spat." Mattie followed Geri up the walkway as Peter disappeared from their line of sight.

"Hold on I forgot my phone. I've got to sign off on a few advertisements." Geri backtracked to her sports utility vehicle.

"What time is it; she's not making us late."

"9:15, so we got time." Geri said before opening Cindy's front door.

. . .

"You spend too much damn time with them! Every time I can do something, you running the fuck off with them broads or are you fucking around on me bitch!" Peter's voice echoed throughout loudly that the wall's vibrated.

"Get your damn hands off me and get the fuck out my house! I don't tolerate no drunk, punk-ass little boys who act like they grown men!" Cindy's voice was heard coming from the living room. She was meeting Peter's energy head on.

Geri and Mattie moved quicker through the foyer to stop them from escalating the argument any further.

"Bitch, I leave when I want to!" His voice bellowed out before they heard Cindy screaming bloody murder.

"You fucking hit me! Get the fuck out!"

"I don't give a fuck! You're not going with…" Peter was saying as Geri and Mattie ran into the living room.

Cindy was standing her ground when her friends appeared.

"All y'all some fucking bitches!" Peter's words slurred but he said them with force.

Cindy was no longer rational. She picked a lamp up to hit him, but Peter shoved her down and advanced. Geri ran and tried jumping on his back, but he caught her and threw her across the room, slamming her back up against the glass coffee table.

Mattie had already started moving towards him as he threw Geri across the room. As he turned to face her, he was too late as she cracked the apple juice bottle across the side of his head breaking it in pieces.

As he staggered backwards, Cindy had the lamp in her hand and hit him squarely in the face. The blood gushed out his nose and mouth before he fell over Geri's body who was trying to get out of the way. He crashed down onto the glass coffee table, breaking it in into pieces.

Cindy took the lamp and slammed it down on him again, and Mattie went to kick him in the head, but Geri grabbed her.

"Call the police Cindy!" Geri screamed.

Cindy was bleeding from the corner of her eye from where she had been struck. She was dazed so Geri picked up her cordless phone and dialed.

"I need the police! There's been an assault!" Geri gave the address.

Peter was incoherent and moaning as his body lay inside the frame of the broken coffee table.

"Don't let his ass up!" Cindy screamed as Mattie stood over him.

One of the benefits of living in an upscale neighborhood was the police came when they were called. Two patrol cars were pulling up when Peter started to regain consciousness. Geri greeted them at the door.

"We were called about an assault?" A female officer was first to enter, followed by a male police officer. Geri escorted both into the living room.

"He attacked us!" Cindy pointed towards Peter. She held a cloth to the side of her eye as a compress to stop the flow of blood. She felt angry and embarrassed. The emotional damage weighed heavier than the physical violation. Her heart and mind were not on the same page. She wasn't sure if she could ever trust herself with a man again.

Geri was rubbing her shoulder still dazed. She was grateful that they arrived when they had, but even more so that Mattie hadn't escalated the altercation after Peter fell into the glass table.

Peter was trying to get up, but he staggered and fell back down before cutting his hand on some of the shattered glass. The second officer helped him up, checking the severity of his wounds before handcuffing him.

"So, what happened?" One of the male officers asked.

Cindy told him that Peter showed up seemingly intoxicated but explained that she didn't think he drank anymore because he was an alcoholic. She said he started yelling at her and then it escalated to him grabbing her, punching her, and knocking her down.

"I tried to stop him, but he threw me across the room," Geri added. She was clearly in business mode.

"Ok… ok and what happened next?" The female officer asked.

"Well, I reacted seeing them getting assaulted by hitting him and then he fell into the coffee table," Mattie said shakily, leaving out the part of the apple juice bottle. She didn't want the officers to think she had escalated the attack.

"We're all pressing charges against his ass! This muthafucka gon' put his hands on me and my sisters, and she is pregnant!" Cindy was still riled up and tried to reach around the officer trying to hit Peter again.

"Ma'am, don't… we got it under control." The second male officer shielded Peter from Cindy.

"Can you get his ass out of my house? Ol' sorry excuse for a human being!" Cindy threw Peter's suit jacket to the female officer. The jacket landed short and as she picked it up, a small vial fell to the floor.

"Is this your jacket sir?" The male officer asked Peter, who had still not regained his full faculties.

"Yeah... yes, that's my coat. They jumped me!" Peter attempted to stand on his own two feet, but the officer secured him. They addressed the gash from Peter's wound while waiting for the paramedics to arrive and learn if the injury required him to be transported to the hospital before going to jail.

"So, this is your jacket? And this also belongs to you, Mr. ... Handford?" the lady officer asked as she checked his wallet for ID, indicating the vial of powdered substance.

"If you all are able to follow us to the station to get your statements, we can go as soon as we get medical advice," the officer asked as she removed the cloth from the side of Cindy's face to see what type of damage had been done. "You're probably gonna need a few stitches." She placed the cloth back on her face and told Cindy to keep it there.

Always thinking responsibly, Geri had pulled her phone out to take pictures of Cindy's face and the damage done to the house.

"We will have them check each of you first and then we'll get your written statements later," the female officer motioned to the two paramedics being escorted inside by Mattie.

One of them checked Peter's wounds and vital signs. His pupils were dilated, and he blew above the legal limit.

"Peter Hanford, we are placing you under arrest for assault and battery. Anything you say can and will be used against you in a court of law...."

FROM BAD TO WORSE

CHAPTER 24

"What!" Kendal's voice carried anger over the phone.

"Yeah, you heard me, baby, we had to jump him. He punched Cindy pretty damn hard; her eye is all black and blue, and she had to get stitches. I can't believe it myself. Then they found a vial of cocaine in his jacket. You just never know nowadays." Mattie explained everything about the altercation.

"I swear, baby, if I ever meet him…"

"No forget about it, we're all going to be fine," she interjected; there would be no need for retribution. Peter was now in the hands of the city prosecutor.

The tour had finished up in Boston, and they had a small break before spending two weeks in Dallas, Texas, another week in Atlanta, Georgia. There would be another small break before picking back up in Charlotte, North Carolina, where Kendal would get a chance to see his older brother. That was almost three months away. So, with the brief layoff, he was flying into Columbus in one day and was spending it with Mattie.

"I'm glad I didn't meet him. Cindy is ok?"

"Yeah, she's angry that she opened up to him and even more upset that she didn't see it coming. She's on an I-hate-all-men tirade now," Mattie replied sitting at her dining room table staring at her engagement ring. She didn't want to talk about the incident anymore.

"I can't wait to wrap my arms around you. I've been taking care of Auntie. She's still lying down; she had a little bug that she's getting over, so she's been resting the last couple of days. Oh… the daycare center may be more difficult than we thought. I've got an inspector to come out in two weeks just to break everything down in black and white because some of the codes just don't make sense." Mattie kept the phone to her ear as she stood up to walk into the kitchen to get another dill pickle out the refrigerator.

"I wish I could be there to talk to them, but I'm sure you all have it under control. What else is new, baby?" he asked as music sounded off in the background.

"My bad, I set the alarm last night to wake me up," he waited for her reply.

"Nothing much… Henry came by the center yesterday, just popping in." Mattie crunched loudly biting down into her pickle.

"He's a good man, giving back to these kids. I heard that they arrested somebody in connection with that murder months ago. I wish we had more officers like him." Kendal was a fan of good law enforcement, and their friend was an exemplary model.

Mattie heard him moving around the hotel and when she heard the faucet running, she imagined him.

"You brushing that hot breath out your mouth. It kinda sounded like you had two dragons up in there when you said good morning." She had grown accustomed to his habits and one was brushing his teeth the first thing he did after using the bathroom every morning.

"Two dragons, shit, more like three, babe." Kendal chuckled.

"I can't wait until we move in permanently," he said out of the blue.

Mattie couldn't wait either, besides always having a person in her home, she wanted to fall asleep and wake up with him the rest of her life. For Mattie, things couldn't get any better.

"That makes two, well three of us," she referenced their baby.

"So, you taking care of Junior, eating and sleeping?" Kendal asked.

"Uh, yeah of course." She was eating better but her sleep had been sporadic. Plus, last night she barely got any rest because of the hospital visit and pressing charges against Peter. They hadn't gotten home until almost four o'clock in the morning as much of the time was spent in the hospital waiting room. Evidently people arriving by ambulance got priority treatment.

Cindy had to black out on the charge nurse after waiting over an hour with blood running down the side of her face.

"Hold on, baby, somebody's calling." Mattie answered the other line not knowing exactly who it was the display read "unknown caller."

"Yes." Mattie said. She had stopped saying "hello" completely.

"Madison, hi this is Detective Roberts, John Roberts… Henry's partner." The voice was familiar.

Mattie tried to think what business they could possibly have with her, but no adequate reason surfaced.

"Yes, hi Detective," She replied.

"Hey, I'm just calling because my buddies told me about what happened up in their neck of the woods last night. I know you all and Henry are like family. He would've called but he's been tied up in the prosecutor's office since seven this morning. I didn't want to bother you so early, but I know it was something on his mind when he left. I hope I didn't wake you," John finished.

Mattie was relieved it had nothing to do with the case of Mark Floyd.

"No intrusion, but I have my fiancé on a long-distance call on the other line. Please tell Henry I said thanks for checking on his little sister," Mattie said with finality to the call.

"You're welcome, ma'am, have a nice day."

Mattie clicked back over.

"Baby, I'm sorry that was Henry's partner. I guess they have some friends from that precinct we were in last night," Mattie stated.

"They say it's a deep brotherhood." Kendal replied.

"I put some thought into what your aunt asked, about having the wedding down south. I think it would be a great idea! My family and friends would travel with adequate notice, and we would be able to meet more of your relatives." Kendal was already planning their ceremony.

Mattie hadn't expected him to agree with her aunt.

"I don't know, the money for people, the distance? I don't know anybody down there really; most of my friends are here," Mattie voiced a few reasons.

"Well, honey, like I said whatever you want, but I do think it's a good idea," Kendal told her. "But it isn't something we needed to dive deep into right now." He changed the subject.

"So, what are your plans for today? I know you have to help Frances with Mr. Jackson taking a vacation day. Do you think we should hire one more person? We are getting more kids every month," Kendal was speaking to her when he heard another voice.

"Madison… Mattie…" Aunt Penny's voice carried into the dining room.

"Hold on, baby," Mattie asked Kendal.

"Yes ma'am?"

"Oh, there you are," she said, turning the corner from the kitchen into the dining room.

"Can we go by the site today? I need to visit her," she asked in reference to Grandma Redd's resting place.

"Of course… Kendal says hi," Mattie added, she appreciated her aunt's presence more now than before.

"Tell him I said hi, and I been praying for him! Can we go early before it gets too hot?" she asked.

"Yes, ma'am, in about an hour?" Mattie responded making sure that was sufficient.

"That be fine." Aunt Penny walked away from the dining area humming a song that her grandmother often sang.

"Ok, baby, I'm back." The conversation didn't last much longer because Mattie felt sick to her stomach.

"I hate this part."

"I hate it for you. Go ahead and handle your business. I hope you feel better, baby, just call me later." They exchanged "I love yous" before hanging up.

Mattie walked quickly to her bathroom and bent over the toilet feeling sick to her stomach, but nothing came up.

Thank God, she thought before undressing to take a shower. She noticed that there was spotting in her cotton panties and after taking a shower she put a pad on in case the blood kept coming. She made a mental note to call and speak with Sheila later about the spotting when they returned.

"Auntie, you ready?" Mattie knocked on Aunt Penny's bedroom door.

297

"I'm in the front room, baby. You hungry? I've got some boiled eggs ready." She asked her young niece as Mattie walked to greet her.

"No ma'am...I ate already."

The cramps in her stomach came back but not as intense, the last few days her lower back burned from time to time. She wished her aunt knew how to drive a manual because she wanted to sit back and just ride.

She decided not to tell her aunt about last night until right before they arrived at the cemetery. Aunt Penny was a bit emotional standing over the grave site of her sister.

"I miss you so much." The older woman held a steady stream of tears falling from her eyes.

Mattie wore sunglasses and behind them she felt the same emotion her aunt was feeling. Her grandmother would still be alive had the back door been locked, but Mattie had come to terms with God calling her grandmother home. Her only wish was to find out who broke into her house that day.

A sharp pain in Mattie's lower back made her go back to the car and wait.

Aunt Penny took another five minutes before joining her inside the car.

"Ok, I'm ready baby…are you ok?" She recognized Mattie was in discomfort.

"Oh yeah, just tired. I didn't get much sleep last night because of what happened at Cindy's house." Mattie went on to give the whole account from the altercation to the waiting in the hospital and then to filing charges.

"How is she?" Aunt Penny asked.

"Well, she's got a black eye and stitches and pissed as hell." Mattie realized she had just cursed.

"I'd be pissed as hell, the only man that ever hit me…well he ain't never hit nobody else." Aunt Penny said as a matter of fact.

"You need to get some rest…is Geri ok?" the elder woman asked changing the subject.

"Yes, she's ok, her back is a little sore from being thrown across the room." Mattie answered.

"You have to stay out of stuff as much as possible…" Aunt Penny had concern in her voice.

"…I know they're your friends and I would've done the same thing but remember you're pregnant and that baby is going to be special."

Mattie didn't respond because she knew the older woman was right on both accords, she hadn't thought when she reacted last night.

"We need anything before we go back home?" Mattie asked because she wanted to lay down uninterrupted.

"Not that I can think of." Aunt Penny answered.

"Good." Mattie thought, trying to push the pain out of her back.

Mattie laid down when they got back to the house while her aunt began cleaning the greens she was going to make for dinner along with baked fish, macaroni and cheese and sweet bread. Aunt Penny then texted both Geri and Cindy to invite them over to eat. She even showed Cindy affection in her text.

"Baby I'm so sorry about last night, come be around family for dinner…no is not an option child." She finished the text with a smiley face. After seasoning the fish and putting it in marinade she went to lie down in the bedroom because she hadn't fully recovered from her bug.

…

Mattie hadn't been sleeping for long when she woke with excruciating cramping in her stomach. At first, she thought it was from only eating pickles but that quickly passed as she felt something wet beneath her. She wondered if she had wet the bed accidentally but that too faded as her stomach cramped again curling her up into a small ball.

She forced herself to pull the covers back and saw the red liquid soaking into her sheets. She didn't fully comprehend what was going on, but then she knew for certainty that something bad was happening.

She stumbled out of bed with blood flowing down her legs.

"Auntie!" she bent over walking down the hall from her bedroom door to her aunt's room.

"Auntie!" she yelled again hysterically.

The older woman opened her bedroom door.

"What, baby?" she saw the blood on Madison's legs.

"Ok, baby… ok." She moved quickly back into her bedroom before coming out with a blanket to wrap around her niece.

"Sit down, baby… just sit down." She called 911.

The ambulance arrived and the paramedics put Mattie on a gurney before rolling her out. Aunt Penny rode with them in a night shift and jacket wrapped around her holding Madison's hand all the way.

Mattie didn't say one word as she still felt the blood coming out from inside her, but her eyes couldn't hide her emotions.

She was scared; afraid that something was terribly wrong with her baby. She was in shock as the ambulance pulled into the emergency room, taking her directly into a room where doctors and nurses had already been waiting.

When she was stabilized, the doctor told her she had had a miscarriage. Mattie tried holding back the tears, but it didn't work as both she and her aunt cried. As they rolled her away, going into a regular hospital room, she looked back at all the blood on the sheets with Aunt Penny carrying a bag of her belongings behind them. She realized that her life would never be the same.

THE FIRST STEP
CHAPTER 25

Mattie slept on the couch instead of her bed since she had miscarried three weeks ago. She had drawn into herself and wanted to be left alone. Her friends had called her daily; sometimes she answered the call but many times she let it go to voicemail.

Aunt Penny decided to stay longer, but the older woman gave her niece all the space she needed.

Mattie hadn't showered in four days and had eaten sparingly.

Kendal had come home for a week in between shows but even his presence had no effect on her. In fact, his face was a constant reminder of how she had fallen short of being a mother. She needed him to leave. She found herself being bitchy with him, making him stay at his condo instead of with her.

She went back to drinking Pepsi, but as her depression set in, she began to drink liquor inside her home regularly. She found that being intoxicated temporarily made her feel better. Her sleep was still rare and her dreams of having a child shattered each time she remembered the blood covering her lower body.

Lying on couch now staring at the ceiling, she grew angry at every thought that surfaced.

I need to get an appointment sooner, she thought in regard to seeing Dr. Stevens. He would understand her when no one else did; he had been there through all her turmoil as a teenager.

She picked up her cell phone to call his office, hoping that someone had cancelled, and she could replace that appointment slot. But when the receptionist informed Mattie that this was his week of vacation, she got an attitude and hung up the phone on her.

Mattie felt like she was dying inside; she felt that the miscarriage was entirely her fault, regardless of the doctors and Sheila saying it could've been a birth defect as most miscarriages were. She didn't care about what most miscarriages were; she only found sadness in the one she had.

Mattie crossed her arms across her chest and fought back the tears. Unable to sleep in the past ten days, her 20-minute power naps did nothing to take the edge off.

"Good morning." Aunt Penny walked into the kitchen to brew some coffee.

"Morning," Mattie replied dryly. There was nothing good about this morning or any other morning the way Mattie saw it.

"How are you feeling?" The older woman stood in between the kitchen and the living room. Wisdom had told Aunt Penny to let things run their course with Madison, but being the only constant person around she saw the strings loosening with her niece's mental awareness.

"I'm ok, Auntie, just resting right now."

Aunt Penny walked down the hall back to her bedroom.

Mattie's cell phone rang, and she looked over to the coffee table to see who it was. Kendal was calling her for the third time this morning, but she had ignored each call. She wanted to answer but each time she simply let it ring.

What could I possibly say to him? Why does he still want me? she thought.

He told her before leaving that nothing else mattered to him in this world except her health and her heart. She told him that both had been broken and to give her space and time. Reluctantly, he left to rejoin the tour because she forced him to leave, telling him that she wasn't going to see him if he stayed.

She turned over on the couch, propping her pillow up and dozed off only to wake up 20 minutes later when she heard Aunt Penny in the kitchen again.

Mattie got up and went to her bedroom. Everything looked the same with the exception of an empty bed frame because she had her mattress and box spring thrown out; she didn't need a constant reminder of the night she lost her baby.

Taking her clothes off, she smelled the must on her body and forced herself into the shower.

"What's wrong with me?" she asked standing in front of her mirror. She was getting dark circles under her eyes due to the lack of sleep. When looking closer into the mirror as she toweled off, she noticed she had lost weight.

"Who cares?" she asked aloud before getting dressed to go sit back on the couch in the living room.

"I made some grits and sausage," Aunt Penny said. She didn't tell Mattie to eat or force her to do anything she didn't want; all she ever did over the past two weeks was inform her niece of things.

"Thanks, I'll eat a little later," Mattie said before adjusting her pillow and blanket again. Mattie hadn't felt like this ever before in her life... not as bad as this. She wanted to yell, to scream out at God for being so cruel. She wanted to hate Him for taking her child away, for destroying her happy ever after. But she didn't.

She believed it was all her fault for taking a life and now God required payment. Mattie didn't know what to do, how to fix herself.

Sheila was the first to find out about her losing the baby and with years of nursing experience, she didn't push Mattie to talk or express her emotions. Sheila told Geri and Cindy to let Mattie have her space, something Mattie had appreciated.

"I'm going to go see Sheila," Mattie told her aunt as she slipped her blue flip flops on.

"Ok" was all the older woman replied.

This was the first time she had ventured outside the house since leaving the hospital that following morning.

Halfway to her hospital, a man swerved into her lane, almost forcing her into head on traffic. Something clicked inside her and she sped up to catch the vehicle that almost made her crash. She cut in and out of traffic and pulled up beside the Honda Accord. She reached into her center console as the man rolled his window down cursing at Mattie.

"What the fuck you gon' do bitch?" he said, acting like he was going to ram her car again.

Mattie rolled down her passenger side window and pulled her 9mm handgun out and pointed it at him.

The man's expression on his face changed instantly as he tried to speed up, leading him past a red light into traffic where he hit the rear end of a minivan spinning it out of control.

Mattie had stopped in time and rolled her window back up like nothing happened before continuing to the hospital to see her friend.

Mattie had to wait for Sheila. She was helping a doctor with a patient who had recently suffered from cardiac arrest. The older man was complaining about chest pain, so Sheila along with the doctor ran additional tests.

When Sheila was finished with the patient, she had to reprimand a new nurse for not dispensing the correct amount of medicine into an IV drip, which had adverse effect on the patient.

"I love my position but can't seem to get all of my staff on the same page, I'm gonna grab something from the cafeteria. You hungry?" Sheila asked Mattie. Mattie had not had an appetite for quite a while.

"No, I'm good," Mattie answered yawning.

"Can I wait for you in your office?"

Sheila was signing off on a chart for another patient to be released from the hospital.

"Yeah, it ain't much of an office," Sheila replied as they walked down the hall before making a right turn through double doors. Sheila took her keys out and opened the door.

"You sure you don't want something? You look like you're losing weight," Sheila asked again.

"No, I'm fine I ate earlier," Mattie deliberately lied.

As Sheila walked away, Mattie sat down and slouched in the chair. She heard the walkie talkie on her friend's desk going off about two people being transported from a car crash. One of the injured was a woman complaining about neck pain. The other was a man who suffered broken ribs and arm, with abrasions on his face from the glass giving way when impact occurred.

Mattie knew that it was the accident that she witnessed. She wasn't going to take responsibility for the after affects because she didn't run the red light.

His ass shouldn't have tried to run me off the road, she thought, believing he deserved every injury. She did feel remorse for the woman.

But again, I didn't hit her, she thought.

Mattie wondered would she have shot at him if no one was around and then she got sad again.

Sheila walking back into the room with a grilled cheese sandwich and French fries did nothing but aggravate her for some reason.

"I gotta shove this down," Sheila said.

"We've got two buses arriving in the next ten minutes…" Sheila paused taking a closer look at her friend.

"Have you talked with Dr. Stevens to get you something to sleep?" she took a bite of her sandwich.

"No, his ass is on vacation, just my luck." Mattie realized she needed a visit with him when he got back.

Sheila unlocked her computer to see what psychiatrists were on call. She knew her friend was struggling with life, and she would do anything to help her.

"I've got a friend, a psychiatrist that I can get to fill you a script. She'll want 15 minutes to ask a few questions. I think it may do you some good," Sheila added hoping Mattie would take her up on the offer.

Mattie folded her arms in front of her.

I don't need any help from anyone, Mattie thought but she knew that was the pain speaking; that was the sadness inside her.

"That's fine, Sheila," Mattie said in a monotone voice.

Sheila sent a message through the internal hospital cue and received a message back immediately.

"Send her up."

"Ok go to the fourth floor and to room 421. Her name is Dr. Hughes, she's a good psychiatrist, the same one I spoke with when James and I divorced," Sheila said taking two final bites of her sandwich.

"When you're done, meet me back here," Sheila said before hurrying off to the emergency room for the arrival of the car crash victims.

Mattie found herself just going with the motion. She took the elevator up to the fourth floor. After locating Dr. Hughes office, she walked in expecting to be greeted by a secretary or receptionist but instead it was the doctor waiting on her.

"Madison?" she asked.

"Yes, Dr. Hughes?" Mattie forced a smile.

Dr. Hughes was a few inches taller than Mattie, and she styled her hair short like Geri. She wore diamond stud earrings and Mattie thought her dark skin complexion was flawless with her white teeth as the perfect contrast.

"Well come on back," Dr. Hughes said opening the door to the back room where her office was located.

"So, Sheila tells me you're having trouble sleeping." She noticed the dark circles formed under Mattie's eyes.

"Yeah, it's been a little while. I fall asleep but wake up 20 minutes later," Mattie answered.

"Well, I just wanna ask you a few questions before writing you a prescription."

She asked Mattie a variety of questions from allergies to any headaches or pain… general questions.

"And what else, if anything would you like to share?" Dr. Hughes asked with already enough information to give her a script for Ambien.

Mattie understood the question and when she started answering it, she couldn't stop.

"I hate my life… I hate the fact that I couldn't carry my child to term. I hate that when I look at myself in the mirror, I get disgusted… I hate knowing that my fiancé wants children, and I miscarried. I hate being around people. I cry for no apparent reason. I'm depressed. I'm so depressed that I lay on my couch and do nothing but stare out the window and cry. Little things upset me and I'm tired… I'm so damn tired that if I didn't have strong values I don't know if I could manage anything," Mattie said staring at the doctor before she bent over and started to cry.

Dr. Hughes sat back in her chair and let Mattie cry. She knew depression when she saw it, and it would take more than sleeping aids to make her better. Hearing Mattie insinuate without actually saying that she had thought about harming herself threw up a red flag. It was her duty to get her proper medical treatment.

Dr. Hughes typed something on her computer and then gave Mattie tissue to wipe the tears away.

"It can be rough, Madison. So many thoughts, feeling like the ground is giving way under your feet. You feel alone even when there is family and friends to support you... with your permission I'd like to help you," Dr. Hughes said standing from her chair as Sheila knocked on her door.

"Come in," she said.

Mattie looked up and couldn't control her crying.

"Madison, I'd like to admit you to the hospital. I think it's in your best interest. We can tackle your issues, and I don't think you should be alone," Dr. Hughes said.

Sheila stood there wondering what had just happened. She sent Mattie up to get a prescription, and now Mattie was at the worst she had ever seen her.

Mattie heard everything that Dr. Hughes said. She wanted to stand up and walk out of the office refusing the request, but she couldn't find the support in her legs. She thought about losing her baby and then Grandma Redd. She thought about how withdrawn from life she had been, how she was forcing Kendal away, and how her temper had caused trauma to two different people being treated in the emergency room.

Sheila went to say something, but Dr. Hughes motioned her against it.

"That's fine, I'll admit myself," Mattie sobbed in between each word.

"We can take you upstairs now if you're ready," Dr. Hughes said as Sheila held her hand out for Mattie to take a hold of.

"I'm ready," Mattie replied taking the box of tissues off the desk.

"Will you tell Auntie?" Mattie asked Sheila.

"Of course I will, but don't worry about that… we're gonna make sure we get you the best care to make you all better, that's what is important right now," Sheila answered as they escorted Mattie out the office and up to the ninth floor, walking into the psychiatric ward.

VISITING HOURS
CHAPTER 26

After the intake interview, Mattie was given a menu to order dinner, breakfast, and lunch for the following day along with more paperwork to read over. She lay in her room on a single bed. The staff kept checking in on her, but there was nothing that she could harm herself with. She was given a robe to put on as she was stripped of all of her garments save panties and bra. There was protocol to follow.

She wasn't suicidal, although at times over the past three weeks she had wanted to run away and get out of the country, far away from everyone.

Her roommate was an older woman in her late fifties, and she sat on her bed roughly four feet away reading the Bible, rocking back and forth.

I'm in the nuthouse, Mattie thought, depressed about her life.

The psych ward was vastly different than what she had imagined. She had visions of people running up and down the hall being chased by staff or in locked up padded rooms, staring out the small glass window with blank expressions and drooling down their mouths. She was greatly wrong.

The ninth floor was calm. Patients interacted with each other, and the staff made frequent rounds just as an oversight.

"God is good… God is good." Mattie's roommate Betty wasn't speaking directly to Madison, but she kept repeating the phrase.

Mattie didn't look up. She just laid on her back on the bed with her arms folded under her head to prop herself up. How and why, she allowed herself to be admitted still evaded her. Some small voice in the recess of her mind made her do it. Whether or not she would get sleep and the help she needed was still left to be determined, but she was here for at least the next three days.

Dr. Hughes did a more extensive, comprehensive history. She assured Mattie that each day, even on the weekends, that she would check on and monitor her medications to be dispensed. She had started Mattie off with a newer mood stabilizer called Abilify and to help her sleep she gave her five milligrams of Ambien.

"I just want to get better," Mattie swallowed the pills unenthusiastically.

Sheila would give Aunt Penny the rundown on what had happened and where she was.

"Dinner will be up in ten minutes," one of the staff members named Connor said peeking his head into the room.

"Oh yes… yes… food… food." Betty said.

The male staffer was grinning, but his true emotion couldn't be read. Pale skinned with red hair and a moderate build. His hospital uniform protruded slightly around his waist but other than that he looked in decent shape.

"Yes, Betty food! I'm sure you ordered something good to eat." His voice was light.

Betty stood up and put her Bible on the table, situating it directly in the center of the desk.

"I'm coming with you Conner. I'm coming with you, ok?" Betty slid her feet across the floor instead of lifting them up as she walked.

"I'm walking if you're coming," Connor replied, motioning Betty forward.

Mattie didn't move, she did make eye contact with him to let him know she acknowledged what he said. Mattie didn't want to walk around in her hospital gown. She felt uncomfortable in it; the last time she wore such a garment, she had lost her baby. That thought saddened her again, but she was determined to control her emotions.

Walking down the hallway to the dining area, she caught people looking at her, making her feel uncomfortable. The dining room had all its seats filled. Conner sat in a chair nearest the door, keeping order but making sure the patients received their dinner tray.

"Madison." He handed her the tray from the cart before pointing to a spot at the far end of the dining space. "There's a seat."

Mattie sat down and lifted the top of her plate— a hamburger and fries with fruit. She wasn't hungry, but she forced herself to take two bites before returning her tray. When she walked back into her room, she found her sweatpants with the elastic string taken out and her t-shirt laying on the bed.

"Thank you, Jesus." Mattie vocalized her prayer.

She laid back down and dozed off until she was awakened to receive her nightly medications. That night she slept for a few hours on end until she woke to find Betty standing up, staring at the ceiling, and waving her hands above her head.

"What the fuck?" Mattie was still groggy but trying to stay awake. The combination of medicines, however, forced her back to sleep against her will.

. . . .

"Breakfast is here." A different voice came through her cracked door.

Betty was already showered, dressed, and reading the Bible again.

"Breakfast... breakfast." Betty repeated her same actions of the night before.

Mattie rolled over to place her feet on the floor. The medicine still influenced her as she slowly stood up. The sun was shining through her window bars, but she couldn't gauge the time until she saw one of the clocks mounted on the wall: 730.

"Madison, after you eat, your friend Sheila brought you some items," Conner said standing behind the long nurse's desk where the employees were separated from the patients.

"Ok, thanks," Mattie replied.

She felt more tired than when she fell asleep last night as she took her breakfast tray from the cart. The woman who had woken them sat in a chair doing a crossword puzzle, glancing up every now and then. After eating, Mattie retrieved her bag to be informed that group sessions would begin at 9 a.m., and it was highly recommended that she attended each one.

Mattie took the bag of clothing and asked where she could take a shower. Another woman on staff directed her, unlocking the door.

As Mattie waited for the temperature of the water to warm, she stripped naked. With the water being barely warm, she washed quickly and changed. When she returned to her room, Betty told her to come to the group session.

Mattie wanted to lie back down but instead followed the older woman.

"We have a new friend joining us today. What we do is just ask your name and if you want to share anything about yourself you are welcome to." A different staff member welcomed her as Mattie took the last remaining chair.

"I'm Madison, and I think I'll just listen today," she replied, wondering what each of the 15 other people were in the psych ward for.

"Well today we're going to go over relaxation techniques," the man said. He put on an audio CD of natural sounds and went through various breathing techniques.

Mattie was grateful when she saw Dr. Hughes entering the hallway from the locked double doors.

She motioned to Mattie, who had already stood up excusing herself.

Walking into a different room, Dr. Hughes began speaking before they sat down.

"Did you sleep better last night?" she asked.

"Yeah, a little, I guess... how possible is it to be moved to a different room? My roommate is... was... standing up swatting at the air last night." Mattie replied.

"I'll see what I can do," Dr. Hughes answered.

After a brief 10 minutes discussion, the doctor advised Mattie that part of her release was contingent upon attending as many group sessions as possible.

"Many of them deal directly with depression. I still believe we're shooting for Monday, maybe Tuesday of next week. We should have your meds leveled out, and you can make your appointment with Dr. Stevens," Dr. Hughes commented, pulling out a medical release form.

"Thank you," Mattie said after signing the form.

"You're welcome."

Mattie decided not to go to anymore group sessions for the day. She spent most of her time in her bed waiting for her room change.

"Madison, you have visitors," A different female nurse said.

This wasn't expected, Mattie wondered who it was but as she made her way to the visiting room, she could see Aunt Penny sitting with Sheila.

"Hi, baby." Aunt Penny gave her an enormous hug.

"I think you're doing the best thing to get yourself better," Sheila whispered into Mattie's ear as she hugged her too.

"Don't be upset, but I told Geraldine and Cynthia... oh and Pastor Morris. I'll let you tell Kendal when you're ready." The older woman was aware some things were left up to her niece.

Mattie was happy to see her aunt and to have her support. She didn't feel as crazy as before; she was getting help. After visiting hours, Mattie attended the last group session of the day.

The next two days went like this, with the one exception that Mattie found her way to all the group sessions. She found valuable information about depression and warning signs. At the end of each day, she watched the evening news with her new roommate Sarah. This evening, the police had to be called to the ninth floor as one of the newer patients became violent.

"Madison, you have a visitor," Conner told her, pulling her away from the television set. Visiting hours were over, so Mattie figured it was Sheila using her position as Head Nurse to come see her, but when she walked into the room, she was surprised to see Pastor Morris standing in regular clothing.

"Sister Parks." He reached his hand towards her.

Mattie felt embarrassed at first but gathered her wits and greeted him.

"Hi Pastor, I hope you didn't expect to see me in a strait jacket," she laughed to make light of the moment.

"If you only knew," he paused. "You're getting the medical help you need from what Aunt Penny says. You know the doors are always open and we support you, Madison. Spiritually, we all struggle at times, but that struggle is an opportune time to build our relationship with God. My wife sends her love and prayers." Pastor Morris talked at length about points in his life where he struggled. Before leaving, he left Mattie with a scripture from the Bible to read—Isaiah 59:1-20.

Walking back into her room, her new roommate Sarah was just standing looking out the window. She had suffered from an eating disorder her entire life and was recently diagnosed with bipolar disorder. Sarah had been there for nearly two weeks as they struggled to find the right combination of medications for her. It appeared her emotions were under control.

"I'm going home soon." She turned to face Mattie.

"Well, that's good." Mattie walked to her bed and sat down before laying back onto a pillow.

Sarah smiled and left the room.

Mattie decided to read the scripture Pastor Morris had left for her. Afterwards, she understood much of her depression was not only from having a miscarriage but from the turmoil of killing a man. She decided that on her next visit with Dr. Stevens she would disclose that information to him.

As promised, Dr. Hughes had Mattie discharged on Tuesday. Sarah was standing at the nurse's station asking when her doctor was coming because she was also supposed to be released. When they told her not until the following day, she did not get upset and walked away.

Sheila was waiting with Mattie to finish the final paperwork.

"You look one hundred percent better," Sheila mentioned in passing.

"I feel better, sleep does a body good," Mattie said mustering up a small grin.

"Ok, that's it, we're done here," Dr. Hughes said waiting for Conner to hit the button to open the electric doors of the ninth floor.

Mattie felt relieved to be leaving. She was happy to be going home to sleep in her own bedroom. The one thing she was unsure of was Kendal. He had called her friends and Aunt Penny repeatedly but was not given any information about her. Mattie had picked up the phone in the hospital to dial his number numerous times, but each time she didn't complete the call. She would wait until she was out of the hospital.

When she got home, she dialed his number.

"Hello." Kendal's voice sounded but it went to his voicemail.

"Hi, first I want to apologize. I was in a bad place mentally, and I hope you will forgive me. Please call me when you get this message." She was anxiously waiting for his call.

BROTHER TO BROTHER
CHAPTER 27

Kendal had waited patiently to hear anything from Mattie. Her friends were still kind to him, but their loyalty belonged to her. He was forced to deal with similar emotions that he had overcome when Janine passed away.

Kendal never believed his heart could be filled with so much love and joy again until Madison, but now he was struggling. He had two more days before flying back out for the tour, yet he wasn't sure how he could commit to anything.

He spent a large portion of his time at the center staying busy. A new program for writing had begun. He was using his platform to attract young creatives into the space. When he could focus, he taught a few classes.

He worked out extensively daily to help his energy, which was sporadic at best. He was hurt by the way Mattie had pushed him away after the miscarriage, even as he tried to see it from her perspective.

It fuckin' kills me too! His thoughts contained pain, anger… uncertainty, as he hit the heavy bag in the gymnasium of the center.

Boxing was great exercise for staying in shape. Mattie had introduced Kendal to a few colleagues in the mixed martial arts community. Jennifer Kerns had provided lessons to him in her MMA studio.

The day had faded and only a small glimmer of sunlight remained when Frances watched the door to the center open. A group of six men entered dressed in black fitted suits. Two of the men remained by the door and it caused France's concern.

"Hi, how can I help you?"

One man separated himself from the rest of them.

"I am looking for Kendal, is he here?" His accent was heavy, and his question was direct.

"I can check if he's available, we don't have any appointments scheduled for today. Would you like to tell me what your visit is about?" Frances, although nervous, would make sure she got what the unannounced visit was about.

"Frances, I am Roberto, and my sister Madison has told me you are a great asset, but I have come to see Kendal, 'perhaps' my soon to be brother-in-law."

Frances knew this was one of Mattie's "siblings" as she put two and two together.

"We weren't expecting anyone, but I can take you to him. He's in the gymnasium down the hall." Frances moved to walk from behind the desk to lead them. As they approached the entrance of the gym, one of the larger men stopped her.

"We will take it from here." Roberto motioned with courtesy for Frances to remain behind as he walked in by himself.

Kendal was shadow boxing when the doors to the gymnasium opened. He knew there were no assigned classes, so he wondered why the gentlemen was taking off his tie and suit coat.

"Thanks for coming out but we don't have anything scheduled until next week. We can get some of your information and…" Kendal got cut off.

"You know in my family, when one of us needs help, we are there without pause. Everything else becomes secondary. Why aren't you with my sister, making sure she is ok?"

Kendal surmised that this was Roberto. His voice was more baritone than bass, and also because he looked like David, but older than 35.

"Roberto, I take it. Welcome brother, I spoke to your father and…" Kendal attempted to make pleasantries but was cut off again.

"Yes, yes, I know but we aren't speaking on that. Why aren't you at her side?" Roberto had taken off his button-down shirt to only reveal a black wife-beater. He walked towards the ring, eyeing a pair of grappling gloves laying on a bench before slipping off his shoes.

Kendal wasn't sure where this was headed but he didn't like the line of questioning. He had already been on an emotional roller coaster and a surprise interrogation wasn't welcoming.

"Brother, you probably have more insight into your sister this past month than I have." Kendal paused watching Roberto slip in the gloves and step up onto the apron of the ring.

"Roberto, why are you here?"

Roberto slid through the top and middle ropes and stepped into the ring. He bent down to kiss the mat.

"I need to know what type of person you are. Are you a poser or a man, Kendal?" Roberto stretched his arms and placed his gloves up in a defensive posture.

330

"I'm not boxing you." Kendal was making it clear that he had no intention of sparring with Mattie's older brother.

"No, no of course not. You'd rather let life punch you in the face." Roberto threw a mock jab.

Kendal stepped away from him but kept his eyes on him intently.

"My sister means everything to me and my family. Perhaps you don't want to spar, but words mean nothing." Roberto closed some of their distance and jabbed him again with a one two, one combination.

Kendal didn't like where this was going, but he was a man. If words were insufficient, then action it would be. He put his hands up and readied himself.

"I don't want to do this with you, Roberto." Kendal dodged the same combination, but Roberto ended it with a calf kick that landed soundly.

"But you must," Roberto answered. He was a little taller than Kendal with about the same reach. As Roberto advanced again, Kendal took the offensive and kicked him in the chest to get distance.

"Good, good now we can see what type of man you are."

. . .

Mattie saw the running group starting to gather at the park when the streetlights came on. She hadn't run with them in quite some time, so she slipped on some sweats, a long-sleeved shirt, and her running shoes and headed over to meet them.

She looked for the mayor's political aide, but Bianca wasn't with them tonight.

Mattie nodded at a few runners she had met before. As they started, she hung towards the back. Her lungs were burning within the first seven minutes and when they were done, she literally fell to the ground sucking air into her lungs. It took her longer to gather herself to make it back across the street. She started cramping with the first step walking into her building.

Mattie grabbed two water bottles and drank them quickly before moving slowly to the living room couch.

Her phone kept ringing in her bedroom but whoever it was could wait. She laid her head back and inhaled deeply when her phone rang again. She ignored it until she couldn't.

Making her way down the hallway, Aunt Penny looked like she had had enough of Mattie's phone too.

"Can't you put it on vibrate or something?" she asked, following Mattie into her bedroom.

Mattie had bought a new bed frame and headboard. She didn't want any recollection or reminder of her miscarriage, and the new bed helped.

"David and I have been trying to get a hold of you!" Camille's voice came abruptly through the phone when Mattie answered. Mattie didn't have time to greet his sister-in-law because Camille had stress in her voice.

"I left my phone…"

"Roberto is going to speak with your fiancé! He's been upset after finding out he hasn't been there to support you. Their flight landed less than an hour ago. David found out he's going to the school… the center." Camille seemed frantic.

Mattie was calculating everything being said, and if Roberto flew into Columbus, Ohio, unannounced, this wasn't business. This was personal.

"I pushed Kendal away bec…"

"You're not listening! Roberto is going to go and have a talk with Kendal about why he isn't by your side. Whether you pushed him away is irrelevant. El Chaco is with him."

Mattie's stomach dropped. She grabbed her car keys and ran out the back patio door. Kendal would be at the center, and she needed to get there before her brother.

…

Frances was standing at the desk when Mattie pulled up to the door, leaving her car door open with it running still.

When she entered the center, she pushed the two guards at the door out the way and ran towards the gymnasium where El Chaco stood guard.

"Senora Mattie," he attempted to greet her, but she ordered him aside.

He obliged.

When she pushed the gymnasium door open, Kendal and Roberto were in the middle of the ring facing each other. Kendal hadn't seen her in weeks and in the temporary lapse of focus, Roberto rushed him and took him to the ground. Kendal fought for position, using his feet to push Roberto's weight off balance and moved to frame himself for better position, Roberto stuffed the attempt and rolled away.

"You should've been protecting her!" Roberto yelled while pointing at Mattie.

"If you don't know your sister by now, she does what she wants and neither, you, nor me can change that!" Kendal readied himself.

"What the fuck are you two doing? Stop it! Just fucking stop, or I'll kill the two of you idiots right now!" she yelled as she rolled herself into the ring.

"This is what you think I would want? For the two of you to be in conflict?" She pushed Roberto squarely in the chest.

"He tried to be there for me! He fucking stalked me even after I lost his child! I pushed him away. Did you even think to pick up the phone to call and speak with me?" She shoved Roberto again.

Her emotions were taking over, and she wasn't sure if it was anger or sadness, but she began crying as she explained to Roberto the emptiness inside her that she had to overcome, that she believed she could be redeemed by giving birth, but the Creator took that from her.

Roberto's facial expression showed that he recognized he had made an error.

"Hermana, lo siento pero…"

"No buts, my dear brother. Violence doesn't resolve everything. Comprendes?" She couldn't stop her tears.

Roberto stared into Mattie's eyes and shook his head that he understood before Mattie turned and walked towards Kendal.

Kendal's lip was bleeding, and his face bruised but he was still standing.

"I'm sorry" was all she could muster taking his gloved hands into hers.

Kendal couldn't think straight as he stared into Mattie's eyes. His adrenaline was still flowing, and he was more confused than when the day began.

"I wasn't stalking you. I wanted to support you, but you stopped talking. Your friends stopped talking to me. You made me feel like I was unimportant to you. I know you're sorry, but I think I need to take a shower and clear my head."

Mattie heard the pain in his voice, and all she thought about was the New York City debacle.

She shook her head that she understood while staring into his eyes. She wiped the blood on his lips before leaning forward to kiss him on his cheek.

"I am sorry," she whispered before he excused himself and walked to the locker room.

Roberto watched silently. He removed his gloves and waited for Mattie. He was certain that she wasn't done with him.

Mattie understood her family and Roberto even more because in more ways than not, they were kindred spirits and family meant everything to both. She watched Kendal leave before turning to face Roberto.

"I love you, brother, and I thank you for doing what you thought was best, but I am the one to blame, not him. He's the best man I have ever known and the man I love. You have to respect this."

Roberto's simply nodded he understood before Mattie hugged him and told him to get dressed. She made them leave while she waited on Kendal. She told Roberto she would come to the suite he had secured in a few hours. For now, she needed to make amends.

Kendal came out dressed shortly after and was reluctant to speak so he listened to everything Mattie shared about the loss of the baby and seeking help. He asked her to give him the night to think about everything. She agreed because she had no other choice.

QUICK FOLLOW-UP
CHAPTER 28

"I didn't do it; I'm telling you, y'all got the wrong muthafuckin' person!" the fair skinned black man yelled being hauled down the hallway to central booking with his hands cuffed behind his back.

"No, we've got the right people; you still had the stolen merchandise in your vehicle, idiot." One of the two uniformed police officers laughed sarcastically.

"They read your rights to you; you probably just want to shut the hell up." The woman who was walking next to him said.

Henry looked up from his desk and saw both people being led away. He always found it funny that guilty people pled their innocence even when they were caught red handed. He had grown accustomed to being lied to when he interviewed suspects; that was one of the main reasons he was so diligent in connecting evidence to a crime.

Henry was bent over his desk looking into a manila folder that contained phone records.

The captain had been adamant about leaving the Jimmie Fredericks' case closed, but for Henry things didn't add up the way they were supposed to. The prosecutor's office had a confession, forced by the hands of Henry and his partner. The captain had forced them to tell Mark Floyd that the death penalty would be on the table and the only way to take it off was to confess and ask for a plea bargain.

Reluctantly, he confessed hoping the prosecutor's office would honor the plea bargain to save his life. Now Mark Floyd was recanting his confession.

Henry didn't believe much in coincidence; he would let the evidence lead him to wherever it would take him and so far, if he were a betting man he would wager that there was a different suspect connected to the death of the victim.

Luckily, the phone log of Jimmie Frederick had been pulled prior to Mark Floyd confessing and now as Henry went down the list he was hoping to find another piece of the puzzle.

"Hey, partner I'm going across to the deli, you want something?" John asked him.

"No, I'm still kinda full from the breakfast Michelle made." Henry slowly closed the manila folder.

"You are working on the Huntington case?" John followed up.

Henry didn't want John to know about what he speculated, so as he put the manila folder into his briefcase he responded.

"We're gonna catch a break on it, and I'm coming with you. I'll grab a corned beef sandwich for later." He straightened up.

Henry had noticed a phone call on the log report from Jimmie's cell phone to Global Communications just days before he was murdered. He knew he would have to get a subpoena to listen to that specific call. He also knew that his captain wasn't going to sign off on that request.

He hoped that what he was putting together was purely fictional, but the power of evidence kept leading him down a road he didn't want to travel.

Coincidence, Henry thought, walking into the delicatessen across the street from the police station. His ringing cell phone forced his mind away from drawing the same conclusion.

"Hello, Detective Jenkins," He answered.

"Henry, what's going on brother... its Kendal," the voice on the other end replied.

"What's going on with the tour is the bigger question? Michelle said a few shows were cancelled in Philly, everything alright?" Henry asked.

"Yeah, we're good. Patricia ran into some issues with the promoters not wanting to pay what they owed so she had to do what she had to do," Kendal paused. "Listen, I've got a huge favor to ask you."

"Shoot," Henry responded.

"Can you and a few of your brothers at arms show up to the youth festival? We've had a few threats from a local gang saying we're infringing on their territory by recruiting some of the kids for our program. One of my boys got jumped after leaving the center a couple of nights ago," Kendal finished.

"I'll see what I can do. When is it?" Henry needed the details.

"This weekend. I know it's short notice, but I'm hoping the presence of law enforcement will show that we're dealing with a strong hand. The boy's mother made her son tell who did it, so charges are being pressed. But we received two letters saying, 'Snitches are already dead.'" Kendal responded.

"I'll make sure our presence is felt. How's Mattie?" Henry knew that she was going through a lot of changes.

He felt at odds calling because of his speculations and didn't want his personal connection clouding his judgment.

"She's doing better, thanks for asking."

In his own way, Kendal still had issues about being forced away by Mattie, but he understood that his fiancé felt personally responsible for the loss of their child.

"I'll have Mr. Jackson give you a call in a couple of days. I wish I could be there, but we've got shows all weekend. Tell Michelle I said hi, and make sure you take Jay." Kendal thanked Henry again before hanging up.

"Hey, I'm going to run a few errands." John paid for his order.

"How long?" Henry asked knowing his partner was going to see a woman because he had bought two sandwiches.

"Oh, I'd say about an hour and a half... two at most," John said smiling.

Henry paid for his sandwich and walked back into the station. When he got off the elevator, he saw the mayor was sitting in the captain's office and the conversation they were having seemed to be a friendly one.

Henry decided two hours was enough time to put a composite of photos together containing pictures of female felons, police officers, and Mattie to see if the shop owners could identify the person who had bought the wigs. He knew it was a long shot since it had been nearly six months ago, but he wanted… needed to rule Mattie out.

He was skeptical as he pulled up to the hair shop; he had been ordered to leave it alone, but he needed closure. As Henry walked into the store, he noticed a group of women picking merchandise off the shelves to stuff into a large purse.

The male shop owner must have sensed something and approached the women.

"What can I help you find?" he asked the woman nearest.

"Uh, we jus' looking, we gon' be braiding hair so we gon' need some Yaki Deep twists," the woman said.

"Well, that's up at the front counter." The Asian shop owner waited for the trio of ladies to go up front.

Henry decided to get involved.

"I'm sure your intent is not to go to jail today," he said flatly showing off his badge.

The youngest woman's eyes widened because she was the one carrying the purse with the stolen items inside.

"I'd put everything back while I speak with him and then buy what you need," Henry finished.

"I don't know what you're talking about, sir," the other woman interjected.

"You are stealing from me... my store?" The shop owner said now knowing they were shoplifting.

"I won't say it again," Henry stared at all three women.

The young woman with the purse turned around and emptied the items back to their proper shelves.

"You steal from me... get out... get out!" the Asian man said, forcing all three women out his store.

"Don't you ever come back here!" he yelled.

"I knew they steal from me, thank you." He recognized Henry.

"Oh, detective how did the wigs work for you?" he smiled.

Henry was amused with the question and laughed with the older man.

"Fine... just fine. I was wondering, do you think you can pick the woman out who bought those wigs if I showed you some pictures?" Henry asked.

"I don't know, it's been long time... she was very pretty though," he answered, shaking his head up and down.

"Well, I tell you, just take a look and if you recognize her just let me know," Henry responded.

The back door of the store opened and out came the shop owner's wife.

"Ah, detective, you are back... you need more wigs?" she asked.

"No, no more wigs, but I was hoping that you both could take a look at some photos and tell me who purchased those wigs," he responded, pulling out the composite with eight different photographs of women.

The husband studied the pictures but wasn't sure.

"She looks familiar," he said, pointing to a photo of a woman already serving time.

"No... no... I think it was this one or maybe this one." He was confusing himself.

His wife snatched the photo array and looked deeply at each picture.

"It one of these two."

One of them were of Mattie.

"Are you able to narrow it down?" Henry felt his stomach drop his suspicion was nearly confirmed.

"No narrow down, but the woman looked like one of these two." She handed the pictures back to Henry.

Henry felt numb because all it had done was add more questions to be answered. The one answer he needed could only be found on the conversation that Jimmie Frederick's had with Global Communication.

He walked out of the store, contemplating how he could get a copy or transcript of that call or how to determine what representative the victim had spoken with. Suddenly, he remembered that a unit had been called out to Jimmie's house a few days prior to his death. Henry decided if he could pull the incident report, he might be one step closer to finding out the truth.

"Wherever the evidence takes me," he spoke out loud, feeling leery about the course of action he was taking but the truth would not evade him. It was his job to seek it out.

GOES A LONG WAY
CHAPTER 29

"He'll come around; he needs time to heal too, just like everybody else." Cindy was walking away from Mattie and Geri, barely able to speak while her two friends continued jogging on the treadmill at the gym. It was two days after the altercation at the center, and Kendal had not responded as quickly as Mattie would've liked. Roberto and his men had flown out early in the morning for a business meeting with a politician in Utah that failed to meet his responsibilities.

He had the men sleep in Mattie's basement while he took the guest bedroom. He and Mattie talked all night, and she ended up forgiving him.

She adored her older brother, but he had made a situation that was already strained, worse. Kendal had called only to inform her that he had left to rejoin the tour; the departing conversation between him and Mattie was superficial. She was coming to face facts. She fucked up again.

Mattie was easing her body back into shape, but Geri decided to push her harder today than she had the past two weeks simply because she knew Mattie needed to be challenged. Having Roberto show up unannounced, for her benefit or not, made her face so many issues head on. The revelation that Senor Rojas gave his blessing for the marriage was new. She had no idea that David got Kendal in contact with the patriarch before the engagement. What else didn't she know?

Mattie knew that Kendal still loved her; he hadn't called off the engagement. But she couldn't blame him for taking time to get his emotions under control. She had been the one forcing him away as she dealt with her own demons.

"I guess I could've told him, but I wasn't thinking straight… and Roberto, I hope he didn't ruin everything." Mattie checked her heart rate on her Fitbit as an announcement came through the gym's surround sound speakers that the pool was now open.

After an additional 30 minutes on the treadmill, Geri paused her machine to walk away and returned with a damp paper towel to wipe their cardio equipment down.

"Let's go relax with ya, girl." Geri led the way to meet Cindy in one of the gym's three hot tubs.

Cindy had already dressed by the time they walked through the women's locker room. She was standing in front of a mirror putting makeup on. The swelling around her eye had gone down and now she waited to see if Peter would take a deal for a lesser charge. Either way, he still faced time in jail and had lost his job.

Geri decided to rule the hot tub out, so they showered and changed while Cindy took a few phone calls in the lobby.

Cindy was waiting on them with protein shakes in her hand as Mattie and Geri walked towards the exit of the gym. For the first time in the three weeks since leaving the psychiatric facility, Mattie felt like the fog was lifting.

"This shit ain't so bad! You said it was nasty." Cindy waved the bottle in front of Geri's face and laughed.

All three women drove separately because they were each off to a different destination. Geri was going to her office, Cindy to pick up Darrion and Samantha, while Sheila and James had an outing.

Mattie had done laundry at Kendal's condo the week before she admitted herself, so she was going to pick her clothes up and hopefully speak with him on the phone. He had stopped calling and texting her as frequently as before when he returned to the tour. Having a busted lip and black eye didn't stop him from performing. It was the uncertainty of where he and Mattie stood that was truly bruised.

Now when they communicated, she could feel the distance between them.

When she pulled into his garage, his older neighbor appeared, standing behind her car as she got out.

"Hi, Madison." The older woman, in her late sixties walked with a cane.

"Hi, Mrs. Warner! How are you today?" Mattie asked while pulling her gym bag from the back seat.

"I'm well…" she paused and looked over both of her shoulders before continuing.

"Do you know if Kendal has signed the petition that the condo board sent out? A lot of residents are fed up with the drainage system still not working properly. When it rained, it didn't adequately move the water which left standing water that created havens for mosquitoes, and no one wants to get sick. They say two people in the development have come down with the Nile virus."

Mattie smiled and shook her head affirmatively. Mrs. Warner was the one neighbor who knew just about everything because she was in everyone's business. She was also the president of the condo board and took her position seriously.

"Yes, he's signed it. Give me a second, and I'll bring it over to you." Mattie kept showing kindness; she understood the older woman found a bit of pride in her position in this community.

"Oh good…good enough." Mrs. Warner attempted to look inside Mattie's car, but Mattie politely closed the door and reaffirmed she would walk the petition over within the hour.

Mattie closed the garage door behind her before walking into the house.

She still believed that Kendal loved her. Just like she needed time to sort through some things, he did too.

She looked through the mail that had accumulated and found the petition before taking it to Mrs. Warner. Afterwards she lay down on Kendal's couch and took a nap. Her phone sounded off. "There Goes My Baby" by Usher let her know that it was Kendal calling her.

"Hi honey," she said answering the phone.

"Hey," he replied with hesitancy in his voice.

"Mrs. Warner came by asking for that petition, so I signed your name and gave it to her. How's your day?" Mattie forced herself upright on the couch.

Their conversations had not been as fluid as they once were, both of them thinking before speaking, attempting to find the right words.

"My day's been good. Just been doing a bunch of writing and a lot of thinking. Doug Jr. says hi. He flew in for the show," Kendal kept his voice steady.

The tour was moving to Charlotte, and Kendal was going to be staying at his older brother's home in the guest house.

"Oh, tell him I said hi, and one day soon we'll meet," She spoke in the future tense; she wanted to be Kendal's wife, and she held onto that idea.

"Ok, I will. I was thinking about everything and… I want you to know that I love you with all my heart but every time you close up and shut down, I feel left out when I'm supposed to be your greatest support. If we are extensions of each other, we have to include each other. Baby, I will not go through any of this shit again… so if you think there's the slightest possibility that you will shut me out again… then…" Kendal stopped talking.

Mattie didn't know what "then" consisted of, but she didn't want to hear what came next.

"Baby, I am so sorry that I forced you away. Sometimes I feel so alone when problems surface. I've been this way since I was a teenager. It's hard opening up when I'm unsure or my emotions are all over the place." Mattie paused to make sure what she said next was true.

"But I will never leave you out, even if it's hurtful to deal with. I will always include you. This I promise," Mattie finished.

Kendal didn't say anything immediately, but she could hear him letting out a small exhalation of air.

"I want you and Aunt Penny to fly down here next month when we hit the Carolinas. I want you to meet the rest of my family and I miss you... I miss you so much," Kendal exclaimed, finally expressing emotion.

Mattie was sure she would go but she was uncertain of her elder family member.

"I'll come for sure but who knows what Aunt Penny will say."

"She already said yes, baby. You guys just need to buy the tickets and be here by the third Thursday next month. I love you, Madison, and I always will. One more thing, don't ever take my ring off again," he said with conviction in his words.

Mattie had put her engagement ring back on the minute she left the hospital.

"Honey, I won't, and we'll be there by that Thursday, but you and my aunt better stop keeping secrets from me," Mattie referred to the last time they surprised her with Kendal coming home.

"To be honest with you, coming to Charlotte was her idea. She's got a stubborn streak inside her, and I see where you get it from," Kendal couldn't help but chuckle.

"Hey this is mom calling, so I will call you later. I miss you and love you, bye," Kendal waited to hear her say it back before taking the other call.

Mattie got her clothes out of the dryer, dropped the form off to Mrs. Warner, and drove home.

"Auntie!" she called out after putting her basket of clothes into her bedroom. She called out a second time as she walked down the hallway to find Aunt Penny.

"Auntie," she said knocking on her aunt's bedroom door.

"Oh, come in, baby." Aunt Penny responded.

"So, we're flying to Charlotte?" Mattie asked smiling.

"Yeah, we are. Kendal said he wanted to see you, and I don't feel like being here by myself again so I told him we would come… you don't mind, do you?"

"Of course, not but you all need to stop keeping secrets from me. Y'all act like best friends forever." Mattie walked over and kissed her elder on the cheek.

"Well, I bought some tickets already. We will leave that afternoon and don't worry; I didn't use your credit cards you have in the second drawer of the dresser. I paid for them," she finished.

For once, Mattie wasn't upset that her privacy was invaded; she overlooked it walking out the room to go unpack her clothes she washed at his place.

Kendal still loves me and wants me. Her smile couldn't be contained.

CLOSER TO THE TRUTH
CHAPTER 30

Henry sat at the desk in his basement looking over the incident report from the last visit the police had been at Jimmie Frederick's home.

"Woman said she wasn't abused, although physical marks were present. No charges to be filed," it read.

Henry wasn't so interested in what the conclusion had been but what actually started the whole run of events for that day.

The report said the law enforcement was contacted by the asset protection department of Global Communications indicating a possible assault at the residence. The only indication that a representative had taken the call was the internal ID number that was used to identify the company's employees.

Another dead end, Henry thought. The door opening from the top of the steps startled him.

"Baby, dinner is ready! You've been down there for hours," Michele said as she came into view.

"Why don't you come upstairs and join us? I'm sure whatever you're doing can wait a little bit." She stood opposite him.

The basement had been the family entertainment room, but when Henry received his gold shield it slowly became his work study.

"Yeah, I'm coming up." His mind was still working on how to find a way to either get the specific call from the communications company or at least identify the employee so he could rule Mattie out as a suspect.

It just doesn't make sense, he thought as he followed Michele back upstairs.

Michele had cooked lasagna and garlic bread, Jay's favorite. With Darrien spending the night, she had made enough for dinner and the following days lunch.

"Mom, can me and Darrien eat in the living room? Wakanda Forever is still on, and we won't make a mess," Jay pleaded.

"No, you cannot. I'll record it, but you know the rules: we eat at the table," Henry answered.

The young boys ate their food fast. Henry would've told them to slow down and chew their food, but his mind was elsewhere.

"It's supposed to rain tomorrow, so what time do you think we should come to the festival?" Michele asked.

Henry had gotten 12 officers to volunteer their time for the festival. He knew the visual sight of uniformed officers would ease the minds of those in attendance and prevent gang members from going through on their promise.

"You guys can come around noon. John and I will be there until about three o'clock," he answered.

"I made some peach cobbler, and there's vanilla ice cream in the freezer." Michele rinsed off the boy's plates before placing them in the dishwasher.

"I'll get some in a bit. I just need to finish something, babe." Besides, he was stuffed and needed time to let his food settle.

"Boys, you want dessert?" Michele called out as Henry closed the basement door behind him.

Henry looked in another file at the information of Jimmie's workers to see if the same woman who had been identified on the scene of the last police visit was one of the same women he had interviewed the night of the murder.

Sharlene Chase. He read the background information on her. Various arrests for solicitation, one charge of drug trafficking and then he saw that she was the mother of a teenage girl, who was in the custody of her sister. Henry felt bad for the daughter; hopefully being in the custody of her aunt was better than living with her mother.

So, she didn't press charges, but I wonder if she knows about the call, Henry thought. He sat in the basement wondering if he should interview Sharlene again and take the risk of being suspended by his captain. Henry knew it would have to be an "unofficial" interview. As the idea flowed into his mind, he knew it was the closest thing he had to getting the information he needed.

He was going to invite them to the youth festival as an unofficial guest. He searched for a contact number but when he dialed it the recording said it was disconnected. Henry had one more option he could take, so he called his friend Carla from Child Protective Services and asked for a favor.

After getting the number to Sharlene's sister, he called, identifying himself before inviting her and the child to the festival. Luckily the sister had heard about the event on the radio and decided she would attend.

"One more thing. The number we had for Sharlene has been disconnected. Do you have a more recent number?"

He got the new number and dialed it, this time getting an answer.

"Hello Sharlene, this is Detective Jenkins," he began, and then explained about the youth festival and that her daughter was attending. He told her that the youth program at the center was a viable way to deter kids from making bad decisions and as parents they should give a positive influence.

Sharlene wanted to come but didn't have a vehicle. Henry offered to pick her up with his partner, and she agreed.

Henry thought that his deception was balanced out by the fact the perhaps her daughter would indeed take the opportunity to join the program at the center.

He walked back upstairs to heat up the peach cobbler before putting two scoops of vanilla ice cream on top. Sitting down at the table, he wanted to rule Mattie out as a suspect but much of the evidence he gathered pointed in her direction.

But what possible motive could she have? he thought before moving into the living room with the boys to watch the remaining part of the movie.

Tomorrow… tomorrow I will know more.

. . .

The day of the festival started off slow. It had rained throughout the early morning, causing vendors to hold off setting up their booths. As the day progressed, the smell of food and the sound of people spread throughout the park.

Henry and John had picked Sharlene up on time. She looked like she had had a long night, but she was happy to be able to see her daughter.

"I usually try to stay away from cops, no offense. But most of the time I'm getting harassed," she laughed.

"Well today, we want you to enjoy the festival with your family, but more importantly, I want you to speak with one of the youth coordinators to see if your daughter can join. They have a great program," Henry said as they pulled into the event.

John hadn't said anything or asked why they were picking up Sharlene. Henry hoped it stayed that way.

"There they are," Sharlene said pointing towards her sister and daughter.

"Hi, Mommy!" the teenage girl said hugging her mom.

"Peaches, you are so pretty! Auntie braided your hair?" Sharlene asked.

"Yes ma'am, can we get some cotton candy?" her daughter responded.

"Of course we can." Sharlene reached for her hand.

Kira, Sharlene's sister, looked like she was about to say no but thought against it.

"When I find one of the programs coordinators, I will call your cell but for now enjoy yourselves." Henry watched them walk away.

"Man, you're like the Good Samaritan," John said as they walked through the thick crowd. Most people in attendance seemed to be having a good time. Kendal would've been excited at such a turnout.

"Michele is here." Henry said after checking his texts.

"I'm going to grab a couple of bratwursts; I'll meet you in a few," John excused himself.

"Daddy!" Jay exclaimed when he saw his father.

"What's up my young prince… hi Darrien. You and Jay are going to have a crazy good time. There's lots of stuff to do." Henry motioned to a few booths.

"I just love a man in uniform!" Michele kissed him on the cheek.

"There are all types of vendors here with food, jewelry, books. The games are at the far end. I'll be walking around for a bit… if you see Frances or Mr. Jackson tell them to call me. I have someone I want them to meet," Henry said before making his way back into the crowd.

Shortly thereafter, he received a call from Frances that she had time, so Henry found Sharlene, Kira, and Peaches eating candy apples and introduced them to Frances. After a 20-minute talk, both mother and aunt decided the program would be beneficial for the teenage girl.

"Henry, you do a great job. That was a good deed helping them out; I can see why Kendal speaks so highly of you," Frances told him.

"One child at a time." He felt like this was the best time to speak with Sharlene again to see if she could remember anything about the call Jimmie had with the communications company. So, as he pulled Sharlene aside, he began an easy line of questioning.

"You've been through a lot; is there anything else we can help you with?"

"Naw, you guys have done more than enough. My baby will learn new things today." She seemed relieved.

"Yeah, they say it takes a village to raise a child. I know that before when Mr. Frederick's was alive sometimes you didn't find yourself in ideal situations." Henry waited for a response.

"Yeah Jimmie… Jimmie had his ways, but he wasn't so bad all the time," Sharlene responded.

"I couldn't help but wonder what made us show up at his house a few days before he was… you know," Henry hesitated eluding to the murder.

Sharlene didn't look like she was going to respond at first but then she began.

"He got so pissed off with the phone company. He was cussing and threatening the girl on the phone. I can't believe she stayed on the phone that long trying to help me, but Jimmie could be an asshole when he smoked and drank. He probably would've hurt me even worse had the cops not shown up."

"How so…" Henry was asking before Sharlene interjected.

"Not to be speak ill of the deceased, but yeah, he hit me and threw me around. I was so scared and so happy that she didn't hang up," she finished.

"So, the lady at the phone company tried calming him down?" Henry asked, trying to lead her into speaking about it more.

"Yeah, but Jimmie kept cussing at her and threatening her. 'Madison in Columbus' this, and 'Madison in Columbus' that. I would've just hung up on him," she responded.

Henry's worst fear was now staring him in the face. The evidence was getting conclusive and now that he knew somehow Mattie was involved, he had one final question left: why? The only person that could answer that question already had her life turned upside down. Henry had to find a way to get the truth without causing more turmoil.

BONDING
CHAPTER 31

Charlotte Douglas International Airport wasn't busy at all. Mattie and Aunt Penny were glad to be off the airplane finally. Riding in the car with Kendal's sister-in-law Trisha was better than being stranded on the runway for an hour waiting for the weather to clear. They stopped at a Bojangles to eat.

"You know Trisha, the last time I was in North Carolina the traffic was atrocious," Mattie said as they pulled into the driveway.

"Oh, it's still bad, we're just missing rush hour. Sometimes when I'm coming back from the shop, I sit on I-77 for hours pulling my hair out," Trisha responded. She was older than Mattie, a little shorter, thin, and dainty, but she kept a youthful appearance. Her hair was frosted blonde, but her ethnicity shined through with cowry shells around her neck and wrists.

"Wow this is nice," Aunt Penny said looking at the main house and noticing the guest house off to the side.

"Thank you," Trisha said as she put the car in park. "The closest neighbors ain't even in shouting distance," she finished.

Mattie smiled as she saw Kendal cutting the grass on a riding a lawn mower—nearly three acres of land surrounded the houses. As Mattie stepped out the car, Kendal stopped the mower and jogged towards them with his shirt wrapped around his head.

"Hi, baby," he said with enthusiasm not caring if his sweat was getting on her as he hugged her.

"I missed you like crazy, Kendal Abraham Scott."

"Auntie, how was the trip?" Kendal asked.

"The plane ride was ok; it could've been better if we weren't stuck for an hour," she answered.

"So y'all finally made it in." A man's voice was heard coming from behind them.

"Doug, this is Madison and Aunt Penny," Kendal said introducing them.

"Aunt Penny, nice to meet you…" Doug paused.

"So, this is the woman that my brother keeps talking about? Madison, he didn't give you justice! You're much prettier than he let on. My mother says you know your way around the kitchen. My momma got her way, I'm so glad you can cook, ain't that right, baby," Doug said before smacking Trisha on her butt.

"Y'all go ahead inside, me and Captain got this," he said pulling the suitcases from the trunk.

"Captain?" Mattie asked.

"Oh, he didn't tell you? He's Captain Caveman. When we were kids, he watched it so much that we just started calling him Captain," Doug Jr. answered.

"No, only you and Janine did. Baby, don't listen to a word he says," Kendal said kissing Mattie on the lips. "We'll be in shortly," Kendal promised as they rolled the luggage away.

Mattie could see a small pond on the backside of the property with a tire hanging from a tree. The land was nice and as they walked into the house, two small Pinchers came out and sniffed her and Aunt Penny.

"Mary... Jane... go lie down," Trisha said.

"Mary Jane, how cute," Mattie said.

"Yeah, leave it up to my husband; a big Rick James fan," Trish said with a smile on her face as she showed them into the living room.

"Something to drink? We've got water, lemonade, and iced tea?" she asked. Mattie took water and her aunt asked for iced tea.

"I love your ring," Trisha said taking Mattie by the hand.

"Thanks, I love it too," Mattie replied.

"I never thought in a million years Kendal would remarry. You must be a special woman! Welcome to our family," Trisha stated before walking back into the kitchen.

"Ok, we have everything set up for you," Doug Jr. said walking into the living room.

"Captain is taking a shower; he has the show tonight. I can't wait to see him on stage being all Aristotle and Plato," he said laughing. "If you all want, we can go a little early and grab something to eat before the show," he finished, wiping the sweat from his brow. Trisha had returned from the kitchen with two bottles of water for him.

"No, we just ate some chicken, if we can rest up a bit first," Mattie said standing up. She missed her man and was heading to the guest house.

"Something smells good in here, baby," Doug Jr. said.

"I'm just cooking a little bit before your mom gets here."

"Your parents are coming?" Mattie asked.

"Yeah, Captain didn't tell you? They decided to get out of Cleveland for the week. They're flying in tomorrow," Doug Jr. answered.

Mattie was excited about being away, but it would be the first time she saw Kendal's parents since she miscarried.

"Mom loves you, don't look so worried," Trisha added.

"Oh, I'm not worried, I just didn't know," Mattie responded.

Mary was at Aunt Penny's feet smelling her again.

"Well come on," Aunt Penny said tapping her knee to invite the dog into her lap. On cue, Mary jumped right up.

"Wow! She never does that! She's usually afraid of people," Doug Jr. said before excusing himself to clean up.

Mattie walked out the door, heading to the guest house.

Kendal had already showered and was walking around in shorts and sneakers when she walked in.

"Come here," he said as Mattie walked towards him. He kissed her passionately. "I never want to be away from you."

"Me either, and I will never keep you out or force you away again. I swear to you," Mattie replied, kissing him again.

"You wanna ride with me to Piggly Wiggly? I need to grab some stuff." Kendal pulled his t-shirt over his head.

"I don't know what that is, but I will go anywhere with you," Mattie answered.

"Oh, it's the grocery store, Super Wal-Mart is too far away," he replied.

"Do I have time to take a quick shower?" she asked.

"Ten minutes, baby, I'm on a tight schedule. I thought y'all would've been here earlier, but I know shit happens... 10 minutes, baby. I'm going up to the main house. Your room is here, and auntie's is over there, so hurry up, sexy." Kendal finished kissing her again before walking out.

. . .

The next day came a lot quicker than imagined. Mattie was still shaking the cobwebs off from not sleeping the whole night through.

"They should be pulling up any time now," Trisha said to Mattie as they sat in the kitchen finishing brunch.

Aunt Penny had gone back to the guest house to lie down. She wasn't used to being up so late after attending

Kendal's performance. She was pleasantly surprised to see Kendal on stage, but it was Doug Jr. who shouted out, "That's my brother!" as his performance came to an end.

Doug Jr. was so proud that he kept everyone up talking about it to the wee hours of the night. Doug Jr. and Kendal had gone to the airport to get his parents, and now Trisha and Mattie were sitting at the table drinking coffee.

"You and Kendal plan a date for the wedding yet?" Trisha asked before ordering Jane out of the kitchen.

"Not an exact date, but we both want a summer wedding," Mattie answered.

"Well, that's almost a year away! You know mom and dad didn't have a huge ceremony. They said only a few family members and friends were there," Trisha replied.

"I never thought I'd be getting married. All the men I dated didn't fit the bill, if you know what I mean. But Kendal took his time to know me, and I needed that," Mattie replied.

"Yeah, he is a good man and he's been through more than his fair share, but I think you two make a perfect match… they're here," Trisha said watching the dogs run to the front door.

Both Mattie and Trish walked outside to greet them.

"Ah, my favorite daughter-in-laws." Doug Sr. said hugging Trisha and Mattie.

Mattie felt proud to be included as a genuine family member although she had not said "I do" yet.

"Trish… Mattie, we gon' need some time away from the men today," Gloria said kissing each one on the side of their cheeks. "Junior, we're taking your car too," she followed up.

Doug went to protest but his father shaking his head was enough warning to just agree.

"Where's Aunt Penny? I sure would love to meet her," Gloria asked.

"Oh, she's lying down, we got home late and then had to be up early. Trisha made a huge breakfast… well, brunch," Mattie answered.

"Well, I'm starving! We're gon' carry this stuff inside and I'll be in the kitchen, honey," Doug Jr. said.

"And me and the ladies got some catching up to do! Don't eat it all up, big daddy," Gloria replied before walking around to the back of the main house.

A few birds scattered away as the ladies got closer to the pond while a few fish surfaced from the water.

"So, Mattie, you like it down here? A lot quieter than the city, right? The first time I came down here I couldn't believe my son had become a country bumpkin. But after a week I saw why he chose Charlotte," Gloria said.

"It's not so bad. The city is less than a 30-minute drive, and the coast about an hour or so away," Trisha said as they walked to the bench at the far end of the pond.

"How deep is it? I know y'all take dips whenever it gets too hot down here?" Mattie asked.

"Doug Jr. says about 12 feet, but he doesn't know. It was here when we bought the property, and he doesn't go in there a lot after seeing a few snakes in it. Just last week he was out here firing the shotgun at a few wolves drinking from it." Trisha answered.

"That boy just likes shooting stuff. He used to teach Kendal when they were younger with BB guns. They would shoot squirrels eating out my garden, but Kendal gave it up after shooting a pigeon, killing it. He always followed in his older brother's footsteps," Gloria said.

"They seem so different," Mattie added.

Gloria laughed out loud as they sat down.

"Well, I'll say this Junior ain't as hard as he makes himself, and Kendal's got a mean streak something fierce. That's why I love 'em both," she hesitated.

"Madison, I'm so grateful that you two found each other. Things won't always be so easy, but love makes it better. Lord knows me and their daddy have had our fair share of difficulties," Gloria finished.

Kendal walking out of the back of the house broke the conversation up.

"Aunt Penny is up, and I gotta get going. They're going to be filming some behind the scenes stuff today, so I gotta go…" he said bending down to kiss Mattie.

"I love you, honey."

"I love you too, Captain," Mattie responded, and Gloria laughed.

"So, I see Junior has already told you that story," the older woman said.

"Before she had even walked into the house, mom," Trisha said laughing with her.

"Ha ha ha; it's all fun and jokes until somebody gets hurt…" Kendal said pausing as he laughed too.

"What are you all getting into today?" he asked.

"Shop, shop, and more shopping," his mom answered.

"Oh, and we gotta stop by to see Reverend Brown," Trisha added.

"Oh yeah that's right," Gloria replied.

"So, we have a full day ahead of us?" Mattie asked, hoping she would see Kendal again before the show.

"A full day... a full week." Gloria said making eye contact with Kendal like they shared a secret between them.

Trisha stood up first and they walked back into the house.

Doug Sr. and his son were sitting at the kitchen table finishing the rest of their food.

"I'll get Aunt Penny ready and let her know what's on the agenda." Mattie said walking out the front door with Kendal.

"Damn, I wanted to see you before..." she started to say.

"Don't worry, baby, we have the rest of our lives. I'll call you in a bit," he said as he kissed her. He hopped in his rented Chevrolet Impala and drove away.

After being introduced to Aunt Penny, Gloria ate and changed quickly. The four women shopped for nearly four hours before driving to Trisha's church to meet with Reverend Brown.

Reverend Brown was nearly 80, but his mind was still sharp. He spoke with the ladies at length about marriage and family and then he turned his attention to Mattie who was reading another text message.

CINDY: What you doing down south, redbone?

Mattie was being polite to Reverend Brown, but she was getting tired of answering questions and she thought it was odd to be having such a conversation with him.

"I can remember the first time I met your husband, Trisha. He was so sure of himself. Big professional athlete but beneath the exterior he was like every other man— searching for purpose, looking for the meaning of life," Reverend Brown said.

"We all seek the answers to life," Gloria added.

"But we have to have the right questions. Madison, have you taken Jesus Christ as your Lord and Savior?" he asked straight forward.

Mattie didn't know where the question came from or why he even needed to know, but she was clear with her answer.

"One hundred percent yes, Reverend Brown," she answered before her cell phone vibrated again.

"Good… good. God is good indeed. You have such a beautiful family, Sister Scott. Aunt Penny you all have dun good with her," he said referring to Mattie.

"I will see everyone tomorrow and make sure all the men folk come. I'll be speaking directly to them about their roles as husbands," Reverend Brown finished bidding them farewell.

MATTIE: I'm down here getting grilled by Reverend Donald Lee Brown about my life. 😊

"I'm worn out," Aunt Penny said. She had bought a few items, but it was Gloria who had the bulk of items.

"I am tired too; we should just go relax for the rest of the day. It's supposed to be a nice day tomorrow so after church maybe we can do something outside and just relax a little," Gloria added.

"Yeah, that sounds good," Mattie's aunt responded.

"Well, me and Mattie will drop you two off. I need to go to Super Wal-Mart for a couple of things for dinner tomorrow," Trisha replied.

Mattie was happy to be around everyone, not long ago she had closed herself off from world and now it seemed that the universe was opening up again and she could marvel in its beauty.

SURPRISE SURPRISE
CHAPTER 32

Mattie wondered why Kendal didn't make Sunday service with the rest of the family. Doug Jr. had left early without giving a reason, but Trisha took it all in stride. She loaded everyone into her minivan and drove back home.

"Reverend Brown preaches like my pastor back in Georgia," Aunt Penny said as Trisha pulled across the grass, directly to the front of the guest house.

Mattie thought it was strange because the paved driveway was a better route to take. She figured that Trisha was minimizing the walk for Aunt Penny.

"He's a good Reverend; he's been at it for nearly 40 years. My family grew up in that church… well the old one, but the congregation is nearly the same," Trisha added as she opened the electric sliding doors to the minivan.

Gloria followed Aunt Penny and Mattie into the guest house.

Mattie had been so amazed at how down south felt; she contemplated spending at least two months out of the year somewhere in the southern states. No longer did she feel anxious or sorrowful. She felt the love that Kendal's family had extended to her.

"Aunt Penny, is this kinda like Georgia?" she asked as the older woman sat down on the couch with Gloria.

"Georgia is a little hotter but the land your grandma left you is beautiful like this. Maybe a little more wooded areas, but there's a stream that runs through your property," she answered as Trisha excused herself to go to the main house.

"Mattie, you haven't been to Georgia yet?" Gloria asked.

"Uh, no… I kept telling grandma we could go but something always came up," Mattie answered.

"I keep telling her that her kin folk would love to see her," her aunt interjected.

Mattie walked away to use the toilet in the bedroom, but when she opened the door, she was confused. Lying on the bed was a garment bag with an envelope on top addressed to her in Kendal's handwriting. When she opened the envelope, she stood in awe as she read the question.

384

"Will you marry me at four o'clock today?" Beneath the question were two boxes, one marked "yes" and the other for "yes" as well.

Aunt Penny and Gloria were now standing in the doorway. Gloria had an ink pen in her hand, extending it to Mattie.

Mattie checked "Yes," and Gloria took it to the main house with a huge grin on her face.

"Well, alrighty woman, we gon, have to get you all cleaned up and pretty," Aunt Penny paused.

"Go take a shower and then we'll do your hair and makeup," the older woman finished.

Once again, Mattie felt butterflies as she showered. She loved the fact that Kendal was a risk taker.

He knew I would say yes, she thought before toweling off.

"I'm getting married today," she said aloud walking out of the bathroom. Mattie was surprised to see Trisha back with blow dryers and curling sets, but what made Mattie more elated was to see her three closest friends sitting on the couch in the living room. What amazed Mattie even more was Senora, Camilla, Simone, and Carmelita were pouring glasses of wine for the group.

"Hermana, I told you she knows before we do," Simone hugged Mattie before anyone.

"Ain't no way in the world we was gon' let yo' ass tie the knot without us! We go back like peanut butter and jelly, sand and water, greens and hot sauce." Cindy was second to hug Mattie.

"I'm so happy for you," Sheila said.

Geri looked like she had already been crying.

"You're gonna be a great wife. Kendal is lucky to have you," Geri added.

"So y'all all knew once again? Well, I'm done with the surprises," Mattie said smiling.

"Ok we ain't got time to be talking," Aunt Penny said as Trisha began doing Mattie's hair.

"Kendal was up there sweating bullets. He wasn't sure that you would say yes, even though we kept telling him not to worry," Geri said.

Mattie got nervous suddenly.

"His ring… I don't have his ring. I didn't finish paying on it," she said anxiously.

"Oh, you paid for it; I used your credit card," Aunt Penny said pulling his wedding band from her purse.

Mattie smiled and felt relieved.

"Reverend Brown will perform the ceremony," Trisha said as she made the final touches to Mattie's hair.

"So that's why he had 50 questions yesterday?" Mattie asked.

"Yeah, he needed to make sure you were ready. You'll have to sign the marriage license beforehand. Pastor Morris sends you his congratulations," Aunt Penny added.

For the next two hours, Mattie prepared. Her wedding dress fit her perfectly as Sheila had taken one of Mattie's formal gowns to use as a base. Her friends had gone to the main house to change and when they returned, they each wore peach color dresses.

"We're all your maids of honor. We tried drawing sticks and playing rock, paper, scissors, but that shit ain't work," Cindy said.

"You all look beautiful," Trisha told them walking back into the guest house.

"Damn Mattie, you look so beautiful," Doug Jr. said walking in behind his wife wearing a black tuxedo.

"Thank you," Mattie said, feeling a bit nervous.

Aunt Penny was walking out of her bedroom putting a pink hat on her head to match her ensemble.

"Aunt Penny, I'm here to escort you," Kendal's brother said.

For the first time, Mattie looked outside and saw multiple vehicles lining the driveway and front lawn.

"I'll call you when we're ready for the bride," he said taking Mattie's aunt by the hand to escort her. Trisha walked out with them.

Mattie's palms were sweating; she realized she was much more nervous than she believed.

"I'm getting married today," she said without emotion.

"Yes, you are Pocahontas," Cindy said.

"I need something to drink," Mattie replied.

Geri opened her black bag and pulled out two bottles. One bottle of Hennessey cognac and a bottle of vodka.

"Hennessey," Mattie said choosing the darker liquor.

Sheila pulled out glasses from the kitchen cabinets and as Geri poured the liquor Trisha walked back in. The look on her face couldn't be read, but when she added a fifth glass to the mix, Mattie knew she was indeed family.

"So, they're ready. You all will go first and then I will bring her." Don Rojas stood in the doorway with a huge grin.

Shortly after Mattie's friends and family left it was her turn. As she walked toward the main house, she saw Kwame standing there with something in his hands. When Mattie got closer Kwame had begun rolling out a white liner for her to walk on.

Mattie's knees felt light, and she was surprised once again to see nearly 100 people standing from their chairs surrounding the pond. She marched forward to *Here Comes the Bride.* Unable to see Kendal yet, her heartbeat faster.

She could see many people that she had just met at church earlier that day and as she got closer, she saw Patricia Kearns and Stephen Blue along with the other poets on tour.

Kendal stood upright with his eyes fixed on Mattie with a smile across his face. As she stood across from him and his brother as best man, Kendal spoke.

"You look stunning," he grinned from ear to ear.

She smiled and slowly turned to face Reverend Brown.

"We are gathered here today to bring these two children of God together in holy matrimony. As God created the moon and the sun, He created man and woman to stand together. Marriage is a sacred union as many of us can attest to…" Reverend Brown went on for nearly 15 minutes before he asked them both to share their wedding vows.

Mattie was unprepared but as she went first, she decided to speak from her heart.

"I had searched an entire life for purpose. I had prayed that God would shine His love down upon me. Not knowing what or why, I had only been given glimpses of happiness, never knowing the true meaning of unconditional love. But I know I search no more for in God's grace—He has given you to me. I am not perfect, yet I am perfect for you. I am your friend and your lover, as a wife I will honor and cherish our commitment for eternity. As you have submitted to The Creator, I too, submit to you. I will obey as a wife and helpmate according to God's will, and I do it freely without hesitation. You are the air I breathe. As the sun rises, I will rise with you and stand side by side with you atop the highest mountain peak or in the valley of the shadow of death. My heart has always been yours, and I give my life to you, Kendal Abraham Scott," Mattie finished staring at Kendal.

She heard sniffles coming from behind her. If she had to guess, all three of her friends were crying.

Doug Jr. stood next to Kendal attempting to hold back his emotions as Kendal began.

"That was beautiful, honey. I had thought about writing a poem but instead I want to speak about loving you in the words of Pablo Neruda," Kendal said before he recited Sonnet XVII

I don't love you as if you were the salt-rose, topaz
or arrow of carnations that propagate fire:
I love you as certain dark things are loved,
secretly, between the shadow and the soul.
I love you as the plant that doesn't bloom and carries
hidden within itself the light of those flowers,
and thanks to your love, darkly in my body
lives the dense fragrance that rises from the earth.

I love you without knowing how, or when, or from where,
I love you simply, without problems or pride:
I love you in this way because I don't know any other way
of loving
but this, in which there is no I or you,
so intimate that your hand upon my chest is my hand,
so intimate that when I fall asleep it is your eyes that close.

I will honor you, protect, and provide for you. I will lead with love and compassion, and I will love you through each heartbeat that propels my walk of faith. I too have searched heaven and earth for you. You are my soul mate, and I am not whole without you," Kendal finished.

Reverend Brown finished the ceremony and as they kissed most of those in attendance was wiping their eyes including Kendal's brother.

"Ladies and gentlemen, it is my great pleasure to introduce to you, Mr. and Mrs. Kendal Abraham Scott."

CORNY
CHAPTER 33

Sheila and Geri were already up and dressed when Mattie walked up to the main house. Trisha was standing out back watching the dogs. Sheila had just finished speaking with James, making sure he would be on time to pick them up from the airport later.

"Good morning, Mrs. Scott," Geri said, sitting at the kitchen table eating waffles.

"Trisha made some waffle batter; you want me to make you some?" Geri asked Mattie.

"I can do it," Mattie answered as she poured a glass of orange juice from the pitcher sitting on the table.

"James will pick us up… what time did you get back last night? I didn't even hear you come in?" Sheila asked Geri.

"Not too long ago, and no, he still didn't get none," Geri answered.

"Huh, what… who didn't get none?" Mattie asked walking over to the waffle iron.

"Kwame, I spent the night with him. I was torn up from the floor up last night and couldn't drive back from the hotel, so I stayed with him. He didn't even attempt to get none, but when I woke up this morning, he had showered and was walking around the room with only a towel on," Geri said.

"Oh, so he was acting like he ain't want it. That's the classic, 'Act uninterested to get them panties' move," Cindy said as she walked into the kitchen.

"Great Scott, it's Mattie," she concluded.

Sheila shook her head with a frown on her face.

"That was corny… real corny," Sheila added.

"Yeah, it was…" Cindy agreed with her. "What time y'all driving down to King's Plantation?" Cindy asked.

"King's Plantation? I thought you guys were headed to Myrtle Beach?" Sheila interjected, kinda confused.

"King's Plantation is where we'll be staying at Myrtle Beach. My husband said he wants to leave around 1:30," Mattie answered.

"Your family being here surprised us. David wasn't sure y'all's dad would make it, but we wouldn't say a word even if we knew for sure," Geri offered before making another statement hesitantly.

"So, we're leaving before you then. I mean, you'll be back for Peter's hearing?" she finished.

"I'll be back on Thursday; his hearing is Friday. But I thought he took a lesser charge?" Mattie answered, adding butter and syrup to her waffle.

"The prosecutor's office called before we came down and said Peter's attorney didn't accept the plea bargain, so we might be going to court. I can't believe I got y'all all caught up in this mess," Cindy said.

"The way you told me, if they hadn't been there, who knows what could've happened," Sheila said as Trisha walked back in.

"I gotta keep an eye on them so they don't become breakfast for some critters," Trisha said closing the sliding door behind her.

"Were those wolves I heard howling last night?" Sheila asked.

"Yeah, we got wolves somewhere in those woods. Doug said he's going to build a fence, but he been saying that for years," Trisha answered.

"Well, good morning, sister-in-law! Your ceremony was so nice," Trisha added.

"Thank you, sister-in-law," Mattie responded.

"Now that's corny," Cindy said as everyone laughed.

Mattie's friends had packed their luggage into the minivan after eating. They said their goodbyes before being driven to the airport.

"Aunt Penny, you're in good hands; we'll only be gone a few days," Mattie said as she packed her suitcase for the drive to Myrtle Beach.

"Baby, don't worry about me; I was just thinking about home. I really want you both to come visit," the older woman said sitting down on the couch to finish crocheting.

"How about we come with you when you leave?" Kendal said walking into the guest house after pulling the rental car to the door.

"That would be good, son. Y'all get a chance to meet some relatives, and I'm sure you'll be surprised at the land. But can you go down in two weeks? What about the tour?" Aunt Penny asked, concerned there would be a conflict.

"Atlanta is in ten days, so if that's good for you, it's good for me," Kendal responded.

Mattie didn't care when they left. She was happily married and after spending time in North Carolina she was ready to see what Georgia was like.

"That will be perfect, now get out of here, and enjoy your honeymoon. Me and your mom are going to spend time together and Trisha said she would fancy my hair up," the older woman said, giving them hugs before they drove away.

Over the next three days, Mattie's aunt and Kendal's mom shopped heavily, so much that Gloria had to buy extra luggage to take the newly bought items onto the plane. Luckily, everyone was flying out on the same day, saving Doug Jr. and Trisha multiple runs to the airport.

"You all have to come to Cleveland before you leave, Auntie," Gloria said as their boarding pass was called.

"I promise to try. I gotta give my bones a rest," Aunt Penny responded.

Kendal was shaking his father's hand while Mattie returned from the restroom.

"I'm proud and happy for you and Madison," his father said, reaching down to hug Mattie.

"Aunt Penny, it was truly my pleasure," Kendal's father said.

"Well come on, big daddy, they're waiting for us," Gloria said as the flight attendant called over the intercom system.

Shortly after Kendal's parents flew out, Kendal and Mattie boarded their flight.

Geri was waiting on them when they touched down in Columbus.

"So, the flight was good?" Geri asked as Kendal loaded the luggage into her SUV.

"Yeah, I took a nap," Mattie said, opening the front door for her aunt.

"Baby, I want to go by the center a little later," Kendal told Mattie on the ride home.

Mattie didn't object because he needed to see the changes at the center, and she knew he missed his students.

"Don't forget, tomorrow morning at nine, we have to be downtown at the courthouse," Geri said as she pulled up to Mattie's home.

After unloading, Aunt Penny went to lay down.

"Baby I'm hungry… you hungry? Kendal asked.

"Kinda, you wanna order something or grab something on the way to the center?" She was being flexible.

"You know what, let's order pizza and have it delivered to the center. I'll call Frances to let her know to expect it," Kendal answered.

When they walked into the center, there were streamers and poster boards welcoming Mr. and Mrs. Scott. Kendal was smiling as Mr. Jackson saw them first.

"Welcome back, good people," he said standing from behind the front desk.

"Mrs. Scott, so good to see you again." Mr. Jackson said laughing out loud.

"Frances is in the back office, and we took the liberty of hiring someone to run the computer room. Her name is Adrienne," Mr. Jackson said.

As Kendal and Mattie walked through the doors of the gymnasium, a few boys were playing basketball. The ball bounced off the rim and rolled towards Mattie's feet.

"Mr. Scott!" one of the boys exclaimed.

Mattie knew the impact Kendal had on many of the boys.

"Hey Kevin, Terrence…. and I don't think we've met," Kendal said reaching his hand out to the third young man.

"I'm Gregory, sir," he said shaking Kendal's hand.

"Well Gregory, I'm Mr. Scott and this is my wife. How long have you been coming?" he asked.

"This is my second week, sir," Gregory answered.

"Well Greg, I'm going to be spending some time with you but for now…" Kendal paused as he took the basketball from Mattie. "See if y'all can get range like this," he said as he shot the ball.

"Air ball… air ball," Mattie said as his shot fell short of the rim.

The boys laughed and started playing with each other again.

Kendal decided to see Frances first before going to the computer room.

"No… no… no, we've paid for all the textbooks with the last payment. I'm staring at the invoice. It's not my fault your salesperson forgot to turn in his copy. I'll fax… no, I'll fax it over right now." Frances's voice was heard before she was seen.

"It's coming now," she said before hanging up.

'Hey you two! Congratulations!" she said as they walked into her office.

"Problems?" Kendal asked.

"Not a problem for us," Frances said loading the fax machine to send the invoice.

"I saved you all some cheese pizza, it's on your desk. The kids tore through the other boxes. So how was Myrtle Beach?" she asked.

"Frances, it was so beautiful! We relaxed on the beach, and when we didn't eat out my husband cooked for me," Mattie responded.

"So, I see we got some new faces, and Jackson said there's a new hire," Kendal said.

"Yeah, we had to hire someone. The kids love the computer room, and someone had to manage it. Have you met her yet?" Frances asked, sending the fax through.

"Not yet we're going to eat really quick," Kendal said.

"Oh, the check for Henry is on your desk, just sign it before he picks it up," Frances finished.

Mattie thought back to the last time she was at the center and Henry had stopped by. She had forgotten all about the videos of Samantha, but she didn't think much of it after she cut up and discarded the wigs. The case of Mark Floyd had gotten regional news coverage, so Geri had one of her writer's interview Henry and John about the case.

In the interview, Henry talked about evidence being the "truth" for all. The Mark Floyd case had gone to the jury and now everyone was waiting for the verdict.

Mattie's phone rang as Kendal stood up to run to the computer room to meet the new hire and see the facility.

"I'll come down in a second honey," Mattie said before taking the call.

"Yes," she answered.

"Ms. Parks, this is Dr. Steven's office, reminding you of your appointment tomorrow at three o'clock," the woman's voice came through.

"Oh ok, thank you," Mattie said before hanging up.

She opened the small refrigerator in Kendal's office and opened a bottle of Pepsi.

Tomorrow my husband will learn more about his wife… I'm going to tell him all about my parents, she thought, squishing her face as she swallowed her first sip of Pepsi in a while.

REVELATION
CHAPTER 34

"The prosecutor says Peter still isn't going to take a plea bargain. He's upset about attacking us and getting his ass whooped... and I guess he can't hear out of his left ear," Cindy said as they waited for their case to be called from the docket.

Peter sat with his attorney on the opposite side of the courtroom only glancing periodically at the trio of ladies.

Mattie and Geri didn't say much; they were observing the cases before court.

"You must've broken his ear drum," Geri whispered in Mattie's ear.

Mattie thought about the way the bottle had shattered against the side of Peter's face, and she had to agree that the impact had to have caused damage.

After an hour of waiting for their case, the judge finally called them forward. It didn't take long for their case as Peter's attorney pleaded not guilty to the charges and a date was set for trial.

"All that time for that! I could've stayed in bed." Geri led the way as they walked out into the hallway.

There were all types of activity with camera's taking pictures and news crews interviewing people. Much more hectic than when they arrived.

"We believe we built a strong case against Mr. Floyd, but the jury didn't," an older gray-haired city prosecutor was answering a reporter's question.

"Do you think the circumstantial evidence lacked?" the reporter followed up.

"The older prosecutor shook his head and kept walking without verbally answering.

"Mr. Floyd... Mr. Floyd. How does it feel to be acquitted of all the charges?" another reporter called out.

"It feels good to see the justice system working for a change." He quickly made his way through the crowd.

"What they fuck? They found him not guilty?" Geri said, knowing how much work and time Henry and his partner had put into the case.

Mattie was quiet; she remembered seeing him that night in the bar. He looked different dressed in a suit and groomed but he was the same man she passed on the way out the back door.

"Henry... Henry!" Cindy called out loudly, waving her hand to get his attention.

"So that's one for the bad guys." Geri couldn't hold back her disgust.

"Yeah, I guess so, we thought with the length of time the jury was sequestered it would be in our favor, but honestly, I didn't think the evidence pointed his way. I guess the confession we got was out of duress," he paused. "What are y'all doing down here?" he asked.

"The case against Peter came to court today. Can you believe that he didn't want to accept a plea bargain?" Cindy was bewildered.

"Even when people are wrong, they can't see the error of their ways..." Henry replied.

"How's the married life treating you? It was a beautiful ceremony," he directed his attention to Mattie.

"It's absolutely fabulous. I didn't want to come back," she responded.

"I bet, Kendal said he got spoiled. Michele and I would love to take you both to dinner. I'll be stopping by the center later, so run it by him and let us know when's good for you," Henry looked like there was something else on his mind. "Will you be there this evening? I have a couple of things to run by you too… nothing big," he asked Mattie.

"More than likely, after 4:30. What's up?" Mattie was curious; she wanted to get a hint of what the topic was.

"Oh, nothing much. Listen, I've gotta get to the station. I'm sure the captain has something to say about the case." Henry concluded before walking away.

They followed the hallway leading out of the courthouse. The sky was cast with clouds and as Mattie got into her car, she worried about whatever Henry wanted to talk to her about.

I'm gonna deny it 'til my death, she thought, feeling slightly anxious. She had a three o'clock appointment with her psychiatrist, a session Kendal would sit in on.

She had made up her mind to use this as a forum to talk about the night when her life had changed. Kendal would know the reason her family had been torn apart. Mattie stopped at home to change out of her dress and blouse to throw on some jeans and a black t-shirt.

She texted Kendal to make sure he knew where to go and to tell him about Henry's dinner offer. Mattie walked down the hall, stopping in front of her family picture.

We were so happy, the thought faded.

She grabbed her purse and keys and headed back out into traffic.

THE LUCKY MAN
CHAPTER 35

Mattie felt nervous about the appointment. For the first time in her life, she would be telling someone else her side of what happened.

Kendal was already there when she pulled up, waiting by his motorcycle.

"Hi beautiful!"

"Hi, hubby, you ready?" she asked.

Kendal nodded his head as they walked inside the building.

"Mrs. Scott to see Dr. Stevens." It was different using her married name, but she enjoyed saying it as they checked in.

Shortly after, the doctor opened his office door to let them in.

"Kendal, this is Dr. Stevens," Mattie introduced them.

"So, this is the lucky man!" Dr. Stevens and Kendal shook hands firmly.

"Well, have a seat. Anything to drink?" he offered.

Both Mattie and Kendal declined.

"So, first off, congratulations! How's it feel to be married? Madison, the last time we talked it was quite some time away," Dr. Stevens asked.

"Well, the timing was right. There's no better time than the present, right?" Mattie gripped Kendal's hand.

"No there's not; when you know it's right you just know. Kendal, I've heard a lot about you… all good things, of course," Dr. Stevens switched direction.

"Well, I hope so," Kendal said smiling.

"So, Madison, I thought I would leave it up to you on what we talk about today," Dr. Stevens offered.

Mattie cleared her throat and started.

"You know my father died and my mother is serving the last few years of an 18-year sentence, but you don't know why…" she paused as Dr. Stevens sat back and she faced Kendal.

"When I was 14 years old, my father, who was taking tainted drugs, tried to rape me and my mother shot him. She didn't kill him, but she did paralyze him. Later, he died from infections and complications of the paralysis. My mother shot him to prevent me from being harmed, but the court didn't see it that way. They painted her as a calculating battered woman getting revenge after years of enduring abuse. For much of my life, I witnessed how he treated her. I was afraid of him when he drank. I haven't spoken to, seen, or heard from my mother since the day they walked her out of the court room in handcuffs. The only person she allowed to visit or write was my grandmother... her mother... and since she passed, it seems Aunt Penny has taken that role. I don't know why that is, but I resent it. I hate that they found her guilty, but I hate her for leaving me alone. I used to accept the blame for that night. Had I locked my door or slept in pajama bottoms, maybe nothing would've happened. But with years of therapy, the guilt has lessened. I think forcing you away was purely a defense mechanism, but as I promised to you, I will include you in all aspects of my life," Mattie stared into Kendal's eyes.

Kendal simply reached over and took her hand.

"Thank you, honey," he said softly.

Dr. Stevens was writing in his folder when Kendal continued.

"That's a huge burden to carry. I'm here to support you no matter what, 'til death do us part. You're much stronger than you think," Kendal finished.

"You know I was thinking the same thing. Strength isn't always measured in tangible terms. What I've come to learn over the years is that strength and weakness really aren't opposites. Instead, they both come from the same strand of substance, and it's our perception that determines what portion of the strand we recognize. I think it very brave of you to talk about this to your husband. It shows growth, Madison," Dr. Stevens said. "I believe your mother is scheduled for release sometime in the next year or two. What then?"

Mattie hadn't thought about it. She figured she would cross that bridge when she got to it.

"I don't know. No one's talked to her since grandma died, at least I don't think. If she wants to see me… us… then we can. If not, oh well," Mattie answered feeling disconnected from her words.

"Honey, I think we should see her. It may help you find relief to some things…" Kendal paused.

"Realize it may open some old wounds, but I agree with Kendal. If you want, I can send correspondence on your behalf?" the doctor offered.

Mattie took a moment to think about it all. Was she really prepared to face her mother? She had questions, but the answers might not be what she wanted to hear.

"That's fine. If she wants to see me when she gets out, then I will."

"I think this is the most you've talked in years," Dr. Stevens said as he pulled up his appointment availability on the computer.

"Two weeks—before you even ask," Mattie said lightheartedly changing the tone.

"Kendal, you have a great wife and person," the doctor said handing Mattie the appointment card.

"Yes, I know," he shook the doctor's hand before walking out.

"Baby, can you run by the condo and grab my bag by the front door?" Kendal asked Mattie as he started his motorcycle.

"Yeah," she answered.

"Come to the center afterwards. I've got some paperwork to catch up on, and Henry has to pick the check up to pay for the police working the festival hours," he was grateful for the law enforcement presence.

. . .

Frances had the music playing louder than usual as Mattie entered the center.

"Yall got these funky little dances nowadays, but this is classic!" She saw Mattie and motioned her over to do the line dance with her. Mattie stepped in for a few rotations before laughing with the kids.

"I'll have Mr. Scott come out and show you his breakdancing skills."

Henry and Kendal were sitting in the office when Mattie walked in. Whenever Kendal had more than two days in a row off from the Spoken Word tour, he came home to see his wife. He knew what his priority was.

They were talking sports—football to be exact. They didn't root for the same NFL teams and were ragging on each other.

"Dallas still has the one big problem they've had for years," Kendal said with his arms folded behind his head. He was ready for any rebuttal.

"What Jerry Jones?" Henry leaned forward in his chair.

"Well, I forgot about him. But I was thinking more Dak Prescott. He'll get you the statistics, but he can't win the big game," Kendal laughed out loud.

"I'd take Prescott over any Cleveland quarterbacks. Stefanski may have taken over the helm of the ship, but it's still Cleveland," Henry reminded Kendal how dismal his hometown NFL team was.

"We're playing decent ball at least; we've already won three games so far… hey baby!" Kendal said as Mattie walked in.

She walked over and kissed him before greeting Henry.

"Alonzo has some of the boys outside running. He said he was in charge of physical fitness today… you may want to check on them cause a few of them don't look so good," Mattie shook her head before sitting down.

"They're alright, I gave Alonzo the workout plan: two times around the field and then push-ups and sit-ups," Kendal added.

"So, have you guys picked a day that Michele and I can take you guys to dinner as a married couple? We would've stayed longer at your ceremony, but my case load is piling up and the Floyd case was coming to an end." Henry had received accolades on closing a few cases, but the Mark Floyd verdict was a strain on his captain.

Mattie cringed inside when she was reminded about the Mark Floyd case, it was like a bad migraine that wouldn't go away… always bringing memories of Jimmie Fredericks.

"If you want, tomorrow is fine? We don't have anything planned, do we? I don't have to be back on tour for the next few days," Kendal responded before asking Mattie what her schedule looked like.

"Nope tomorrow is good!" Mattie had some errands to run with Aunt Penny in the morning and nothing else set in stone.

"Well, we will make reservations for eight o'clock at the Ocean Club. I'll let Michele know to get Jay dropped off by six." Henry wanted to add clarity.

"That's right, it's Sheila's turn for the weekend," Mattie added knowing Darrien and Jay had another sleepover scheduled; they were developing a close bond.

"They play really good together, you should see them playing basketball. Jay is Anthony Edwards and Darrien is Lebron James," Henry shook his head in earnest.

"All this sports talk," Mattie interjected as Frances walked in.

"Hi Mattie... Henry." She greeted them both.

"Adrienne is leaving in 20 minutes. It was her day off, but she came in to cover for a few hours. I still been dealing with that company on shipping the books out. They'll be arriving by next Friday finally." Frances paused to get back to the reason she entered the office.

"But she's leaving in 20 minutes. Can either of one of you take over for the last hour? We still have 11 kids signed up to use the room," she asked.

Mattie took that as a hint to say yes, so she could put off Henry for a while. She wasn't sure if he remembered wanting to speak with her or not and didn't want to give him space to maneuver.

"Yeah, I will," Mattie touched Kendal on his shoulder before she walked away.

"Baby, before you take over can you run to Dairy Mart and grab a pint of chocolate chip cookie dough ice cream? I'll probably be here for a couple of more hours," Kendal asked.

"Two pints," Henry added.

"Yeah, I got you guys covered. Frances, you want anything?" Mattie also had a sweet tooth.

"Oh no, my stomach is fine just the way it is. Lactose intolerant over here." She pointed to her stomach and squished her face.

"Well, I'm outta here, so I can get back and let Adrienne go home."

When she got to the parking lot, she saw that Alonzo had the kids doing jumping jacks.

"That wasn't on Kendal's workout list," she thought.

As she drove out, she noticed three older boys were walking into the parking lot. They wore khaki pants and white t-shirts and hanging out of their back pockets were purple bandanas, but she didn't even think twice about them. Often, kids jumped the fence as a shortcut to the neighborhood.

Her mood was light and easy as she drove into the Dairy Mart. She got the ice cream and a box of popsicles for the kids when they got done with their workout. Low on gas, she also filled her tank up. She blasted her music as Gov White's "32" was being played on the radio station.

"Today has been a good day." She thought as she put her blinker on, but that idea was quickly erased as she pulled into the parking lot. Her mind still hadn't completely figured out what her eyes were seeing.

Alonzo was pressed up against the wall by one of the three boys she had passed on the way out with a knife to his throat. Kendal was standing with his arms raised as another male had a gun pointed at him. Henry had his badge in one hand and his weapon drawn in the other hand pointing it at the third male who extended his pistol towards him in return.

"Put your weapons down, there's no need for any of this to go any further." Mattie could hear Henry say loudly as she lowered the music. One gun for three delinquents was not enough, Mattie surmised.

"P. Mo, dawg, he's a cop." The one facing Henry was fidgety and kept looking to the older member for direction.

"I don't give a fuck; this is our hood. What you thank he jus' gon' let us dip and shit? We in it now homie," The male in charge of the group responded with the gun pointed at Kendal.

"These muthafucka's think they better than us! Giving pipe dreams to all these nappy-headed little fucka's that go here." His dreads were shoulder length. As he made eye contact with the one holding the knife, Henry's voice became louder.

"This can end one of two ways." Henry lowered his badge but kept eyeing the boy with the pistol pointed at him.

"Lower your weapons!" he repeated with more force.

"Look, we're trying to save these kids from the streets. Give them a chance to have more than what they got." Kendal took a step closer to the leader of the trio with his arms still raised above his head. He kept attempting to de-escalate the situation.

"Don't fucking move! Move again, and I'll split yo' fucking wig right the hell open!" P. Mo held no hesitation in his tone.

The boy holding the knife on Alonzo was losing his nerve. He seemed to be on the side of dropping his weapon, but P. Mo was the alpha male of the bunch, and he pressed the moment.

Mattie had already parked and started to get out of the car.

"Baby, stay in the car!" Kendal yelled after seeing her door open.

"Yeah, stay you ass in your ride, bitch!" P. Mo sounded cocky, like they had everything under control even if Henry was a police officer.

Mattie took that as a sign that the three males were not going to back down. As Mattie walked around her car, she had already put one bullet in the chamber of her 9mm and pointed it at the leader.

"Don't worry, I'm a licensed to kill yo' ass type of bitch!" It was the only thing that she could think of.

"Look lower your weapons and leave. We can do this another time, but by now I'm sure there are more units on the way. Take the smart way out, young brothers," Kendal remained rational.

"P. Mo let's dip, dawg. He's a cop!" The boy with the knife let Alonzo go and started backing away.

"Stupid fucks! That's the second time you've used my name, so they know who I am now." He took his eyes off of Kendal for a split second to address the youngest kid with them.

"I ain't going back to jail!" P. Mo blurted out.

Kendal was nervous but he was sure that P. Mo had made up his mind to take his chances because he could be identified. Kendal knew he had to act. He stepped forward and quickly took hold of P. Mo's shooting hand and as the gun discharged all hell broke loose. The bullet flew past Kendal's ear.

Henry's body jerked as a second round was fired from the male holding the gun on him. Henry had taken a round in his left shoulder.

Mattie shot Henry's assailant in the chest twice. He fell forward towards her. She stepped closer to kick his weapon away and turned to face Kendal and his assailant.

Henry staggered backwards but kept his balance even though he had been hit.

Kendal was still struggling with P. Mo as a second round was spent from the aggressor's gun. The discharged bullet ricocheted off the pavement and into the center's front door, shattering the glass without hitting anyone inside.

Mattie couldn't get a good shot on P. Mo without taking a chance of hitting Kendal or Alonzo, who was now free from the knife but had not fled. Alonzo's attacker had also frozen when the first shots were fired.

Henry fell to one knee with his gun still in hand and took aim as P. Mo separated himself from Kendal.

P. Mo had Kendal at point blank range, but as he squeezed the trigger, his gun jammed. Both Henry and Mattie fired. One bullet went into his abdomen but the other pierced him through his head. The blood splattered across Kendal's face. He looked at Madison and then turned his attention back to Henry who was bent over one of the gunmen.

Henry checked his vitals, but P. Mo was dead. The second assailant was clinging to life, his breathing was labored as the blood extended past his lips.

Police sirens could be heard as Mattie kept her gun pointed at the one boy remaining.

"My shoulder," Henry said as Kendal ripped Henry's shirt open. He removed his belt and used it as a tourniquet.

"It don't look bad... it don't look good either," Kendal said as four police cruisers pulled quickly into the parking lot.

"Take my badge and identify me as a detective." Kendal did as he was told.

422

Multiple ambulances were called out along with the coroner for P. Mo lying dead in a puddle of blood. A television crew was setting up to get footage for the evening news as a crowd started to form around the center.

The crime scene investigators were mapping out the area with yellow tape.

P. Mo's body had already been lined with chalk before the coroner ruled on his death. All the guns were confiscated as evidence, along with the knife.

Henry was being checked by a paramedic he was familiar with. He nodded towards Mattie who had made eye contact with him.

"The bullet went through your shoulder, missing all your vitals. You'll recover, no problems, but you're going to be sore detective," The first paramedic relayed to Henry who reached out and took hold of Mattie's hand.

"Mattie, I think you saved my life; all of our lives," he said as they put him in the ambulance.

Mattie was in shock, not realizing how things had gone from bad to worse. It was beginning to dawn on her that indeed, all three could have been the ones dead had she not pulled up when she did.

"The Universe doesn't make mistakes," Mattie went to say, but hesitated after seeing Henry's phone light up with a picture of Jay on the ID.

"I'll call Michele," she looked at Kendal but was speaking with Henry.

"No, give me a second to regroup. She's going to have more questions than I have answers for right now." Henry shifted his body in pain as the paramedic told him what hospital they were being transported to.

Mattie kept thanking God that Kendal wasn't shot. P. Mo had a dead aim on her husband.

"The chamber jammed... or I'd be..." Kendal couldn't get the words out; he was still slightly shaken up.

Alonzo was standing by himself next to a police cruiser waiting to be interviewed. Mattie didn't know what to say.

"Are you ok?" Mattie held her composure together so Alonzo could vent.

"Yeah... I mean, yes, ma'am. Is Detective Jenkins going to be ok?" He was concerned with others even though he was clearly in shock.

"Yes, he's going to be fine," Mattie answered with assurance.

"I... I saw them coming and made the kids hurry inside, but they stopped me. Mr. Scott and the detective came out when... when..." Alonzo tried saying before Mattie cut him off.

"It's ok, you did everything that you could have. Alonzo, you're a hero to those kids. You saved them. Just tell the officers what happened," Mattie encouraged as she saw John, Henry's partner, getting out of his car. Her eyes then traveled to Kendal who was giving his statement to an officer.

"What the hell happened?" John pushed up on one of the investigators. He needed answers as to why his partner was sitting on a gurney with a bullet hole in him.

"Just piecing it together right now, but it seems the Royal Thugs were trying to make a statement. Your partner is fine; he had a through and through. But we've got one suspect in custody, one dead, and the third sent to the hospital, fighting for his life," the investigator relayed.

"Henry Jenkins, you can't be getting into a gunfight without me! Kendal, are y'all good?" John was genuinely concerned.

Henry nodded his head. Kendal was slow to respond.

"Man, I'm glad you all are ok. The gangs were leaving the center untouched like it was Switzerland until the eyewitness stuff came about. I'm heading to the hospital to keep an eye on you."

"I was going to call Michele," Mattie interjected.

"No, I'll call her." John understood the ordeal they had just gone through and felt hearing the news from him would be best.

"We're coming to the hospital when everything is done here." Kendal tried to gain his composure.

John walked away, leaving Mattie and Kendal alone for the first time since the shooting took place.

"You should've stayed in the car." Kendal hesitated because as much as he wanted to be her protector, she saved them all. "But they were really going to shoot us regardless. Are you ok?" he asked as she reached out to hug him.

"Yeah, I'm ok because you're ok… Alonzo is pretty beat up about it though," she gestured towards the younger male sitting in the back of a police car with the door opened. Kendal excused himself and joined Alonzo for support.

"Mrs. Scott… Mrs. Scott," Mattie saw the same investigator who had interviewed Kendal walking towards her. She was so relieved that her husband wasn't lying dead. P. Mo had taken dead aim at him and wouldn't have missed at that close of range.

By the grace of God, she thought as she began telling her side of the story to the investigator.

LIBATION
CHAPTER 36

Henry had been at home for almost a week now after the shooting incident. He still had his arm in a sling and was taking medication to manage the pain. Michele had calmer nerves than was expected. She was more grateful, knowing her husband was alive and was recuperating under her care.

The investigation was still underway since it was an officer involved shooting although it was pretty cut and dry.

"Baby, Kendal and Mattie are here to see you," Michele said, standing in the doorway of their bedroom.

"Ok, I'll be down in a second." He found his slippers and put his robe on.

Mattie and Kendal were sitting at the table when he walked into the kitchen.

"How are you, brother? I know you're not letting that little bullet keep you down," Kendal asked lightheartedly with genuine concern.

"I'm good! I just have to wear this sling for another week," he answered.

"Well, I won't be saying another bad thing about Dak Prescott." The two men grinned.

"Madison, I can't thank you enough. A lot of people would not have even gotten involved. Henry says you made the difference." Michele stood up from the table to retrieve some bowls.

"Who wants ice cream?" she continued.

"Yeah, we brought your pint of chocolate chip cookie dough," Mattie motioned towards the kitchen island.

"If you don't mind, I'll take a scoop or two." Kendal seemed more relaxed than he had been.

As they ate the ice cream, Henry told Mattie that P. Mo had a record as long as his arm and had no doubt he would've shot all of them if he had the chance.

"So far, it looks like it was my discharge that put P. Mo down," Henry acknowledged.

Mattie felt better knowing that no other options were really left to be taken the day at the center. When Henry was shot, she instinctively took out the first threat. The second threat, P. Mo, was killed by the head shot from Henry's weapon.

"Enough talking about it; all of you are safe. Baby, they wanted to take us out for drinks. Sheila has Jay until tomorrow, and I think it would be good to get out the house," Michele said.

"I thought we were supposed to be taking y'all to dinner," Henry was genuinely confused.

"Yeah, well we kinda been stuck at home and the center all week. Your partner has had cruisers driving by frequently. He said the Royal Thugs have been in a power struggle since the shooting and that we have nothing to worry about..." Kendal paused.

"So, you can still take us to Ocean Club tomorrow, but before you even think about saying no, we're doing the driving and treating tonight!" Kendal finished.

Henry didn't respond immediately. The truth was, over the past week he had slowly dealt with being shot and killing someone.

"Yes, we're going... go get showered and dressed. I'll iron some pants and a shirt for you." Michele was not taking no for an answer.

"You guys can wait in the den or living room; we won't be long," Michele finished as she helped her husband up and out the chair.

"He looks ok, right?" Mattie acknowledged while flipping through television channels.

"For a man taking a bullet," Kendal said with a grin on his face.

"Smart ass." Mattie bumped his shoulder playfully.

"You guys ready?" Michele asked as Henry waited by the front door.

"Absolutely! I've already got my mind on a strawberry mojito." Kendal and Mattie followed them out the door.

After being seated on the patio of the restaurant, the couples ordered drinks and appetizers to share.

"Does it hurt?" Mattie asked watching Henry grimace adjusting his posture.

"Not much. Just when I move a certain way, I can feel it in the muscle. The doctors said I was lucky that it missed my clavicle completely," Henry answered.

"Well, here's to the good guys," Kendal said lifting his glass just as the evening breeze gently pushed across their table. They talked until their food arrived.

Henry and Michele were adamant about still taking them out for dinner, offering to foot the bill for the present night. Kendal told them this was a business dinner, and the center was paying for it.

"The least we can do for providing security to the kids. I had to reinforce to a few parents that unlike other programs, we have a visible police force. We had counselors come out and speak with the kids about that day. Alonzo showed real courage and wisdom making sure all the children he was responsible for got inside," Kendal added.

"Well tomorrow, if you all are not busy, we can go to the jazz spot after Ocean Club." Henry felt better after a couple of drinks.

Mattie and Michele were having their own conversation about their husbands.

"So, I'll be driving home tonight," Mattie said as Kendal and Henry ordered their third round of alcoholic beverages.

"We should make them both sit in the back seat." Michele leaned into Mattie.

"Well, if we're sitting in the back," Henry said waving the waiter over.

"One more for me and my brother."

"I'm already drunk. This is absolutely the last one."
Kendal slapped Henry on his good shoulder. They toasted
to family as Mattie took care of the bill.

Both men sat in the back seat on the drive back and
were extremely quiet, and it was Mattie's cell phone going
off that startled her as she pulled into Henry's driveway.

"Yes," she answered the phone when she saw it was her
aunt calling.

"Hey, can you get me some ginger ale?"

"Look in the pantry, Auntie. There's a 12 pack of
Canada Dry I brought for you. We're going to stay at the
condo tonight." Mattie was learning her aunt's little
nuances.

Mattie parked and got out to help Michelle get Henry
out the backseat while Kendal shuffled to the front
passenger side.

Mattie still listened to her aunt speaking on the cell
phone.

"Oh, thank you Lord. My stomach is so upset."

"Kendal has some Prevacid for acid reflux in the
medicine cabinet. Take two of those, they should help."
Mattie pulled back onto the street.

The alcohol was in full effect and Kendal dozed off on the 15-minute ride to the condo.

She was glad to be taking care of him while he had a brief break from the tour. They were going to be flying to Atlanta in less than two weeks and then driving up to see her property and family with her aunt.

"Come on baby, we're home," Mattie urged Kendal out of the car.

He hurried inside, kicked off his shoes, and passed out on the sofa.

Mattie placed her purse on the counter and saw she had received a group text from her friends.

CINDY: So y'all went up to Easton and ain't tell nobody?

Cindy's light sarcasm was coming through.

MATTIE: Yeah, the married couples hung out lol. 😜

CINDY: Are you going to the gym in the morning with us?

Mattie wasn't sure; she wanted to sleep in with Kendal. If she had her way, she was going to be taking advantage of him in his drunken stupor tonight. Kendal sat up quickly from the couch and stumbled a few feet.

"Oh God," was all he could muster before staggering into the downstairs bathroom to expel the contents of his stomach.

"Baby, you ok?" Mattie heard him before she even walked into the restroom.

"Yeah…" he tried to respond but he began throwing up again. He removed his shirt as sweat poured off his body. Falling to one knee, he gripped the side of the toilet bowl.

Mattie got him a cold compress to put on his neck and helped him to bed, undressing him first. She thought about how horny she was but decided to let him sleep it off. She walked back downstairs and reheated her leftovers and sat down on the couch. Her phone vibrated again.

GERI: Don't go getting lazy on us.

MATTIE: I'll be there.

I'm going to take all this pinned up energy out on them, she thought twisting open a bottle of Pepsi to drink with her leftover food.

THE TRUTH SHALL SET YOU FREE

CHAPTER 37

Mattie felt tired but invigorated after the morning workout. She had pushed both Geri and Cindy to their breaking point. All three women were on the floor. Geri and Cindy were sweating and breathing heavily while Mattie was stretching. She was winded too, but her two friends were sucking in oxygen.

"You're a beast," Geri groaned, laying back with her arms folded on her forehead. She was paying for trying to keep up with Mattie instead of pacing herself. Mattie was getting back in top notch shape.

"My legs are on fire!" Geri sat up attempting to stretch her legs.

"Don't go getting' lazy on us. Ain't that the little message I got sent yesterday?" Mattie joked, forcing a grin onto her face.

"Legs and back used to be my favorite…" Geri paused, "but I'm reconsidering," she concluded.

Cindy rolled over onto her knees and stood up slowly.

"Fuck stretching, I gotta cool off. I'll see y'all downstairs." She started to walk away.

"You need to stretch," Mattie called out.

"No, what I need to do is shower in cold water and go lay my ass down before my appointment," Cindy said using a small gym towel to wipe more sweat off.

"You workin' on a Saturday?" Geri knew it was unlike her friend.

"Yeah, I'm trying to close that property in Bexley close to the mayor's house… I'll see y'all downstairs." Cindy kept moving.

"I'm going to shower too," Geri said following Cindy.

Mattie wanted to go with them, but she had back spasms that she needed to stretch out. By the time Mattie showered, Cindy had already left, and Geri was closing her locker behind.

"I guess I'll catch up with you later," Mattie said, walking away into the shower. After dressing, she purchased a smoothie from the gym's small store.

She checked her cell phone when she got into her car for any messages. Kendal had sent two. The first one informed her that he was at the center, so she should come there. The second message asked her to retrieve a briefcase from his truck and drop it off at Henry's before she came to the center.

"Yes, I'll drop it off first," she responded.

She drove to the condo and walked inside. Even though she had showered, sweat was still pouring out of her pores. She grabbed two bottles of water from the refrigerator before taking the briefcase out of his truck.

Out of curiosity, Mattie tried to open it, but the combination wasn't set.

"That figures," she laughed at herself for being a "nosey Parker" as her grandmother used to say.

It wasn't ten o'clock yet, so Mattie thought it wise to call and let Michele and Henry know that she was on the way. Michele said she was just leaving to take her son some more clothes because he had had an accident, wetting the bed over Sheila's.

"I should be back in 30 minutes, but Henry's up. He's got a killer hangover." Michele told Mattie.

"Well, my husband was praying to the porcelain God last night too," Mattie laughed into the phone.

"Men still have a tendency to be boys... I should be back by the time you get to the house."

Mattie drove on the highway, thinking about how supportive Kendal had been at Dr. Stevens. She thought about God's grace saving him from being shot when the gun jammed. Her phone rang; it was Sheila calling.

"Yes," she answered with her new greeting.

"Hey Michele said you guys are going to Ocean Club and the jazz spot after tonight. Y'all don't mind if James and I come, do you? My brother is coming over to watch the fight tonight," Sheila asked boldly.

"Girl, you know I don't care! The more the merrier. Did Michele leave already?" Mattie asked.

"Yeah, about five minutes ago. Jay was so embarrassed. He got his clothes dirty yesterday, so I made him change into what he was supposed to be wearing today but he fell asleep in them," Sheila responded.

"Well, kids have accidents, but why didn't you make him change into his pajamas?" Mattie asked.

"I fell asleep at eleven, and they were still up. Overseeing other adults can be taxing," she replied.

"Well, let me call you back, I'm pulling up right now." Mattie parked on the street in front of Henry's house so as not to block Michele when she returned.

The front door was open when Mattie rang the doorbell. Henry came and unlocked the screen door. She could tell he was dealing with not feeling so well from the previous night's drinking escapades.

"Those shots put both of y'all under," Mattie said with a grin on her face.

"No doubt... Kendal said he threw up last night. I should've forced myself too because I'd feel a lot better," Henry walked into the kitchen.

"I'll take that." He took hold of his briefcase.

"You want something to drink?" he asked, opening up the refrigerator to get water.

"Yeah, let me have a bottle." Mattie followed Henry down three stairs of the split-level to his desk.

"Michele's on the way back. I had to get her to stop to get some Alka Seltzer. I'm not drinking anything tonight," Henry said with a smirk on his face. He placed the briefcase onto the desk, put the combination into his briefcase, and opened it.

There was an awkward silence as Mattie saw her picture alongside the photos of other women. She saw blown up pictures of Samantha wearing the two wigs she had discarded recently.

Henry shook his head but knew it was too late to hide it. In fact, he didn't want to.

"What's going on Henry?" Mattie asked, trying to confront a problem head-on.

Henry had debated on whether to say something to her over the past few weeks. He had determined after being shot and saved by Madison to end the search for more evidence, but now it was too late to not have a discussion with her.

"Mattie I'm going to be honest..." he paused before removing all the evidence from the briefcase. "This is a photo array I've shown to the owners of a hair shop. This is a description of the woman that Mr. Fredericks had spoken to prior to his death. This is a statement from one of the women that worked for the victim. Your photo was picked out along with another by the shop owner as the woman who purchased the wig we found fibers of..." he showed her the picture of the second woman picked out.

"She's a cop, Mattie. This is the unofficial statement of the woman present at Jimmie Fredericks home the last time the police showed up at his house. The initial call came from Global Communications about possible domestic violence and abuse. What's not in the statement is that she said 'Madison in Columbus' was the representative who stayed on the line trying to help her. I never believed that

Mark Floyd was the guilty party. All I do is follow the evidence."

Mattie hadn't taken her eyes off the information he had laid out in front of her. She was at a crossroad. She believed he already knew the answer to his question. She felt odd finally having a chance to be honest, but initially she felt reluctant to speak the truth.

Henry had always been like a big brother to her, but she knew his job was to seek the truth and justice for victims. She never wanted to compromise him.

Henry took a sip of water and then put his hand on top of Mattie's.

"With all the things that have transpired in your life with your parents… your grandma, losing the baby. And then saving me, your husband, and Alonzo. I know your heart. I was going to question you at the center that day because I needed the truth. I didn't know what I would've chosen to do with the answers you would have provided…" he paused as Mattie looked up at him.

"It's no longer important for me to know, so I won't ask you about it. But you should talk to someone about it. For the past week, I've had visions of shooting him in the head. No matter what I try, I can still feel myself pulling the trigger. I can still see his body locking up before falling to the ground and smell the gunpowder. My job is to protect and serve, but I can't seem to shake it off that I killed a teenager no matter how justified it was," he hesitated again to put all the evidence back into his briefcase.

"It's a huge burden to carry. I can't speak to Michele about it. The shrink the department has assigned to me doesn't work either, because… well, I don't trust him. I guess I'm trusting you right now, Madison."

Mattie was caught and she knew it, but Henry was giving her a free pass. She understood exactly what he was going through, trying to put things into perspective after killing someone even if in self-defense.

"What if someone was attacked, assaulted, and knew their life was in danger? What if they had no choice but to defend themselves, by any means necessary?" Mattie blurted out.

For the first time since the night she killed Jimmie, she was talking about it, and she felt the release of guilt being removed.

Henry sat up in his chair before responding.

"The first rule, the first law of nature is self-preservation. I would expect anyone in a life-threatening situation to defend themselves to the fullest." Part of him wanted to know how it all transpired between Jimmie and Mattie, but the larger portion no longer cared.

"Well perhaps with that we both have answers about dilemmas that keep us up at night. Life threatening

442

experiences don't happen often, and I'm glad that you trust me enough to talk to me about what happened at the center." Mattie had hoped Henry would find consolation in the advice he had just given.

"I guess you're right, Mattie. Sometimes you have to do what you have to do…" he paused. "I'm going to lose everything in this briefcase, because it's no longer important," he said as Michele walked in.

"I got Alka Seltzer and orange juice." His wife carried a plastic bag in her hands.

"Mattie, tonight *we* drink, and *they* drive." She pulled out the headache medicine and a bottled water before bending down to kiss Henry.

"Yeah, I think we can manage drinking without going over our limit like our husbands," Mattie responded as she stood up, taking her water bottle with her.

"Well, I'm going to get out of her and take Kendal something to put on his stomach. What time is the reservation? Mattie asked.

"Eight o'clock," Michele answered.

"Ok, we'll see you guys later." Mattie walked out the front door still thinking about her talk with Henry.

She felt a weight lifted from her shoulders; she understood that Henry was in the same space she had found herself in. Henry knew what she had done without confirmation, and he accepted it. Mattie was ready to face life again without remorse or regret. Her phone vibrated with a text from Sheila, reminding Mattie of the investment event she promised to attend with her. Mattie had completely forgotten, so after dropping the stuff off at the center she went home and changed. Sheila picked her up and when they arrived, she felt underdressed in khaki pants and blouse as others were wearing cocktail dresses or suits.

This oughta be interesting, she thought, watching a bunch of bourgeoise people mingling with each other.

RESURGENCE
CHAPTER 38

S ipping on some homemade fruit concoction was about the high point of this meeting. Mattie didn't know why she let Sheila talk her into coming here. After the first 15 minutes of listening, Mattie had no doubt that this was a good old-fashioned pyramid scheme. No matter how pretty the diagrams were or how polished the speaker was, if it involved giving up money and getting others to give up money, which had pyramid written all over it. The conference room was like any other large space with multiple tables set up next to each other to create several rows.

"What you think?" Sheila asked Mattie sounding a little excited while smiling at groups of other participants standing off in three to five person groups. The smaller tables stationed throughout held finger foods and other hors d'oeuvres and beverages.

"You think it's worth it?" Sheila finished.

Mattie looked around the room and told her she would tell her what she thought when they left.

As the presentation ended, Mattie found her way to a table set up for snacks. Taking some crackers and cheese, Mattie walked around the room more so than mingling amongst the guests.

"We can start you in the program tonight and by tomorrow you will have the benefits of a full fledge member." A man wearing a blue suit said trying to close a couple who had attended. The handshake between both parties had sealed the deal.

Got 'em, Mattie thought looking towards Sheila who was speaking with the presenter.

Looks like she's got her mind made up already, Mattie thought, knowing nothing she would say now or later was going to deter her friend from giving up her money.

"And what about you... do you have any questions about the program?" an older woman dressed in black casual slacks and a gray blouse asked as she approached Mattie. Mattie turned to address her.

"Actually..." Mattie hesitated thinking about whether to be sarcastic, but she decided against it. "I'm ok. It's a lot of information to take in. I'm one of those people that takes a few days to sleep on things. So, I'm good, thanks," Mattie replied.

The woman smiled and walked away evidently knowing Mattie was uninterested, so she began to look for someone eager to sign up.

A younger woman was talking to a group about how her team was making money hand over fist, and it caught Mattie's attention.

"I am building up my team so fast. The program comes with all types of benefits to it. My fiancé got me into it a few months ago, and I love it!" She flashed her watch and a necklace with diamonds.

Mattie shook her head and turned to see Sheila making her way through the crowd to listen to the young lady.

"All you have to do is show the benefits and most people sign up. Then all you have to do is have small get togethers like this. There's mega support with a 24-hour support line. They even give you two websites with your package," the woman said, handing out her business cards.

It wasn't so much that she was surprised to find Sheila snatching up all types of literature, but the bracelet the woman wore had Mattie staring. Mattie walked over and stood next to Sheila just to make sure her eyes weren't playing tricks on her. The bracelet the younger woman wore was undoubtedly the one her father had given her mother, the same one stolen in the robbery.

Mattie felt herself flush and began thinking of what to say.

So, this bitch knows something or someone who knows something, she thought to herself, taking another sip of her drink.

"That is a beautiful bracelet," one of the other women said, complementing her on the jewelry.

"Oh… uh, thank you. My fiancé bought it for me with the money he's been earning," she responded.

She may not know, but I bet her man does, Mattie thought.

"You know what, I'll take a card too… can I call your or set something up if I decide it's something I want to do?" Mattie asked as the young woman extended her card.

"Oh absolutely, call anytime of the day or night! We're here to build business relationships… my name is Earlene, but you can see that from the card. Any chance we could get you started with the program today?" she asked.

Mattie smiled through the anger building inside.

"No, I'll call you if I have any questions," she answered.

The older lady who had approached Mattie first walked by with a look of displeasure on her face.

"Fuck you too," Mattie almost said.

Sheila asking, "What's the minimum I could put down?" gave Mattie an opportunity to walk away.

I'm gon' find out what she knows and if... oh my God... if, Mattie thought only seeing images of her grandmother flash in her head.

"I'm just gon' find out," she said out loud.

"Excuse me?" a man said, overhearing her.

"Oh nothing, just thinking about everything," she replied walking away.

She took the business card back out from her purse and studied it. Earlene Jennings.

Well Earlene, I'm going to get to know you and your man, she finished the thought as Sheila walked up to her with her purse in hand and a folder in the other.

"So... you signed up?" Mattie asked.

"Yes, I did," Sheila was excited when she responded.

"I've got some people at work that will come to a meeting, plus my brothers you know they be after the green. I'm trying to get some of this money too." Sheila was serious.

Mattie was hearing her friend speak but wasn't paying attention to her. She kept scanning the room back and forth to where Earlene was now sitting down at a table signing people up for the program.

Sheila took a cracker from Mattie's plate and ate it with some cheese.

"I'm glad you're eating again. Being married must be good for you. You want me to get some more for you?" Sheila asked but Mattie failed to respond.

Mattie's eyes were fixed on the bracelet, and her mind was still deciding whether to say something right now. She wanted to snatch it off her arm, with or without the wrist still being attached.

"Mattie?" Sheila said again.

"Huh?" Mattie answered.

"Do you want something else or are you ready to go?" Sheila asked, wondering what Mattie had been in deep thought about.

"We can get out of here," she answered.

As they drove off, Mattie sat in the passenger seat thinking while she stared out the window.

"Damn you so quiet… what's up?" Sheila asked.

"Oh nothing, just thinking about everything. I'll probably call that Earlene lady sometime; I just didn't feel like asking a whole bunch of questions. You'll let me look at your stuff, and I'll come to your event too," Mattie answered, hoping it was a sufficient response.

"Yeah, that's nice... I'm about to call my brothers and tell them about it," Sheila said, pulling out her phone.

Mattie started out the window dealing with emotions that had resurfaced.

I'll fuck that bitch up... I swear to God, she thought.

Her grandmother was her life and the way she had been beaten still gave Mattie thoughts of hurting someone like she had done Jimmie Fredericks.

After leaving the event, Sheila couldn't stop talking about who she was going to invite to her meetings and how long it would take her to move up to the second level of achievement. Mattie chimed in when she could, but her mind was on the bracelet and earrings. She had memorized Earlene's contact info by heart.

When they pulled up to her condo, they noticed two black SUVs with two men standing at each.

Mattie got excited, knowing someone from the family was surprising her. The men greeted Mattie with respect as she moved past them. She waved to acknowledge them. Sheila smiled and followed Mattie inside.

"Mama," Mattie exclaimed as she opened the door to her place. She looked around and saw people sitting at the dining room table. Aunt Penny and Señora stood up to greet Madison, but the third person looked hesitant.

"Why didn't you tell me you were coming? I didn't think I'd see you again until next year when David and Camilla get married. How's Papa and Roberto? The twins haven't called me since the wedding…" Mattie hesitated as she noticed the woman standing from the table to turn and face her. When their eyes locked, everything stood still.

Memories flooded back that she had forgotten: love, anger, and all the emotions in between.

"Mom."

"Hey, Mattie Boo…"

ABOUT THE AUTHOR

A. **V. Smith** is an athlete turned writer. During the mid-2000's, he was a featured poet at the Columbus Arts Festival and also won second place during The Great Debaters poetry slam in Columbus, Ohio as Oprah Winfrey's movie was being released nationally.

With a passion for storytelling, he paints with words that draw readers into the story. A.V. writes on an emotional level to empower readers to engage in deeper conversations about their past, their relationships, and their connection with The Universe.

With his first book, *Madison God's Fingerprint 1.618,* Smith won the Author Academy award for Best Romance in 2019. Since then, he has released *Madison: In the Presence of God* and *Madison: Vengeance Is Mine.* He has also written two crime novels, *OHIO 10* and *OHIO 10 Book II.* Each book has earned Amazon's #1 Best Seller Rank.

Smith also wrote a fantasy fiction book titled, *Normal Chaos: Ledoma Book I.* He loves to stretch his own limits of creativity by dabbling in various genres of fiction.

Through life and love, André has learned our journeys are temporary, yet intensely meaningful. This understanding led him to donate a kidney to his younger brother. As the father of three children, his desire is to see his children overcome the fear of success by being the best version of themselves; therefore, he strives to lead by example, at times falling short, but understanding human beings are still a work in progress. When he is not engaged in his passion, you can find him with a fishing pole in his hand, coaching youth level football, or attending a local artist event.

For more information or to contact A. V. Smith, please visit www.warpedwritingandpublishing.com.

OHIO 10

Dive into the gritty, pulse-pounding streets of Columbus, Ohio, where a diverse team of detectives battles corruption on all fronts. **OHIO 10** is a riveting tale of integrity versus power, as good cops take a stand against bad cops amidst a tangled web of crime, politics, and betrayal.

Amid chilling crime scenes, personal struggles, and relentless pursuit of justice, detectives Cole and Everett lead the charge, navigating the murky waters of loyalty and morality. With tension as sharp as the thin wire that left its mark on their latest victim, this story will keep you on the edge of your seat.

Brace yourself for a gripping, no-holds-barred look at the cost of doing what's right in a city where justice feels like a distant dream. **OHIO 10**—because some fights are worth everything.

Available on Amazon.

.

OHIO 10 Book II

The stakes are higher. The corruption is deeper. The danger is closer.

In **OHIO 10 Book II**, A.V. Smith plunges readers back into the chaotic streets of Columbus, where the line between ally and enemy blurs. As the detectives take on a perilous investigation into City Hall and a criminally compromised law enforcement hierarchy, the team faces mounting personal and professional challenges.

Two detectives risk it all on a high-stakes undercover mission—can they stay hidden, or will their cover be blown? Meanwhile, Captain Montgomery battles increasing pressure to halt his pursuit of cold cases, even as he edges closer to uncovering the truth.

With crime bosses pulling strings at the highest levels, the team learns their greatest fight isn't on the streets but within their own ranks. Will integrity prevail, or will the weight of betrayal prove too much to bear?

OHIO 10 Book II—where justice faces its toughest test yet.

Available on Amazon.

NORMAL CHAOS

The battle between light and shadow rages on.

In *Normal Chaos*, A.V. Smith masterfully weaves a tale of epic proportions, where the eternal forces of nature clash and the balance of the world teeters on the brink. Since the dawn of creation, every millennium has brought a new cycle of transformation—each one a battleground between the

greed and dark magic of shadow and the resilience and hope of light.

As the Seventh Age looms, humanity stands at the edge of its greatest trial. The descendants of the Light of the First Mother—the bridge between humanity and the heavens—must rise to protect the Tree of Life. Giants, dragons, and the guardians of the Order of Petals fight to stave off the growing darkness, but even among the chosen, the shadow tempts those who carry the bloodline.

Will the light endure, or will the forces of chaos prevail?

Normal Chaos is a breathtaking journey of power, destiny, and the relentless war for the soul of the Earth. Dive into a world where the ancient and the eternal collide and discover what it means to be both the savior and the storm.

Perfect for fans of high-stakes fantasy and richly woven lore, *Normal Chaos* is the first step into an unforgettable saga.

Available on Amazon.